D0898383

CHOCOLATE
LIZARDS

CHOCOLATE LIZARDS

A NOVEL

COLE THOMPSON

ST. MARTIN'S GRIFFIN ☙ NEW YORK

Book design by Scott Levine

Library of Congress Cataloging-in-Publication Data

Thompson, Cole.
    Chocolate lizards / Cole Thompson.
        p.   cm.
    ISBN 0-312-20052-8 (hc)
    ISBN 0-312-26486-0 (pbk)
    I. Title
    PS3570.H59685C46 1999
    813'.54—dc21   98-47013
                                                              CIP

First St. Martin's Griffin Edition: May 2000

10 9 8 7 6 5 4 3 2 1

THE BEGINNING

EVEN ON A BUDGET TOUR BUS, HE'S AN UNUSUALLY GRUESOME
passenger. Where his left eye should be is a big yellow rectumlike
scar, and what few teeth he has are rotted to brown nubs. White
beard stubble covers his cheeks and neck, greasy gray hair hangs
from under his Dallas Cowboys cap, and his jacket, a navy blazer,
is ridiculously long in the sleeves. He plops down beside me, looks
at me with his bloodshot eye, and nods.

"Hey. I'm Luther."

As I nod and introduce myself, his BO hits.

Yow.

I sit up and look over the lady's hair in front of me to find an
empty seat. To my dismay, a horde of El Pasoans are filing up
the aisle. There are no empty seats. Holy shit.

"Where you headed?" he asks.

"Uh . . . Boston."

He slides his hand out of his sleeve and points to himself.

"I'm goin' home, bo. Tuscaloosa, Alabama." He smiles a
rotten-tooth smile.

Holy shit.

As we set out from El Paso, I put on my Walkman, crank the
Femmes, and look out the window into the darkness. Damn, I wish
it wasn't dark. This was one of the few pluses of this whole trip, getting to see Texas. I think they shot *Giant* out here somewhere.

Luther nudges my shoulder. I turn from the window and he holds up a deck of cards in the overhead light. I click off my Walkman.

"What?"

He jigs his eyebrows and smiles.

"Game fer a hand or two?"

I shake my head.

"No, but thanks."

He frowns.

"Aw, what else we gonna do, bo? Texas is a long ways across." (For some reason he calls me 'bo.' I don't know why. It's not my name.)

I look at the cards and shake my head again.

"Sorry, Luther, but I'm just going to hang out, if you don't mind." I punch my Walkman back on and look out the window. In the corner of my eye I watch Luther produce a roll of cash from the inside breast pocket of his blazer. As he riffles through his roll, counting it, I see that Luther has quite a few ten- and twenty-dollar bills. I click off my Walkman. "Are you wanting to play for *money*, Luther?"

"Heck yeah, bo. Pokuh ain't pokuh if ya ain't got money out they-uh." He shoves his money back in his jacket and shuffles the cards on his thigh.

I have about a hundred bucks, which is more than enough to last three days to Boston. So when I ask Luther what sort of stakes he has in mind, and he says one dollar ante and one dollar bets, with a pot limit of ten dollars per hand, I think, What the hell. I could use the extra cash. I take off my Walkman and stuff it in my backpack.

"Okay, Luther. Let's play."

He smiles.

"Hey, bo. You all right."

Beneath the dim overhead light, the other passengers dozing

around us and the Texas night rolling by outside, Luther deals the cards.

Å Å Å

After about thirty hands I want to scream and gouge out Luther's other eye. The sonofabitch bluffs. Hand after hand he raises the bet past the point where I can reasonably stay, and after I fold, he smiles, buries his cards in the deck, and rakes the pot toward him. Given this is such a small-stakes game, several times after I fold and concede the pot, I show my cards and ask, "What did you have, really?"

"The meek cain't peek," Luther says, smiling his rotten three-teeth smile. "The meek cain't peek."

What an asshole.

About three hours into the game I get a whopper—a full house, three aces, two sevens. It's a cinch winner, but warming to the dramatics of the game, I hesitate as I bet a dollar. Luther calls my bet and takes up the deck.

"How many, bo?"

With a show of head-scratching indecision, I indicate that I want no additional cards, but will stay with my original five.

"Well lookee he-uh," Luther says, "bo gonna stay all the way." He picks up his hand and looks at it. "Not I. I's head-high in the shit sty." He discards four of his cards and draws four new ones. Upon seeing his new cards his eye opens wide. He laughs and slaps his leg. "I be goddam." He takes a dollar from his pile and tosses it into the pot. "I betcha a dollar on this one, bo."

I call Luther's bet, then, chewing my lip and feigning reluctance, raise him a dollar. To my surprise he calls my raise and, in turn, raises *me* a dollar. I know exactly what he's doing, but it won't work this time, not when I hold such a doozy.

"My condolences, Luther, but unfortunately you can't bluff your way through this one."

"You sho, bo?"

"Yes, I'm sure." Matching his raise, I put another dollar into the pot, taking it to its limit of ten dollars. I start to lay down my cards, but Luther reaches up and stops me.

"Hang on, bo." He carefully lays his cards facedown on the seat between us. "Maybe we should ferget our pot limit and play this one big as we want."

I look at my cards again to make sure I haven't misread them—no, it's definitely a full house, aces over sevens.

"I might agree to that," I say. "How much do you want to bet?"

"The bet's yo's, bo. I made the last raise."

"So you're saying on this particular hand, I can bet however much I want?"

"Yes suh. We playin' New Awlens rules on this one. No limit."

I sit back and perform a quick calculation. With aces as the group of three in my full house, it's impossible that Luther can beat me with a full house—he must, at the very least, have four of a kind. And since he discarded all his cards except one from his original hand, in order to have four of a kind, he would've at least had to draw three matching cards to go along with the one he held. I'm not exactly sure what the odds of that are, but I know they're ridiculous, like about one in a million.

"Luther, I will bet you twenty dollars." I take the money from my wallet and lay it in the pot. I'm sure such a beefy bet will snuff Luther's bluffing tactic, but instead he pulls his roll of money from his jacket.

"I'll see yo twenty, bo . . . and raise you . . . two hundred and fifty." He places his roll of cash on the pile of money between us.

My first instinct is to throw in my hand, accept the thirty-dollar loss, and quit the game altogether. But I'm sick of this moron, his ridiculous bluffing and haughty posturing. I remind myself this is a situation of numbers. Cold facts. I rethink the odds. There's no

fucking way. Luther, this stinking hick, is bluffing. Like a gunshot
my resolves quickens. I take all my money from my wallet.

"I don't have two-fifty to call your bet, Luther. I only have
seventy here, but I guarantee you, my credit is good."

He throws back his head and laughs, his three-teeth mouth
open wide.

"Ain't no credit rollin' on a bus, bo. If you ain't tall enough
to call, then that's all." He puts up his hand, indicating this is the
end of the betting, then reaches toward the pot to gather up the
money. I grab his hand.

"You liar. I know you're bluffing. You've been bluffing all night."

He jerks his hand back and stares at me with his one eye.

"You really wanna see my cards, bo?"

"Yes, I do."

He looks down at the stack of money in my hand.

"How much you got they-uh?"

"I told you. Seventy dollars."

"All right, bo. I'll draw down my bet to seventy, and you put
in yo seventy, and we'll just turn 'em ovuh."

"Okay. It's a bet."

He takes 180 dollars from the pot and I lay down all of my
remaining money.

"Fo fo's," he says. He turns over his hand and fans out his
cards. There they are, four fours. Staring in stunned disbelief, my
head swimming with panic and outrage, I slam my hand down on
the pile of money between us and close my fist around my stack
of bills. Instantly he grabs my wrist with one hand. With the other
hand, from somewhere in the long baggy sleeve of his blazer, he
brings out a switchblade knife.

Click.

He flicks it open and presses the blade to my throat.

"You let go uh that money or I'll cutcher fuckin' throat."

I stare at his eye and release my grip on my money. Holding
the knife to my throat, he wads together the money and stuffs it

inside his jacket. He takes away the knife, folds it up, and slips it back into his long sleeve.

"No hard feelin's, bo, but don't evuh fuck with my money."

He licks his lips, leans back in his seat, and looks away.

THE WIND HOWLS THROUGH THE STREET, SWINGING THE traffic lights in a loopy yellow-blinking ballet. As the bus pulls away, a tumbleweed comes blowing down the sidewalk. Bounding and rolling in the wind, it bounces off my hip, then blows down the street beneath the swinging traffic lights, bounding and rolling.

Light glows in the windows of a restaurant across the street. Several pickup trucks are parked in front under a red neon sign: Wildcat Cafe. Suitcase in one hand, backpack in the other, I duck my face from the blowing dust and walk across the street.

It's not even dawn yet, but already a half-dozen men sit at a big round table near the door, drinking coffee and talking in low mumbles. Some wear their cowboy hats, others have set theirs on the table before them, revealing short, neatly oiled and combed gray hair. Their faces are tan and creased with wrinkles. They stare as I walk past. As I sit at the counter I hear one say, "Got off the bus over 'ere while ago."

A gum-chewing waitress stops behind the counter, sets a cup before me with a clatter, and fills it with steaming coffee. She lays a laminated menu on the counter, chews her gum, and winks.

"Lemme know when yer ready, doll." She walks away, leaving me with my coffee and chaos.

On the bus, pissed off about losing all my money, not to mention having a switchblade shoved to my throat, I snatched down my suitcase and backpack and got off at the next stop: Abilene, Texas. I guess I could've just starved and rode it out penniless for three days to Boston. But hell, no way was I going to stay on the bus with that stinking one-eyed hick. But now what? Jesus. I don't even have a buck to pay for this coffee. Fuck, what else can I do? I guess I'll have to call home and ask Mom and Dad to wire some more money. God, Dad will go insane. All the stunts I've pulled lately, and now this. Just the fact that he had to send me four hundred dollars to get out of LA was enough—I'll hear about that for the rest of my life anyway—and now I don't even make it halfway home. Holy shit. Oh well, maybe I'll say I was robbed.

As I mull my situation, a lean broad-shouldered guy in a cowboy hat walks up to the counter beside me. About six feet tall and a lanky 175 pounds, he wears gigantic tan cowboy boots, brown slacks, a belt with a silver-and-gold buckle, a long-sleeved white shirt, and snugly atop his head, a big wide-brimmed straw cowboy hat. I do a double take on his boots. They're *huge*, with massive tall heels and long sharp toes. They must be real Texas cowboy boots. I'm the only customer seated at the counter—there are at least a dozen other empty stools—but he sits right beside me. He turns to me. Under his big hat brim he has a handsome sun-weathered face of about forty-five years. His sky blue eyes are large and searching, his nose is thin and long, and he has a deep crevice in his chin. He nods in a curt earnest gesture.

"Mornin', son."

"Good morning."

"Mornin', Merle," the waitress says.

"Mornin', Faye."

"Looks like another windy one."

"Yep, lil breezy."

Faye puts a cup before Merle and fills it with coffee.

"How's thayngs?" she says.

He pushes up the front brim of his hat with his index finger.

"Aw hell, Faye, I'm goin' broke hand over fist. And now on top uh that, I'm so damn worked up about it, my love-makin' equipment's goin' bad on me."

Faye frowns.

"Well honey, you shouldn' letchurself get all chewed up like 'at." A bell rings and a plate of steaming pancakes appears in the stainless-steel service window behind Faye. She turns, snatches up the plate, and carries it away.

"Yer right, Faye," Merle says, though Faye is gone. "Yer goddam right." He reaches down, slips his hand into his huge elaborately stitched boot, and brings out a flat silver flask (about six inches by four inches). He unscrews its cap and pours a splash into his coffee. He turns and offers me the flask. "Lil hair fer yer monkey?"

"Uh . . . no, thank you."

He raises his eyebrows, as though surprised that I have declined.

"Ar-ight, well, reckon I better have yers." He dumps another splash into his cup, caps his flask, and slips it back into his boot. He sips his cup of coffee/liquor and nods toward my luggage. "Where ya headed?"

"Boston."

"*Boston?* 'At's goddam Yankeeland, ain't it?"

I smile.

"That's my home."

"Oh. Goddam. Where is Boston, anyway?"

"It's in Massachusetts."

He stares at me blankly.

"You know," I say, "New England?"

He keeps staring at me.

Bam.

He slaps the counter.

"Goddammit, 'at's it."

"What?"

"I been sittin' here tryin' to figger out who ya remind me of, and by God, I just did. It's ol' what's his face. 'At movie actor from back in the ol' days. Ya look just like the sumbitch." He snaps his fingers again. "Aw hell, ya know who I'm talkin' about."

I do know who he's talking about. Ever since I was about fifteen, people have told me I look like Montgomery Clift, the Hollywood star of the fifties. And I guess it's true. My eyes are blue and I have big eyebrows like his. And my hair's brown and pretty thick. I know in a way it's a plus—I do get a lot of compliments on my head shots—but still, sometimes I get tired of hearing it. Anyway, rather than help Merle put a name to the face he has in his mind, I shrug and play dumb.

"Goddammit," he says. He puts his hand on top of my head and turns my face so that I'm looking down to the end of the counter where Faye is stooped over, adding a check. "Hey Faye!" He points to my face with his other hand. "Who's this kid look like? Ya know, 'at ol' movie actor."

Faye looks up from her calculations, chews her gum, and ponders my face. She smiles.

"Montgomery Clift. He looks like Montgomery Clift."

Bam.

Merle slaps the counter.

"By God, 'at's it. Montgomery Clift. Ya look just like the sumbitch." He sips his coffee/liquor and stares at me again. "I'll be damn."

Faye refills our cups, then brings out her order tablet and grabs the pen behind her ear.

"Wanchur usual, Merle?"

"Ar-ight. Why not. Ain't had it since yesterday."

She writes down Merle's usual, flips the sheet over, and looks at me.

"How aboutchoo, handsome? What can I getcha?"

"Uh, nothing to eat, thank you. Just coffee."

She nods, tears off Merle's order, and puts it in the window to the kitchen. As she hurries away with the coffee pot, Merle brings out his flask and dumps another splash in his coffee. I look back out the windows. The sky over the bus terminal across the street has lightened to a soft gray. The wind gusts and swirls clouds of dust past the window. Merle sips his coffee/liquor and sets down his cup.

"How old are ya, son?"

"Uh . . . twenty-one."

"Goduhmighty, twenty-one. What I wouldn' give to be twenty-one again. Joo go to college?"

"Yeah."

"Where abouts?"

"Harvard."

"*Harvard*. Goddam. You must be sharper'n a snake's ass."

I laugh.

"No. Actually I got in because my father teaches there. They had to let me in."

"Yer daddy teaches at Harvard?"

"Yeah."

"What's he teach?"

"Math."

"*Math*. Crap fire. I bet he's a smart sumbitch."

"Well, he's a sonofabitch, but other than that, I—"

"*Ha-ha*." Merle laughs and slaps my back. "I like you, Harvard. I like to hear ya talk."

Faye sets a large oval-shaped platter of greasy food in front of Merle: three fried eggs with bright yellow yolks, an enormous round sausage patty, fried potatoes, and two biscuits. My stomach growls. I haven't eaten since yesterday in Albuquerque. Merle cuts into his sausage and takes a bite.

"Yep, boys and daddies are funny. Ya never know how it's gonna turn out. I got a boy aboutchur age. Be twenty in June."

"Oh? What does he do?"

"Aw, he's in the pen right now."

"Oh. Sorry."

Merle saws off a flimsy strip of yolk-dripping egg and forks it into his mouth.

"Naw, never could do nothin' with him. Hardheadedest sumbitch ya ever saw. Ran off down 'ere to Houston to live with his mama and started snortin' 'at cocaine. They finally caught him with a sack full of it."

"God. That's terrible."

"Yep." He sets down his fork and sips his coffee/liquor. "So, yer on yer way home to Boston."

"Yeah."

"Where ya comin' from?"

"California."

"*California?* Good God, whatcha doin' out 'ere? Ain't nothin' but prune pickers and prick lickers out 'ere."

I laugh.

"Well, actually, I was trying to find a job."

"What sort uh job?"

"Acting. I'm an actor. Or at least I wanted to be. I'm still a *stage* actor. Sort of. Anyway, I was trying to get in the movies."

"I'll be damn. Hey, Faye!"

Faye turns from the coffee machine. Merle points to me.

"Harvard here's a movie actor."

"No," I say, "I didn't say that."

Merle ignores me, and Faye, chomping her gum, walks along the counter to us. She smiles.

"Really? What were you in? Maybe I seen ya."

"I wasn't in anything. That's sort of the whole point. I bombed out. I'm going home."

"Oh. Well, bless yer heart." Faye walks back to the coffee machine. Merle chews a bite of biscuit and looks at me.

"Ya *bombed* out?" he says.

"Yeah."

"What the hell's 'at mean?"

"It means I couldn't get a job. So I'm going back home."

He stares at me and blinks his eyes like he doesn't understand.

"Hell, maybe ya just didn' fight hard enough."

"No, I fought. Believe me. It's just an extremely—"

"What's uh matter, boy? Ya hungry?"

"Excuse me." Without realizing it, I'm ogling Merle's food. I look away.

"Ya look hungry, boy. What's goin' on? Ya out uh money?"

"Uh . . . no. Actually I just . . . uh . . . hadn't thought to order yet."

"Yer lyin', aincha? Faye! Brayng Harvard here one uh my specials on me."

"No, really," I say. "I couldn't accept that."

"The hell ya couldn'," he says.

He continues to eat, and in a few minutes Faye serves me a heaping sausage-and-egg breakfast just like his.

" 'Ere ya go, son," he says. "Get after it."

"Thank you, Merle. Thank you very much."

"Yep." He shovels a forkful of potatoes into his mouth. I begin devouring my breakfast.

"So," Merle says, "wha'd joo do, get on the bus without no money?"

I pause as I chew a bite of sausage. I decide this is a good chance to rehearse my robbery routine for my parents.

"Actually . . . I was robbed."

He looks at me.

"*Robbed?* When?"

"Last night. On the bus. Just west of here."

"Who the hell robbed ya?"

"It was a gang."

"A *gang?*"

"Yeah. There were about eight of them. Young Hispanic guys."

"Goddam. How much they get off ya?"

"About a hundred dollars."

He whistles.

"I'll be damn."

I poke a piece of biscuit in my mouth and nod woefully.

"Yeah, it was pretty bad."

He plucks a paper napkin from the stainless-steel dispenser on the counter and wipes his mouth.

"Harvard, I hate to do it, but I'm gonna call bullshit on ya."

"Pardon me?"

"Yer lyin'. I been robbed a time or two, and you don't act a damn thayng like a felluh 'at's been robbed. What happened? Joo take off broke?"

I stare down at my food.

"I lost my money playing poker on the bus. Then I got pissed off and got off the bus."

Merle roars with laughter and slaps the counter.

"*Ha-ha*. Goddam, I love it. Harvard, yer ar-ight." He sips his coffee/liquor. "So whadda ya gonna do now, boy? Ass-up stranded in Abilene, Texas."

"I don't know. I guess I'll call my parents and tell them I've lost my money. My dad's going to kill me." Dread shoots through me as I imagine Dad's wrath.

Merle takes a bite of sausage and sips his coffee/liquor.

"Harvard, tell ya what I'll do. I could use a hand right now. One uh my crew broke his arm in a bar fight and cain't work. I'll give ya a job and a place to stay fer a week or two, till ya getchur feet back under ya, then ya can shag ass on home with some money in yer pocket."

"What kind of job?"

"Roughneckin' on one uh my rigs. I know ya ain't got no experience, but I'll go on and startcha at eight dollars an hour. Hell, 'at's about sixty-five a day. In a week's time ya arta hair up and heal over perty good, don'cha reckon?"

"Uh . . . yes."

"Well? Ya interested?"

I'm stunned by the abruptness of his proposal, but even this unknown seems better than enduring Dad's scorn. Besides, what an adventure. Roughnecking in Texas. Wow.

"Yes, I'm interested."

"Good," Merle says. "Got us a deal then." He eats a bite of egg and sips his coffee/liquor.

"Excuse me," I say, "but what is your name?"

He sets down his cup and holds out his hand.

"Luskey. Merle Luskey."

TRUDGING INTO THE WIND, I FOLLOW MERLE UP THE STREET
to a huge red pickup truck with a four-door cab and ridiculously
large tires, especially at the back, which has *two* tires on each side
and big bulbous fenders to accommodate them. The truck also
has shiny chrome wheels and bumpers, a chrome grille guard on
its front, yellow running lights above its windshield and along its
wide fenders, and sprouting from the roof, a long antenna wobbling in the wind.

Holding down his hat with one hand, Merle opens the backseat door, takes my suitcase and backpack, and tosses them into
the truck. He slams the door and points over the truck to the
passenger's side.

"Get in!"

I go around and wrestle with the door, wedging my body
against it to hold it open against the wind. Finally I pull myself
up into the cab. The door closes with the force of the wind, leaving Merle and me in quiet stillness.

"Man, this wind is amazing."

"Aw, hell, this is just a breeze." He reaches behind his seat
and brings up a big half-gallon bottle of Jack Daniel's Old No. 7
Tennessee whiskey. He raises his eyebrows, as though surprised.
"I'll be damn. Brand new bottle." He unscrews the cap, pushes
back his hat, and takes a sip. Grimacing and pursing his lips, he

wipes his mouth with the back of his hand. "Aw yeah," he says. He holds the bottle out to me. "Here ya go, boy. Getcha a sip."

I stare at the bottle. I'm not exactly opposed to catching a buzz (although I rarely drink the hard stuff), but the crack of dawn seems like a fucked-up time to do it.

"C'mon now," he says. He wags the bottle. "Getcha a lil taste."

"Uh . . . gosh, Merle. I don't know. It's sort of early, isn't it?"

"Aw goddam, Harvard." He points to the digital clock on the dash. It reads 6:19. "Tell ya what. Yer drawin' pay right now. As uh six o'clock I'm payin' yer ass eight dollars an hour." He knits his eyebrows and scowls. "Now by God, I'm tired uh drankin' alone. Have some whiskey, dammit." He shoves the bottle at me.

Although it seems an incredibly morbid thing to ask of someone, I guess I can't very well refuse a direct order from my new employer. I take the huge bottle and drink. The warm whiskey burns my throat, but I clench my teeth and swallow. I offer to return Merle his bottle. He won't take it.

"Go on," he says, "getcha another. And goddammit, don't play with it. *Drank* the sumbitch."

I nod. With Merle carefully monitoring my performance, I gulp a generous swig. I cough and shudder. He smiles.

"What's uh matter, boy? Don'cha know good whiskey when ya see it?" He grabs the bottle and tosses back another swig.

Ã Ã Ã

Merle drives through a wide street lined with crumbling red-brick and rusty tin-roofed industrial buildings. Their signs, painted on front windows or suspended from poles along the road, advertise tire repair, oil-field supplies, veterinarian supplies, agricultural seed and fertilizer, tractors, propane, and hardware. A mile or so beyond the last businesses, the pavement and chain-link fences give way to red-soil farm plots bordered by barbed-wire fences. I turn and look back at the town. The ground is so flat it's hard to see much: a thin band of green treetops, scattered steeples of churches, and rising solitary from this prairie oasis, one tall modern golden-reflective glass business complex. Merle slaps my shoulder.

"Hey, know what this is?"

I turn from the back window and he flips me the bird.

"I beg your pardon."

"Do ya *know* what this is?" He wags the bird in my face.

"Well, usually it—"

"The Abilene skyline." He smiles. "Get it?"

I do. The one bird finger is supposed to correspond to the one tall building in town.

"Yeah. That's a screamer, Merle."

He slaps the dash and chuckles.

"Goddam, I know it."

"What *is* that building?"

"Aw, 'at's the fuckin' bank."

As I turn and look again at the Abilene skyline, Merle swerves off the road and pulls into a white crushed-rock parking lot. Before us is a bright red trailer house parked on a cement slab. Above the door, painted in white western rodeo-style lettering: Luskey Drilling, Inc. Behind the trailer house, a sprawling equipment yard packed with huge red-and-white machines. With a bank of engines and an operating house on one end, and a long arm of crisscross iron beams extending out along the ground, they look like the giant cranes in the shipyards along the north wharf in Boston. I count them—*one, two, three, four, five*—all in a row, easily occupying the space of two football fields, their engines and operating houses painted red and their long girded arms gleaming white. And across the top of the red operating house of each one, in the same white western style of lettering as on the trailer house: Luskey Drilling, Inc.

"What are those?"

Merle skids to a halt alongside the trailer house and nods toward the machines.

"Those?"

"Yeah."

He grabs the bottle of Jack Daniel's on the seat between us, unscrews the cap, and guzzles a double-gurgling swallow.

"Harvard, ya see 'em thayngs?"

"Hell yes. How could I not?"

He stares out at the machines.

"Ever' damn one of 'em is a two-hunerd-ton anchor tied around my nuts." He swigs the bottle. "Harvard, ya know how hard it is to get around with a thousand tons hangin' on yer balls?"

"Well, I—"

"It hurts, Harvard. It hurts."

"You say anchors, Merle, and I know you're being meta-phorical, but really, what are these, drilling derricks for digging oil wells?"

"They're drillin' rigs, boy."

"Then why are the derricks lying down along the ground like that? Are they designed to drill horizontally? Didn't I read something about that?"

"*Ha-ha*, goddam." He swigs the bottle. "No, Harvard, they ain't designed to drill horizontally. The mutherfuckers are layin' down cuz they ain't drillin'."

"Oh. So were they actually drilling, the derricks would be vertical."

"Yer goddam right. Now c'mon, let's getcha some overalls and a hard hat."

We step from the truck into the gusting wind.

"Hang on," he says. He goes into the red trailer-house office, then reappears carrying a one-piece red overall uniform fluttering from a hanger in the wind. Under his arm, like a football, he carries a dull red construction hat.

"Try it on." He hands me the wind-fluttering uniform. I look around.

"Right here?"

"Yeah."

I look around again. He scowls.

"What's uh matter? Hell, I ain't no frog watcher."

"Okay. Okay."

I strip down to my underwear and loafers. As I step into the uniform I notice the patch on the left breast. It's white with a puckered red border and red cursive letters of machine-stitched thread that spell Luskey Drilling. I zip it closed up to my throat. The sleeves and body fit well, but the legs are a bit long.

" 'At'll be ar-ight," Merle says. From his back pocket he brings out a pair of soft cotton work gloves and stuffs them in my hand. "And most important of all—" He sets the dull red construction hat on my head. "When yer on location, I don't care whatchur doin', ya wear yer fuckin' hard hat, got it?"

I nod.

"Thanks, Merle." I hold out my hand to shake and show my appreciation, but before Merle can take my hand, from the direction of Abilene three white cop cars come creeping along the side of the road. They have Taylor County Sheriff's Department written on their sides and red-and-blue emergency lights mounted across their roofs, and each is occupied by the dark silhouettes of men.

"Goddam!" Merle yells. "Get in!" He dashes for the truck, and I follow him. The sheriff's department cars break their formation and speed toward us. By the time we get in the truck, the three cars have nosed themselves in a fan in front of us.

"What's going on here? What do they want?"

"Hang on!" Merle pushes in the clutch, shifts the stick to reverse, lets off the clutch, and slams the accelerator. We grind backward in a cloud of white dust and rock bits. He slings the front of the truck around toward the road and shifts the stick to first gear, but the sheriff cars scramble and surround us, two skidding to a halt before us and one sideways behind us.

"Ya dirty cocksuckers!" Merle says. He turns the wheel, lets off the clutch, and stomps the accelerator. We jerk to the right.

WHAM.

We hit the front bumper of one of the cars, knocking it back, and charge toward the road. Accelerating up the small slope between the parking lot and road, we launch airborne and crash down—front wheels, then back—onto the road. My hard hat flies off, and pieces of pipe bounce from the bed of the truck and scatter in our wake.

Within seconds the sheriff cars catch our lumbering diesel truck. All three cars follow immediately behind us, sirens wailing, lights flashing.

WEE-OH-WEE-OH-WEE-OH . . .

"What the hell is going on, Merle? What do they want?"

"Goddam bank's tryin' to close on me." Both hands on the wheel, eyes focused on the road ahead, he mashes the accelerator against the floor. Our diesel engine roars as we gain speed. A sheriff car zooms up alongside us on the left and tries to pass. Merle sees it in his side-view mirror.

"Jack! Don't make me fuck you up!"

URRRR.

He swerves to the left, forcing the car across the oncoming lane and onto the dry dirt on the other side of the road. A cloud of red dust rolls up in the sheriff car's wake as it fishtails and swerves back onto the road.

As soon as we swerve to the left, another car tries to get around us on the right.

URRRR.

Merle jerks the wheel to the right and we screech back across the road, sending this second pursuer off the road into a red-dust spinout.

Although I'm scared shitless, once I get my seat belt on tight

I sort of get fired up. I think how completely bizarre life is. One minute I'm bored off my ass in a bus and the next I'm in a fucking king-sized pickup truck in Texas with a hat-and-boot-wearing whiskey-swilling maniac being chased by the sheriff. It's like a western film *déjà vu* or something. I decide to just play the side-kick and go with it. I grab the bottle of Jack Daniel's from the floorboard and take a swig.

"*Yeehai!* Give 'em hell, Merle!"

For several minutes, as we race along at one hundred miles an hour, like darty scissortails harassing a gliding hawk, the three siren-wailing sheriff cars attempt to get around us, but Merle thwarts each attempt, veering his truck at them, forcing them to red-dust spinouts off the road. Then, amid the howling sirens and our roaring diesel engine, a low, powerful sound:

POP-POP-POP-POP-POP . . .

Out of nowhere a helicopter zooms overhead, its white belly, long skilike skids, and buzzing tail rotor only a few feet above us. Tilted forward, it sails down the road ahead of us.

"What the hell is that?"

" 'At's a fuckin' helicopter."

"I *know* that. But who's in it? More cops?"

"Beats the hell out uh me." Merle slows for an upcoming bend in the road. We make the curve and head down into a small red-walled canyon, a steep-sided trench about three hundred feet wide and fifty feet deep etched into the landscape's hard skin. A narrow two-lane bridge stretches across the gap, and there, parked sideways across the bridge, blocking both lanes, sits the helicopter, white with a big gold stripe along its side, its rotors slowly winding to a stop. The sheriff's gambit is obvious, but by the time Merle sees it, it's too late. Our momentum carries us out onto the bridge, where a small sign reads Brazos River. A uniformed man in a straw cowboy hat hops from the door of the helicopter, and the three cars trailing us pull in behind us, block-ing any escape. Merle rolls to a stop and turns off the engine.

"Goddam."

Two men get out of the car behind us and approach our truck. One wears a law-enforcement uniform: dark brown pants, broad black belt with a pistol in a holster, khaki short-sleeved shirt with a star-shaped badge on his breast, and a straw cowboy hat. He's surprisingly short and fat for a law-enforcement official. The other man is tall and bald and wears a black business suit. He carries a black leather briefcase.

The fat uniformed officer appears at Merle's window. He has a pink flabby face, beady brown eyes, and a frazzled greenish brown cigar stub in the corner of his mouth. He holds his hat down on his head in the wind. Merle rolls down his window.

"Mornin', Merle," he says. His cigar stub wobbles as he talks.

"Mornin', Jack."

"How ya doin' this mornin'?"

"Aw, busy. And you?"

"Aw, just here and there. You know how it is. Hey, Merle, I thank Don's got some papers fer ya to sign. If ya don't mind." He nods toward the backseat. "Ar-ight if we get in?"

Merle sighs, lifts up the front brim of his hat, and rubs his forehead.

"Yeah, go on."

The law-enforcement man pushes my suitcase and backpack across the seat and crawls in the truck. He is followed by his well-dressed companion, who sits by the door behind Merle. He has a bullet-shaped head and clear gray eyes. He closes the door and arranges his briefcase on his lap.

"Good morning, Merle," he says.

Merle glances at him in the rearview mirror.

"Don." Merle gestures to me with his thumb. "This here's my new hand. Innerduce yerself, Harvard. This is Jack Nall, the sheriff of Taylor County, and Don Brock, president uh the bank."

I turn and face them over the seat.

"Hello. Actually my name is Erwin. Erwin Vandeveer."

They nod and shake my hand.

" 'Zat whiskey I smell on yer breath, Erwin?" Sheriff Nall asks.

Oh shit. I try to hide the bottle on the seat beside me with my arm.

"Uh . . . no sir, that is . . . probably my cologne that you smell. It smells a lot like whiskey. It's a northern product. I'm from Boston."

Sheriff Nall stares at me with a puzzled expression and lolls his cigar stub. He turns to Merle.

"Merle, ya got whiskey in here?"

"Yeah, Jack, I do." Merle grabs the bottle and holds it up.

"Lemme see 'at sumbitch," Sheriff Nall says. "I may have to confiscate a sip." He takes the bottle from Merle, plucks the nasty wet stub from his mouth, and drinks a swig. "Yeah, Merle, I thoughtchoo's gonna kill me back 'ere."

"Well," Merle says, "I tried."

Sheriff Nall laughs.

"Ya didn' know I's gonna brayng out the whirlybird, didja?"

"Naw, ya got me there, Jack."

Sheriff Nall drinks another swig.

"Yep, we got so much fuel we gotta burn ever' month. Thought I'd brayng it out fer yer ass. Sort of a salute, don'cha thank?" We stare at the white-and-gold helicopter, its long rotors dangling out over the sides of the bridge, wobbling in the wind.

"Well, Merle," Don Brock says, "I guess you know what this is all about."

"Yer a cocksucker, Don," Merle says.

"Merle, I'm sorry. It's just business."

"Bullshit, you know the price uh oil's gonna come back up. Soon as the A-rabs cut back it'll float back up over eighteen and ever'body'll start drillin' again. Just like they always do, Don. I just need a lil more time. Won't kill y'all to ride my note a few more months. Hell, bump my innerst a point. You'll getchur fuckin' money. Don't worry."

Snap.

Don Brock pops the latch on his briefcase and opens it.

"Sorry, Merle, it's out of my hands. The board voted to call you. There's nothing I can do."

"Board my ass!" Merle says. "You tryin' to tell me Dick and Sonny and Fred voted me down? Who's gonna drill fer 'em if I go under? Huh? Jack Savage over in Midland? Shit, he cain't run 'em big rigs fer less'n ten a foot. They need me, Don. So don'choo bullshit me. I know damn well what's goin' on. You got an offer fer my rigs, didn' ya? One uh them slick deals where ya run 'em through the bank and down to Central America where they're doin' all 'at drillin', ain't it?"

A tense pause fills the cab.

"It's just facts and business, Merle," Don Brock says. "Nothing personal." Don Brock reaches a sheet of paper over Merle's shoulder. "If you'll just sign this, indicating that you're apprised that, because of your accrued back principal, you have failed to meet the terms of your loan, and you now have thirty days from today in which to repay the entire balance, at which time if you fail to do so, the bank is eligible to . . . uh . . . claim your assets."

Merle snatches the paper from Don Brock and reads it. The whiskey bottle sloshes in the backseat as Sheriff Nall has another drink. Merle looks up from the paper into the rearview mirror.

"And what if I refuse to sign this piece uh shit?"

Don Brock and Sheriff Nall glance at each other. Sheriff Nall drinks another swig from the bottle.

"Goduhmighty, Merle, I reckon I'll have to take ya in." Sheriff Nall looks at Don. "What's 'at called?"

"Obstruction of procedure," Don Brock says.

"Yeah, obstruction uh procedure. C'mon, Merle, it's all gonna work out. Hell, bankruptcy ain't the end uh the world. You'll be able to keep yer truck and yer house and yer land."

Don Brock opens his eyes wide and glares at Sheriff Nall.

"Oh," Sheriff Nall says, "well, maybe not the land and the

house. But hell, Merle, yer a big boy. You'll bounce back, hoss."

Merle turns and stares out over the bridge, down the red-walled canyon. The sun is up now, casting shadows on the walls and sparkling on the skinny string of river along the bottom. He sighs and holds up his hand. Don Brock gives him a pen.

"Yer a lousy mutherfucker, Don," Merle says. He scratches his signature on the paper, turns around, and points his finger at Don Brock. "I'm signin' this sumbitch, but I'm gonna tell ya somethin'. Ya ain't layin' one goddam faynger on my rigs, or my house, or my land. Ya hear me?" He tosses the paper and pen at Don Brock. Don Brock drops them into his briefcase and closes it.

Snap.

He locks his briefcase, opens the door, and steps out. Still holding the whiskey bottle, Sheriff Nall scoots his humpty-dumpty body across the seat to the door. He drinks another swig, then puts the cigar stub back in his mouth and passes the bottle back to me over the seat.

"Here's yer cologne, boy." He winks at me, then pats Merle's shoulder. "Cheer up, Merle. You'll bounce back."

"I ain't done yet, Jack! I got thirty days, you ass-kissin' sonofabitch."

Sheriff Nall squeezes Merle's shoulder.

" 'Ere ya go, Merle. 'At's the spirit."

"Get out uh my fuckin' truck, Jack!"

"Ar-ight, Merle." Sheriff Nall hops out of the truck. Hand on his head to hold his cowboy hat down against the wind, he leans his fat head back in and smiles. "Good seein' ya, Merle." He looks at me and nods. "And nice meetin' you. Y'all have a good day now. Drive careful."

A WHITE CRUSHED-ROCK ROAD LEADS FROM A BATTERED
mailbox into the ranch—four hundred acres of golden windswept
grassland. Once a cultivated spread that produced wheat and cotton, Merle has, as he puts it, "let the place go apeshit," allowing
the tall dry prairie grass to grow wild. In the middle of this golden
sea of grass rises a two-story white-rock and brown-trim house
with a tall white-rock chimney and three dormer windows along
its roof. A border of mown brown grass surrounds the house, and
in the front yard two small leafless trees bracket the walk to the
front door.

"See my pecans?" Merle stomps to a skidding halt and he
points to the pair of bare trees wobbling in the wind. They're
about ten feet tall.

"Yes."

"Perty lil sumbitches, ain't they?"

I grin. I love to hear Merle's dialect. And the more Jack Daniel's I drink, the more I warm to it.

"Goddam hell yeah. Damn things are beautiful, Merle." I hic-
cup and look at his trees. Merle swigs the bottle, then nudges my
arm with it.

"Here ya go, son."

Although I'm already wasted, I take the bottle and drink. Hey,
this is my job.

After our adventure with the sheriff and the banker, Merle decided that rather than working a tour (pronounced *tau-er*), or shift, on one of his drilling rigs today, I could best serve Luskey Drilling, Inc. by continuing my supporting role as his alcoholic sidekick. So rather than drive out to a rig, for several hours now we have cruised the flat, windblown outskirts of Abilene, drinking from the bottle of Jack Daniel's. But after dozens of screaming, dash-pounding condemnations of the banking industry and violent promises that he will lose "not one goddam bolt" of his rigs, my new employer seems to be winding down. He hiccups and gazes at his two tiny trees.

"Yep, nothin' like a pecan tree. I planted 'em lil sumbitches one Sunday mornin' with my own hands. And I tell ya what, Harvard. I plan on sittin' out 'ere in the shade scratchin' an ol' man's ass when they're a hunerd feet tall."

"Well, Merle, I hope he's a good friend of yours." This is meant to be a joke, but Merle construes it philosophically.

"Me too, Harvard. Me too."

RAAAWWW.

He slams down the accelerator. Tires spinning on the white crushed-rock road, we sling in a engine-roaring rear-skidding arc into his driveway. We come to a haphazard stop, parked diagonally in the driveway between an old baby blue pickup and the open double-door garage. He grabs the bottle of Jack Daniel's, which now is almost half empty.

"C'mon. Getchur crap."

Carrying my suitcase and backpack, I follow Merle through the garage into a big kitchen with white counters and cupboards, gleaming white digital-display appliances, and a floor of large burnt-orange clay tiles. Beside a sunny window, where you would expect to see a breakfast or dining table, two foldout card tables are set up and pushed together. Scattered across the tables: an assortment of wrenches, screwdrivers, pliers, dirty rags, and a white plastic container of swimming pool chemical treatment. Hat crooked on his head, wobbling on his boots, Merle blinks his eyes and hitches up his pants.

"I don't know aboutchoo, son, but I'm about half lit. We better throttle her back a hair." He sets the bottle of Jack Daniel's on the kitchen counter, then bends down, takes the silver flask from his boot, and sets it beside the bottle. He opens the refrigerator and brings out two tall sixteen-ounce cans of Coors beer. "C'mon. I wancha to tell me about Boston, New Anglin'. I might wanna go up 'ere some day."

I follow him into a huge room, about one hundred feet long and thirty feet wide, with beige carpeting, white stone walls, and a high twelve-foot ceiling. To our left, extending down the entire length of the room, mullioned windows and French doors look out onto an empty swimming pool and the surrounding patio of clay tiles. To our right: a white stone fireplace and a walk-behind bar with a mirror on the back wall and rows of empty gold-bracketed shelves. An incredibly large room, it seems all the bigger for its vacancy. The only furnishings in the entire room are down at the far end: a long white divan and a small carpenter's workbench.

"God, Merle, this is beautiful. Are you just moving in?"

"Naw, hell no." He strides along before me, a beer in each hand. "Lived here four years nearly. I built this goddam place."

"Then where's your furniture? Or do you just have a minimalist streak in you?"

"Naw, I got an ex-wife."

"What do you mean?"

"She took the fuckin' furniture, 'at's what I mean. Damn near got the whole house."

"Oh."

As we arrive at the far end of the room, Merle sets one of the beers on the carpenter's workbench, which appears to serve as his coffee table.

" 'Ere's yer beer," he says. He takes off his cowboy hat. His thick jet-black hair is oiled and combed back off his forehead like Elvis's. He arranges his hat upside-down on the carpenter's bench and falls back onto the divan. He cracks open his beer and sips it. He points to my beer. "Don't fergetchur beer."

"I won't. Thanks." I walk over by the window to the back patio, set down my suitcase and backpack, and look out at the flat horizon. For miles and miles beyond Merle's spread of dry grass, nothing but barren red-soil plowed fields. Not a single tree or speck of green anywhere. On the patio by the empty swimming pool, wedged in the rungs of the chrome pool ladder, a tumble-weed wobbles in the wind. "Why don't you have any water in your pool, Merle?"

The wind gusts and nudges against the window.

"Merle?" I turn around. Head slumped back, eyes closed, mouth open, he sucks a crackling snore.

Hkkkkkkkk.

Å Å Å

With Merle in a snoring stupor, I have *carte blanche* to snoop. I crack open my beer, take a swig, and begin with his boots. I've been checking them out all morning, especially after Jack Daniel's got on board. I've seen lots of cowboy boots in stores in Boston and New York, but I'm pretty sure they were knockoffs. These babies definitely look authentic. They're made of blond leather and they're fucking gigantic. They have tall three-inch heels, long pointed toes, and across their tops and up their sides, swirls of elaborately patterned red and dark brown stitching. I kneel down and run my hand along their smooth tops and press their hard toes. Yes sir, these are the real McDeal.

I stand and look around the den, but literally, there's nothing to snoop, only the carpenter's workbench and the divan where Merle sits, head back, snoring. I go into the foyer.

Sunlight pours through leaded-glass windows around the front door onto the floor, which, like the kitchen and patio, consists of large square Mexican-*hacienda*-style tiles. Not a stick of furniture here, either—just a bare length of gold chain intertwined with severed electrical wiring dangling from the ceiling. I guess light fixtures were included among the ex-wife's spoils. To my right, a long dim hallway. To my left, a beige carpeted stairway with a large-spindled banister of dark wood. I go down the hall to a shadowy doorway.

Aha. Merle's study, complete with a big L-shaped oak desk and a high-backed executive chair. On the desk, a telephone, some papers, and a picture frame. I examine the papers. They're letters from companies with names like Knight Operating, High Plains Petroleum, and Lone Star Oil. They describe wells the companies plan to drill, with information such as depth and location, and request that Merle submit a bid to drill them.

I turn to the photograph at the corner of the desk. It's a black-and-white photograph of a young man with a boy astride his shoulders. From the thick shock of black hair across his forehead, thin nose, and dimpled chin, the young man is obviously Merle, and the boy, a smiling burr-headed kid about three or four years old, must be his son.

As Merle continues to saw major wood, I venture upstairs where I find a long carpeted hallway and three bedrooms. The two smaller rooms are completely vacant, no furniture in the bedrooms, no towels, shower curtains, or accessories of any kind in the baths.

In the master bedroom a plain king-sized bed is arranged against the wall, with two pillows, an ivory sheet, and a brown blanket wadded into a tangle on it. Along the wall by the bed, a big pile of clothes. Opposite the bed a small card table stands against the wall. On it: a gray felt cowboy hat, a pile of assorted coins, several leather belts. Beneath it: two pairs of neatly polished cowboy boots, one black, one gray. I squat down and examine them. The black pair is smooth with white stitching across the toes. The gray pair has no stitching, but is made of an unusual pocked material. Both have tall heels and long pointed toes. I swig my beer and run my hands along them and feel their hide. Suddenly I get a whim. I cock my ear and hear Merle's sucksawing slumber, then I slip off my loafers and pull on the black boots. I look down at my feet and walk back and forth along the foot of the bed. They're way too big for me. My socked feet slide back and forth and side to side. Still, I love how they feel and look. What *is* it about cowboy boots? They're ridiculous—the huge heel and long pointed toe—but they're fucking excellent. They must strike some chord from my childhood. I used to be a maniac about westerns. Swigging my beer and swaggering back and forth across the room, arm out away from my side as though about to draw my gun, I quote some lines from the classics.

I do John Wayne in *True Grit*.

"Fill your hands, you sonofabitch!"

Jack Elam in *Rio Lobo*.

"Don't mind if I shoot, do ya? Makes me feel better."

And Bruce Fischer in *The Outlaw Josey Wales*. I draw my gun and aim it at Josey Wales.

"It's Mr. Chain-Blue Lightnin' hisself. Yeah, the one that everyone's so scared of. . . . Well, Mr. Lightnin', move a muscle, twitch a finger, and I'll splatter yer guts all over the wall. Heh, heh, heh."

I AWAKEN TO A GLOWING RED CIRCLE. HUH? THE <u>SUN</u>? I SIT UP
and rub my eyes. Over the prairie a perfect fluorescent red circle
hangs in a pink horizon. Moving upward in the sky, the pink
blends to purple. I shake my head. Damn. Earlier I lay down here
on the carpet while Merle was snoring and I guess I dozed off.
But I can't believe I crashed all afternoon. Of course I hadn't
really slept since LA.

"Hey there, boy."

I turn from the window. Merle sits on the divan, a glass of
liquor in one hand, my head shots in the other.

"*Hey*. What are you doing?" I hop up and snatch my head
shots from him. "You can't just look through my stuff." I gather
my résumé and old playbills from the carpenter's bench/coffee
table and put them back in my portfolio. Merle sips his drink.

"You done a lot uh actin', huh?"

"A little." I shove my portfolio in my backpack and walk back
to the window. "What *is* this?"

"A swimmin' pool."

"*No*, the sky. All the colors. What's happening?"

"Whadda ya mean? Hell, sun's goin' down." Merle joins me
at the window. The brim of his cowboy hat protrudes about eight
inches from his brow.

"But why is the sun red like that? And for God's sake, man, the sky is pink and purple."

He chuckles.

"What's uh matter? Ain'cha ever seen a West Texas sunset?"

"This is *normal?*"

"Aw, this time uh year it is. Windy and dry around here. Get all 'at dirt kicked up in the air, makes ever'thayng red." He sips his drink, then nods toward the kitchen. "I run to town and bought us some rib eyes. I'm gonna fire up the grill and cook us a steak." He nods toward the kitchen again. "C'mon, I'll fix ya a drank."

I rub my forehead. My brain aches with a hangover from this morning.

"God, Merle, I don't—"

"Aw, bullshit. I'm tired uh drankin' alone. C'mon."

I smile and shake my head. This guy's a maniac.

"Whatever, Merle."

He pats my back.

"Attaboy."

I follow him to the kitchen where he makes me a drink of straight Jack Daniel's on ice.

Apparently impressed by my fascination with the sunset, Merle makes an excellent suggestion and together we carry his divan from the den out through the sliding glass door and set it on the patio facing west, near the lip of his empty swimming pool. The wind has calmed to a breeze. We sit on the divan together, sip his gruesome version of a cocktail, and watch the sun go down. As it sinks lower, it turns impossibly redder. Deep rose red. Then I actually see it go down behind the prairie. In its wake, from above, purple overcomes pink, and in turn is overcome by black.

Then, an even more incredible scene is unveiled. With only the tiny strip of Abilene's lights twinkling on the prairie, and not a hill within miles to obstruct it, the night sky unfurls a huge field of stars. From horizon to horizon to horizon, thousands and thousands of stars. Bright. And near. Some blue, some white, some twinkling red and green. I prop my head back on the divan and stare in awe. I've never actually seen the Milky Way, but there it is! A mysterious looming white shroud. And the constellations, so vivid and obvious: the Big Dipper; Orion, the hunter; Scorpio; the Seven Sisters.

After several trips to the kitchen to refill our drinks, Merle brings out the bottle of Jack Daniel's and the ice tray from the refrigerator and sets them beside the sofa. Then, when the breeze gets too cool, he rolls a portable Bar-B-Q cooker across the patio, situates it in front of the divan, tosses in several large pieces of wood, and douses them with gasoline.

Woosh.

He drops a match on the wood and ignites a roaring yellow flame-whipping fire. Smoke and orange sparks rise to the stars. Warmth envelops the divan.

A couple Jack Daniel's on the rocks later, when the flames burn down, Merle sets a grate over the glowing orange cinders and, with a long pair of tongs, places four thick steaks above the fire. They sizzle, drip, hiss, and fill the air with a sumptuous smell.

I offer to help Merle prepare dinner, but he refuses.

"Aw hell," he says, "ain't nothin' to it."

Soon I see his point. From the kitchen he brings out two thick paper plates, two forks, and two knives. When the steaks are cooked to his satisfaction, he plops two on a paper plate and gives them to me, along with a fork and knife. Dinner is served. Steak. No salad, no potatoes, no salt, no pepper, no napkin. Steak. Two of them. I laugh. In my Jack Daniel's-starfield-campfire reverie, this is perfect fare. Merle nods toward my plate.

"Go on and try a bite. See if it's done right fer ya."

I cut into one of my steaks and eat a bite.

Mmm.

Fat, juicy, tender, warm, smoke-flavored meat.

"Well?" he asks.

"*Goddam*, Merle."

He smiles, then removes the grate from the cooker and places several new logs atop the cinders. As flames rise again and dance in the breeze, we chow. Amid the sawing and chewing, our communication consists mainly of grunts and nods.

After our steak feast, Merle produces several toothpicks from the front pocket of his shirt and gives me one. He leans back, sips his drink, and pokes at his teeth with a toothpick.

"Goddammit, Harvard, tell me about Harvard University. I seen on yer lil ol' paper in 'ere you studied drama in school. What the hell is 'at?"

"Drama?"

"Yeah."

I look at him.

"You're kidding."

Face glowing in the firelight under the brim of his hat, he wobbles his head dramatically and points to himself.

"Goddam, son, I'm an ol' roughneck. Ya know how much schoolin' I got?"

"No."

"*Sixth* grade. I mean it. When I's a kid 'at's all ya had to do. Hell, my daddy put me to work on a rig the day I got out uh sixth grade. And 'at's all I ever done till I's about thirty-five and put together my own outfit. But still 'at's all I do, *drill*. I don't know a damn thayng about nothin' else."

"Okay. Well, let's see. Drama. Drama is the art of portraying a story through characters. Live on stage, it's called theater, and on film it's, you know, movies."

He pokes his teeth with his toothpick and sucks his teeth.

"Uh-huh. And 'at's whatchoo do fer a livin'?"

"No, not really."

"Whadda ya mean, *not really?*"

"I mean I studied dramatic arts in school, and acting is what I love to do, but I've never actually been paid very much for it."

"But that's yer dream, ain't it? Bein' in the movies."

"Well, it *was*, but—"

He frowns.

"Aw, *was* my ass. Hell, ya ain't but twenty-one. Yer just gettin' started." He sucks his teeth and points his toothpick at me. "Lemme tell ya somethin,' son. Dreams ain't easy. Ya gotta *fight*. Ya cain't just lay down dead and wait fer some sumbitch to waltz up and hand ya yer dream."

I shrug.

"Maybe so. But whatever I do, it won't be film. I—"

"Aw bullshit. Quit cryin' in yer towel and tell me what happened out 'ere in California. Ya didn' hang no job at all?"

"No, I didn't."

"Well, what happened?"

I cringe at the idea of delving into my Hollywood nightmare.

"Man, it's a long story. You don't want to hear it, trust me."

"Aw goduhmighty, what's uh matter? Ya thank yer the only sumbitch 'at ever took an ass whuppin'? C'mon, spill the beans, boy."

I sigh. I was hoping to repress the whole ordeal, but I don't guess it's any big deal to tell Merle. After all, who's he going to tell? I gulp my drink, kick back, and look up at the stars.

"Okay. Last summer I ran into a friend, Jev Aaronson. He was a film major at the Museum School and I played in a couple of his films. Apparently his uncle is some big exec in New York with one of MGM's distribution companies, and right after he graduated, Jev got on with MGM out in LA as a production assistant. But I hadn't seen him in over a year when I ran into him at the Brattle in Cambridge and he told me now he was doing cinematography for Spielberg at DreamWorks. I couldn't fucking believe it. *Spielberg*." I look at Merle. He sips his drink and stares at me blankly in the fire glow. "You know. Steven Spielberg. *E.T. The Color Purple. Schindler's List.*"

He just stares at me.

"Whatever. Anyway, Jev Aaronson was in town and he asked me what I was doing. I said, Nothing. I'd just graduated and I was working the box office at Cambridge Community and waiting to play Iago in a touring *Othello*, but rehearsals weren't until September. So he said Spielberg's about to start shooting his sequel to *Jurassic Park* and why don't I come out to LA? He said he was in pretty tight with *Steve* and he could probably get me a walk-on, maybe even a line, and that if I got the line, I automatically could get a union card and *bam*, I'm off to the races. He gave me his phone number and address and said I could stay with him until I start pulling down some cash, et cetera.

"Well, about a week later I got into a big fight with my dad—he found out about Iago and the touring *Othello*, which didn't strike him as a real job—so I said fuck it. I packed up that afternoon, cashed in the three-hundred-buck savings bond my grandmother gave me for graduation, and flew standby to LA.

"I called Jev when I got there, but he didn't answer. His machine didn't even pick up. I took the bus to his condo complex in Glendale, but I couldn't get past the security gate, so I hung around at the Denny's restaurant down the street all night long and kept calling him. He never answered.

"Next morning I caught the bus to Hollywood. Lugging my suitcase and backpack everywhere and trying to find the right bus, with literally my last dime I finally got to the DreamWorks studio up in Universal City. The security man, a huge black guy, stopped me at the gate. Unless your name's on the appointments list, you don't get in. But the security man called in for me and asked about Jev. Jev wasn't there, he said. Jev was in Peru scouting locations. And nobody knew how long he'd be there. At least two months, maybe more."

"Aw, hell," Merle says.

"Yeah. Okay, so I thought, Well, what the hell. I'll just dig in and get to work and see what I can do until my ace in the hole comes back from Peru. So I got a job waiting tables at this restaurant called the Cyber Cafe on Wilshire. And I took a room at this flea-hole dump in East Hollywood called the Viva Sol. It was bad, man, but I needed money for head shots and a résumé and clothes for interviews, so it was all I could afford. You know?"

Merle nods.

"Gotta cutchur suit to fitchur cloth."

"Exactly. Well, after a few weeks I got my portfolio together and started calling on agents, but most wouldn't even see me, let alone give me a reading. There's a majorly fucked-up catch-twenty-two in Hollywood—to get a gig you need a union card, but to get a card you have to have a gig. I'm serious. It's the exact same story over and over again. If you don't have a card, see ya. If you even try to *talk* to a casting director and you don't have a card, they get pissed off. And agents won't have anything to do with you, either. Sure, their assistants will schmooze you and take your portfolio, then they just bury it somewhere.

"Out of about forty agents I cold called, I got a reading with one. *One.* This lady named Jane Black. She specializes in kids and TV, but she did at one time represent Tom Cruise, back before he broke out big. Anyway, Jane Black gave me a script and told me to come back for a reading in a week. It was a docudrama based on Susan Smith, that moron in South Carolina who rolled her car into the lake and drowned her kids. It was about to be cast for a Fox-TV production, and Jane thought I had a shot at the role of the husband. I practiced night and day for my reading, then I went in and read. Just the year before I had played Brick in *Cat on a Hot Tin Roof*, so I was gung ho about my southern delivery. I had a gut feeling this was going to be my break, and sure enough, about halfway through my read, Jane Black cut me off.

" 'That's enough,' she said, and she smiled.

"I smiled back.

" 'So you like it?' I said.

"She stood up, took my script away, and ushered me to the door.

" 'Go back to the east coast, Erwin,' she said. 'You belong on Broadway.'

" 'But I don't want to do stage,' I said. 'I want to do film.'

" 'You're too good for film,' she said.

" 'Too *good?*' I said. 'What the hell are you talking about?' But she just shoved me out of her office and slammed the door."

"Well I'll be goddam," Merle says.

"Yeah. No kidding. Well, after about three months of that kind of shit, I finally realized if you don't have some kind of inside angle, there's no way you're going to get an agent. So I formulated a new attack. I researched the hot hangouts and started trolling them. I decided if I could meet an agent on a social level and get to know him—or her—maybe I'd have a shot at breaking in professionally.

"Well, *the* place, at the time, was this superchic Southwestern restaurant/bar in Brentwood called Anchos. According to everyone, that's where the hot agents and big studio people were schmoozing. So I started hanging out at Anchos.

"My second night there I noticed this skinny older chick scamming on me. I was standing at the bar and she was sitting behind me in one of the booths, but she was staring *right* at me in the mirror behind the bar. She had shoulder-length blond hair and sort of a pale moonface, and she was wearing a sleeveless copper satiny cocktail dress. It was weird, man. She just kept staring *right* at me in the mirror from her booth. This went on about thirty minutes, then she got up and came walking along the bar. I turned around and said, 'Hi,' just as she walked by. She stopped and smiled and I introduced myself.

" 'Pleasure to meet you, Erwin,' she said in a strong English accent. 'I'm Tina.' She was about forty and she was pretty plain facewise, but she had a nice body, thin and in shape. And whoever she was, she was obviously flush. She had a magnum rock on her wedding ring, with a bunch of emeralds around it. She set her empty glass on the bar beside me, and I knew if I wanted to scam on her I should offer to buy her a drink. But I didn't know who she was, and I didn't want to burn my only ten bucks on some random married chick. You know?"

"Hell no. Yer waitin' fer an agent."

"Right. And besides, she sort of gave me the creeps. It was like she was in heat or on dope or something. She just kept staring at me with this moony do-me look.

"Anyway, we chatted a little bit, then she said, 'So, Erwin' "— I characterize her English accent for Merle—" 'what do you do?'

" 'I'm an actor,' I said.

She sort of smirked and nodded.

" 'I thought as much,' she said.

" 'How'd you know?" I said.

"She brushed her hair back and shrugged.

" 'My husband's an agent,' she said. 'All our friends are actors.'

" 'Oh really?' I said. 'Who's your husband?'

" 'Al Silverman,' she said. Holy shit. My head almost fell off and rolled across the bar. Al Silverman is like the biggest of the big, Merle. He was a kingpin at William Morris, then he split off on his own and took all his heavy hitters with him. Stallone, Costner, Madonna. Jesus, you know? So 'Hey,' I said, 'can I buy you a drink?'

"She smiled.

" 'Sure, love,' she said.

"So we stood there, drinking and chatting by the bar, and I swear to God, Merle, she was all over me. After like ten minutes she finished her drink and set it on the bar.

" 'C'mon Erwin,' she said, 'let's go somewhere less stuffy, shall we?'

" 'All right,' I said, 'why not?' "

"Aw, goddam," Merle says. "Here we go." He pours himself another drink, then reaches over and fills my glass.

"C'mon, man. What was I going to do? Say no to Al Silverman's wife? Jesus Christ.

"So anyway, the maître d' gave Tina her purse and put this gorgeous long white leather coat on her. Then the parking valet brought her ivory Mercedes around and we hopped in. Now *this* was LA, man. Fuck East Hollywood. We got on the Santa Monica Freeway, cruised out with the top down onto the Pacific Coast Highway, and up along the ocean to Malibu. Tina swung onto a dark road curving up through a canyon, then onto another little dark road through the eucalyptus trees, except it turned out this wasn't actually a road . . . this was her fucking *driveway*, man. The trees opened onto this massive lawn and beautifully landscaped mansion with spotlights shining from the ground cover up across its rock walls and dark wooden eaves.

"So we went in the house into this beautiful rock-walled entry hall with all these magnificent modern abstract paintings everywhere.

" 'C'mon,' Tina said, 'I'll fix us a toddy.' She walked to a stairway leading down to the back of the house, but I just stood there. I was starting to get a little edgy."

"Crap fire," Merle says, "I reckon. Ol' gal's comin' on stronger'n horse mustard."

"Yeah. Right. I mean staring at me lewdly at the bar was one thing, but bringing me straight to her house within a half hour? C'mon. So anyway, she stopped at the stairs and looked at me.

" 'Don't be shy,' she said.

" 'Uh . . . well,' I said, 'is your husband here?'

" 'God no,' she said. 'He's in Argentina. C'mon, love. I won't bite.'

"Well, I thought about it and decided, What the hell. It all seemed a little eerie, but at least it was better than getting thrown out of agents' offices. So I followed her down the stairs to a dark room with floor-to-ceiling windows looking out onto the moonlit Pacific. She told me to get comfortable, then she put some old Rolling Stones on the stereo and made herself a drink and opened me a Heineken. I sat down on a big sofa and she sat beside me and kicked her shoes under the coffee table.

" 'So,' I said, 'what's Al doing down in Argentina?'

"She said she wasn't sure, exactly, that she missed his call and he left a message and said he was on a plane en route from New York to Buenos Aires.

" 'I'm sure fucking Madonna is pissing about something,' she said.

" 'Oh,' I said. 'So Madonna's in Buenos Aires?'

" 'Yes,' she said. 'They started shooting *Evita* last week, and I'm sure by now everyone on location would like to slit her fucking throat. She's bloody impossible.'

" 'Oh,' I said.

"Well, then she opened this little wooden box on the coffee table and brings out a plastic bag full of marijuana."

"Aw, goddam," Merle says. "Ol' gal *was* on dope, huh?"

"Evidently. Anyway, she pulled a joint out of this bag and fired it up. And no kidding, Merle, I swear, I'm not a druggie at all, but hey, I didn't want to hang back from forging a friendship with Tina, then down the line with her husband. So I smoked."

"Aw, fer cryin' out loud, son." Merle swigs his drink. "Drank ya some whiskey, but stay off 'at damn dope, ya hear me?"

"Yes. But listen, man, I swear to God, I don't know what that shit was, but it was strong. I just remember smoking that damn joint, and the Stones playing 'Midnight Rambler,' then everything got totally surreal. It was like I was weightless or something."

"Hell, you were higher'n a goddam kite, I reckon."

"Exactly. Anyway, apparently the pot was the final preparation

Tina needed. After we finished the joint, she took my beer from my hand, pulled up her dress, and swung her leg across me and straddled my lap."

Merle pushes up his hat and frowns.

"Aw hell. Here she comes."

"Yeah. Really. Anyway, she propped her arms on my shoulders and kissed me, which completely freaked me out. So I pushed her away.

" 'What's the matter, love?' she said.

"I told her it was just too much. What about her husband?

" 'Oh, please,' she said. 'He doesn't even know I fucking exist. Anyway, he fucks everyone in town, so . . . there you have it.'

" 'Okay,' I said, 'but what about me, you know? I've got a professional reputation to think about.'

" 'Oh, *please*,' she said. Then she asked me how long I'd been in Hollywood and if I had an agent. I told her no, not yet. 'Of course not,' she said. 'So let's just not bullshit one another, okay?' She put her finger in her drink, swirled it around, and poked it in my mouth. 'Erwin,' she said, 'let me give you a little primer in Hollywood. This town is a game, and one of the tricks of the game is getting laid. It's the great privilege of those on the inside, and it's the key for those on the outside. It's always been that way, Erwin, and it always will be that way. So, my husband's an agent and I personally know dozens of other agents, many of whom I'm sure, upon my introduction, would take you on. So, love, you want gigs, I want to get laid. Now can we do business or not?' "

"Goddam," Merle says. "Ol' gal dudn' beat around the bush, does she?"

"No. Not at all. So I just sat there staring at her, and in my California-doped brain, I decided, Well, if this is the way to the studio, then so what, here we go.

" 'Tina,' I said, 'I'm going to fuck your brains out.'

"She sipped her drink, set it back on the table, then put her arms around my neck.

" 'I hope so, love,' she said. 'I truly hope so.' "

"Goddam," Merle says.

"Yeah. So we did it. And I swear, Merle, it was like she could *not* get enough. As soon as we'd finish doing it, I'd lie back on the sofa breathing like an animal, and she'd start diddling me with her big toe, trying to fire me up for another round."

"Goduhmighty," Merle says. "She's hornier'n a sprayng hare."

I laugh.

"Yes. Anyway, I don't know how long it went on, about an hour I guess, but on about our third go-around, there we were on the sofa, banging away in the buff, when all of a sudden the fucking lights come on."

"Aw, hell."

"Yeah. So I looked up and this short gray-haired broad-shouldered guy in a black jogging suit was standing on the stairs.

" 'Goddammit, Tina!' he yelled.

"Tina looked at him.

" 'Oh, hi love,' she said. 'Back so soon?' Then she started dying laughing. I pulled away and grabbed my underwear and pants. Tina rolled over on her back, pulled her knees up to her chest, and kicked her legs. 'Erwin,' she said, 'meet my husband. Honey, this is Erwin. He needs an agent.' Then she started really laughing."

"Goduhmighty. Crazy bitch."

"Yeah. So Al Silverman turned around and went back up the stairs, and I put on my pants, grabbed my socks, shoes, shirt, and sweater, and ran. But Al Silverman met me halfway up the stairs with a big black pistol and pointed the damn thing right at my face.

" 'You little prick!' he yelled. 'I'm gonna blow your goddam head off, drag you down to the beach, and feed you to the fucking fishes! Do you know who I am? Nobody fucks with me! You hear me? Nobody!'

"Man, I freaked out and started crying and begging, but he

wouldn't let me go. He backed me all the way down the stairs, pointing the gun at my face and yelling. Then Tina hopped over the back of the sofa completely naked, grabbed his arm, and hoisted the gun up in the air.

" 'Just go, Erwin,' she said. 'He won't shoot. The bloody thing's not even loaded.'

"He jerked away from her and *BOOM*, the goddam thing went off and white ceiling chunks fell all over us. She screamed and slapped him and grabbed the gun again, and I dropped my clothes and ran, man. I went back through the kitchen, found a door, and ran out onto this wooden deck. I didn't see any stairs, but right out past the rail was the top of a big eucalyptus tree. I just stepped up on the rail and jumped. I caught the branch I was aiming at, but the sonofabitch snapped and I fell down through the whole damn tree. I hit the ground and took off scrambling down the cliff through the scrubby thickets. Above me I heard Al Silverman out on the deck.

" 'You better run, you little prick!' he yelled. Then *BOOM*, *BOOM*, he cracked off another couple rounds, but I just kept running."

"Well I'll be go-to-hell," Merle says.

"Yeah, but that's not all." I gulp my drink down to the ice. Merle pours us both another splash.

"Okay, so there I was barefoot and naked from the waist up, my stomach and chest scraped and bleeding from falling through the tree. I knew I was too grisly a sight to walk or hitchhike home at night, so I crawled under the deck of a house right above Highway One in Malibu and sat there all fucking night.

"The next morning at dawn I started walking home along the highway, and it wasn't ten minutes until this cop pulled up behind me. I told him the whole story and gave him my ID, and he was cool and gave me a ride to the Viva Sol. But when I got there my goddam door was blocked by this padlocked iron bar. I knew I was sort of behind on my rent, but I had to buy more head shots and a sweater to troll Anchos. You know? So I went to the office and talked to the manager, this old Arabian guy, Ahkman. I asked him what the hell and he said"—I do the Arabian accent for Merle—" 'You pay me last two weeks, you get in.'

" 'What about my stuff?' I said. 'I have to go to work. I need my stuff.'

" 'You pay me last two weeks,' he said, 'you get stuff.'

" 'Fuck you, man,' I said.

" 'Okay, fuck you, too,' he said.

"So then, barefoot and bare from the waist up, my stomach all pink and scabby, I slammed out of Ahkman's office, walked out, and sat on the curb. It was a beautiful LA morning, clear and sunny with a cool breeze. And as I sat there, watching people in cars gawk at me, I got this weird feeling. It was like, Okay, Vandy, you've paid your dues, man. You've been through the goddam gauntlet. *Now* you get your break. I hadn't called DreamWorks and asked about Jev Aaronson in a couple of weeks, and I just had this gut feeling he was back in town. I found a quarter in my pocket and walked down to the pay phone at the Quik-Sak.

"The DreamWorks operator put me through to some smart-ass unit director. I asked if Jev was back in town, and he said, 'I'm sorry, Mr. Aaronson is no longer with us.'

" 'What do you mean?' I said. 'What happened?'

"He just said 'Sorry' and started to hang up, but I said, 'Look, man, please don't hang up. I came all the way out here from Boston on a tip from Jev. And I've been getting fucked over for four months now, waiting for him to get back from Peru. My whole life depends on this. Please, just talk to me for one minute. What happened to Jev?'

"There was a long pause.

" 'Jev ran over Mr. Spielberg,' he said.

" 'Ran over him?' I said. 'What do you mean?'

"He said, 'I mean Jev was supposed to back Mr. Spielberg's

Range Rover up the hill out of the location and go set a light meter, but he fucked up and went forward and ran over the whole unit camp, including Mr. Spielberg.'

" 'Holy shit,' I said. 'Well, where's Jev now?'

" 'He's in Toronto,' he said.

" '*Toronto?*' I said. 'What's he doing there?'

" 'He got a gig in Claymation,' he said.

" 'Claymation?' I said. 'Ah, fuck.' And I just hung up.

"Man. That was it. I just collapsed against the ice freezer outside the Quik-Sak and sat there for about an hour, then finally I said fuck it. I stood up and called Dad collect at his office on campus. Of course he lectured me for about a half hour and made me eat massive crow, but that afternoon he wired four hundred bucks so I could settle my debt at the Viva, get my stuff, and buy a bus ticket home.

"So. There you have it." I guzzle the rest of my drink and wipe my mouth with my hand. "The end."

Face glowing orange in the firelight, Merle stares at me for several long seconds.

"Well goduhmighty. 'At's a hell of a story, Harvard."

"Yeah. Check it out." I pull my shirt up and show him the tree-scrape scabs across my stomach. He looks at my stomach, sips his drink, and frowns.

"Aw hell, I've had worse places on my eye."

"Oh. All right. Whatever." I lower my shirt back down. He sucks his teeth and throws his toothpick in the fire.

"Well, it ain't no secret where ya fucked up, is it?"

"What do you mean?"

"Hell, gettin' mixed up with 'at Tina gal." He pushes up the front brim of his hat and points at me. "Them women ain't nothin' but heartache, boy."

I nod.

"Yeah, she tooled me around. No doubt. But I was probably

toast anyway, without Jev in my corner." I sling the ice from my glass into the dark empty swimming pool.

"Aw, don't take it too hard. You'll do better next time around."

"What do you mean *next time around?*"

"I mean next time ya go out 'ere and give 'em hell."

"Are you crazy? Screw Hollywood. And screw film work, too. I wouldn't—"

"Hey." He points his finger at me. "Don't piss on yer dream, son. You'll—"

"Look, Merle, you—"

"No, *you* look." He leans over, lays his hand on my shoulder, and squeezes. "I like you, son. Now my boy, God bless his ass, I love him, but he ain't worth a shit. Butchoo now, you done gone to college and ever'thayng, and by God, you just listen to me cuz I'm gonna tell ya somethin'." He squeezes my shoulder harder. "I may not be the smartest sumbitch 'at ever pulled on a pair uh boots, but I know a thayng or two about drillin' a hole, and I know a thayng or two about fightin' fer a dream. I come up from a short-pay roughneck all the way to ownin' six uh my own rigs. *Six*, boy. Five National doubles and a Connie-Em triple. 'At's what I always wanted, ownin' my own rigs, and by God I got 'em." He takes an ice-clinking sip of Jack Daniel's. "Now you listen here. If it's in yer blood to be in the movies—and ain't nobody can answer 'at butchoo—then you got a problem, boy. If ya ever wanna be happy in this life, if ya ever wanna be worth yer boots and be able to look yerself in the mirror and say, 'Kiss my ass,' then yer gonna have to fight, son. Yer gonna have to fight like a goddam Mexican bull. Cuz I tell ya, dreams don't come easy. I don't care what it is—bein' in the movies, ownin' a drillin' outfit, or bein' governor uh Texas—*dreams don't come easy.* Yer gonna get kicked in the head and shot in the ass a hunerd times, butcha gotta just stand right back up, swalluh yer teeth, and keep swangin'. Cuz 'ere ain't no other options, see? If ya just give up and try to ignore it and go on, you'll be the sourest sumbitch 'at ever rolled out uh bed and pulled on a pair uh boots."

I bust up laughing. I know it's rude, but I can't help it. The color of his language. God, my kingdom for a tape recorder. Not to mention the irony—being counseled on matters of career by a sixth-grade-educated alcoholic on the verge of bankruptcy with hardly a stick of furniture in his house.

"What the hell's funny?" he says.

"I'm sorry, man. It's just the way you describe things, your way of talking, it's wonderful."

"Well, I ain't meanin' to be funny. Dreams is serious, son."

I nod.

"Okay. I'll remember that."

"And by God, I know I don't have to tell ya again, 'specially after what happened to ya, but I'm gonna tell ya anyhow—*look out fer women, boy.*" He squints his eyes. "They're crazier'n a shithouse mouse and they got but one thayng on their mind—to hurtchurass. I guarantee. I've had 'at split-tail drag me through the courthouse enough times till I finally learned."

I crack up again.

"Okay, Merle. I'll remember that, too."

"Ar-ight. I'll get down off my soapbox now. But I been to the barn and back a few times, and I just figgered I'd pass a lil somethin' along." He leans back and props his feet, one boot atop the other, along the side rail of the Bar-B-Q cooker. Jack Daniel's flowing through my brain, I stare at his big tan boots in the firelight.

"Merle."

"Yep."

"I just have to tell you. Your boots are fucking fabulous."

"Ya like 'em, huh." He lifts a boot up close beside the fire and stares at it. "These ain't nothin' fancy."

"Shit, I think they are. The damn things are massive. That

long toe. And I never realized how tall the heels are on real cowboy boots."

"Hell yeah, boy, ya gotta be able to dig in and get a bite in yer stirrups."

I laugh. He looks down at my loafers and frowns.

"Yep, ya arta get rid uh them goddam thayngs. Hell, 'fore ya leave Abilene you'll have to getcha a good pair uh boots."

I GULP COLD COFFEE AND RUMBLE ALONG WHAT MUST BE THE straightest, flattest road in the world, that between Tuxedo and Sagerton, Texas. The sun, a fluorescent orange ball, rises over an endless plain of arid land. Everywhere, horizon to horizon to horizon, flat red-dirt farm fields. Not a wisp of green anywhere. But along the road shreds of white fluff flutter on the barbed-wire fence—remnants, I guess, of last year's cotton crop. The wind, its fury renewed with sunrise, thrashes the dry grass along the road and drives tumbleweeds across the fields, bounding and rolling until they hit the fences, where they snag in bunches. Scattered here and there across the horizon, big black grasshopper-looking oil-well pumps rock up and down, up and down. . . .

The wind blasts the truck and tries to nudge me off the road, so I drive very slowly, which is fine with me because I'm sort of apprehensive about getting to the rig anyway. I thought for sure Merle would introduce me to my fellow workers and orient me to my new job, but eager to get to the Fort Worth/Dallas area this morning and call upon banks for a loan to refinance his rigs, he has saddled me with Ol' Blue, his standby truck, and sent me out to my first day of roughnecking alone. Ol' Blue's 1979 baby blue body is battered with rusty dents, its motor screeches and coughs white smoke, its cab reeks of dust and grease, and you have to touch two wires under the steering column to start it, but it runs. Barely.

KKKKKKKK.

Static electricity rips through the truck. I jump and spill coffee across the front of my overalls. Then Merle's voice blares at the volume level of a jet airplane:

"BREAK ONE-FOUR, HARVARD. YA GOTCHUR EARS ON?"

I look down at the old dusty citizens-band radio hanging under the dash. The knobs are all broken off and the hand mike lies on the floorboard at the end of a tangled black cord.

KKKKKKKK.

Its speaker, turned to an earsplitting volume, erupts again.

"BREAK ONE-FOUR, HARVARD. THIS IS MERLE. YA GOTCHUR EARS ON, BOY?"

I grab the hand mike, hold it to my mouth, and push the button.

"Uh . . . this is Harvard."

KKKKKKKK.

"TEN-FOUR, HARVARD. WHAT'S YER TWENNY?"

"Uh . . . I beg your pardon."

KKKKKKKK.

"WHAT'S YER TWENNY, SON?"

"My twenty? I don't understand."

KKKKKKKK.

"WHERE ARE YA?"

"Oh. I just went past the cotton gin and railroad tracks about five minutes ago."

KKKKKKKK.

"SHIT, BOY. DRIVIN' AWFUL SLOW, AIN'CHA?"

"It's windy. I'm afraid I'll get blown off the road."

KKKKKKKK.

"AW, 'AT'S AR-IGHT. THEY'RE JUST DRILLIN' OFF UP

'ERE. I'S JUST CHECKIN' ON YA. I'M ON MY WAY OUT RIGHT NOW. I'LL EITHER SEE YA TONIGHT OR TOMORROW, DEPENDIN' ON HOW LONG IT TAKES ME TO RAISE THIS MONEY."

"Okay."

KKKKKKKK.

"MIGHTY FINE. THIS IS MERLE. WE GONE, BYE-BYE."

I keep driving and driving and after an hour or so, just when I'm sure I'm lost, on the horizon, fuzzy with blowing dust, I see a needle, just a tiny dark needle in the distance, and yet it's the only thing of any vertical significance in this entire dust-blown tabletop world. I keep driving. Slowly the needle grows taller and taller and taller, until off to my right, several hundred yards from the highway, a drilling rig towers from the barren landscape like some kind of alien monument. I slow at a gap in the fence, marked by red ribbons fluttering sideways from fence posts, and turn into the field.

God Almighty.

Even in this scene of immense horizons, it's an awesome sight, the derrick rising high and stalwart with its crisscross of iron girders. It's painted like its idle cohorts in the equipment yard—red at the very top, white along the derrick, red on the operating house and ground structure, and stenciled across the operating house wall, in giant white letters, Luskey Drilling, Inc. The rig floor, about sixty feet long and thirty feet wide, stands on struts and braces about twenty-five feet off the ground. The derrick towers from one end of the floor. Right beside it is the operating house, a big steel-walled boxlike room. A huge red spool is mounted in the middle of the rig platform. From this spool a cable feeds up diagonally to the top of the derrick. There, at the top of the derrick, through a system of pulleys, this one cable becomes many cables that dangle down the derrick and feed into a big yellow pulley-block device with a hook on its bottom. The hook of this dangling block is, in turn, connected to a length of pipe that runs down through the rig floor and into, apparently, the earth. Behind the drum spool on the rig floor is a bank of three gigantic red engines. Each spews a black string of sideways windswept smoke from its flapper-lidded exhaust stack. As I approach from across the field, bouncing along the rutted path, the engines' rumble rises.

Raaawww . . .

I park back about fifty yards from the rig, grab my gloves, put on my hard hat, and open the door.

RAAAWWW . . .

The roaring engines grow louder. As I step out into the wind, three men emerge from the operating house, each wearing Luskey Drilling attire—red hard hats and red one-piece overall uniforms. However, whereas my overalls have long sleeves, theirs are sleeveless from the shoulder down. All three of them are smoking cigarettes. They stand up on the rig floor and look down at me, then file down a metal stairway.

Amid the engines' roar, we meet on the dusty ground about twenty yards from the rig. They stop, stand in a line, and stare, each with a cigarette in his mouth. I now see that all of them have torn the sleeves off their uniforms at the shoulders, revealing their round-muscled shoulders and biceps. I smile.

"Hi. My name's Erwin Vandeveer. Merle—"

"DO WHAT?" The one in the middle takes the cigarette from his mouth, cups his hand behind his ear, and steps forward. He's a baby-faced guy, about my age, with big brown eyes and healthy pink cheeks. He's not much taller than me, but his shoulders, biceps, and forearms are huge with muscles. On his right arm, extending from his shoulder to just above his elbow, he has a green tattoo. It looks like some kind of big stalking cat framed by a rectangle of hearts. "YOU A NEW HAND?" He yells to be heard above the engines. I nod and yell back.

"YES."

He nods and smiles.

"I'M SHAY TATUM."

"I'M ERWIN VANDEVEER."

"*EARL?*"

"ER-WIN."

He switches his cigarette to his left hand and holds out his right to shake.

"GOOD TO MEETCHA, ERWIN."

I shake his hand. I'm surprised by its thick callousness. He has such a baby face, but his hand is hard and rough as sandpaper.

"GOOD TO MEET YOU, TOO," I yell. I try to nod back at him, and my fucking hard hat falls off and bowls across the ground. He picks it up and gives it to me. He smiles.

"WHO HIRED YA? MERLE?"

I nod.

"EVER ROUGHNECKED BEFORE?"

I shake my head.

"WHERE YA FROM? ABILENE?"

I smile.

"NO. I'M FROM BOSTON."

"*BOSTON?* WHERE THE FUCK'S 'AT?"

"IT'S IN MASSACHUSETTS."

He stares blankly.

"YOU KNOW," I say. "UP NORTH."

He smiles.

"YOU A YANKEE?"

I smile and nod.

"I'LL BE DAMN, A YANKEE." He pats my shoulder. "WELL, IT'S GOOD TO HAVE YA ON THE CREW. LIKE I SAID, I'M SHAY. I'M THE DRILLER. I'M THE BOSS UH THE CREW." He turns and gestures to a second crew member, a big-bellied guy, about fifty years old, with severely weathered skin and bulging eyes. His face is dark brownish red and creased with deep wrinkles, and he has big ugly features—thick lips, broad nose, buggy brown eyes. His eyes are so bloodshot and tired-looking, he looks like he's been on about a two-week drunk. His arms are covered with green tattoos, but they're so smeared I can't tell what they're supposed to be. His weirdest characteristic, though, involves his uniform. Apparently he's customized it to accommodate his gut. Across the front of his overalls are four vertical tears, each about twelve inches long and splayed open by his round white-skinned stomach.

"THIS NO-GOOD SUMBITCH HERE," Shay yells, "IS VIRGIL BADGETT."

Virgil does not offer his hand to shake. He just stares at me.

"VIRGIL'S GONNA TRAIN YA," Shay says. "HE'LL SHOW YA HOW TO WORK THE FLOOR. 'AT'S WHERE YOU'LL BE WORKIN'."

I nod and smile at Virgil, but he doesn't smile back. He just stares coolly. With his lit cigarette stuck in the corner of his mouth, he leans over and spits in the wind.

"YEAH," he says, "I TRAINED A LOT UH WORMS." His cigarette bounces up and down as he talks. "I EVEN TRAINED A BUNCH A FUCKIN' YANKEES UP'N MICHIGAN ONE TIME."

I acknowledge this statement with a nod. I can't tell if he's just a moronic asshole in general, or if "fuckin' Yankees" is meant to be a deliberate slam.

Shay gestures to the third crew member, a strong round-shouldered guy about thirty years old. His brown eyes are sort of crossed, he has a pimply blank expression on his face, and he stands stiffly with his arms straight down along his sides. He looks like he might be sort of retarded or something.

"THIS HERE'S CARL MILLER," Shay says. "BUT EVER'BODY CALLS HIM MULE." Shay looks at him. "AIN'T 'AT RIGHT, MULE?"

Cigarette clenched in his teeth, Mule nods eagerly without smiling.

"WANNA SHAKE ERWIN'S HAND, MULE?" Shay asks.

Mule looks down at the ground, steps forward, and juts out his hand. I take his hand and shake it. His palm is rough and thick-skinned like Shay's.

"NICE TO MEET YOU, MULE."

He says nothing and withdraws his hand.

"C'MON, ERWIN," Shay says, "VIRGIL WILL SHOW YA AROUND." He turns to walk toward the rig, but bumps into Virgil, who still stands staring at me. Shay steps aside. Cigarette dangling from his lips, Virgil puffs it without using his hands and exhales the smoke into the wind. He stares at me.

"YA SAY YER FROM BOSTON?"

I nod. He props his hands on his hips.

" 'AT'S FUCKIN' YANKEELAND, AIN'T IT?"

My heart starts to thump and my hands tremble.

"YES, I GUESS IT IS."

"I'S BORN IN MISSISSIPPI," he says. "VICKSBURG, MISSISSIPPI. EVER HEAR OF IT?"

"YES, OF COURSE." I fake a smile.

"THEN I RECKON YA KNOW WHAT WENT ON 'ERE."

My heart thumps faster. There's no doubt what he's talking about, but I play dumb.

"I'M NOT SURE I KNOW WHAT YOU MEAN, BUT MY FAVORITE WRITER IS TENNESSEE WILLIAMS. HE'S FROM MISSISSIPPI, I THINK. COLUMBUS, MISSISSIPPI."

Virgil crosses his thick tattoo-smeared arms over his chest, takes another handless drag off his cigarette, and blows out the smoke.

"I AIN'T ASKIN' ABOUT COLUMBUS, YANK. I'M ASKIN' ABOUT VICKSBURG. YA KNOW WHAT WENT ON 'ERE?" He raises his chin and leers at me with his buggy bloodshot eyes. My heart races, my arms and legs quiver, and I start to give up on the possibility of working for Merle. I don't give a fuck. Nothing is worth taking shit from this fat bug-eyed moron.

"YA HEAR ME, YANK?" he says. "I'M ASKIN'—"

"*VIRGIL,*" Shay says, "GODDAM, WHAT—"

I hold up my hand and interrupt Shay. I step forward and glare at Virgil.

"YES, VIRGIL, DURING THE CIVIL WAR I BELIEVE IT WAS VICKSBURG, MISSISSIPPI, WHERE MY GREAT-GRANDFATHER *KICKED YOUR GREAT-GRANDFATHER'S STUPID FUCKING REDNECK ASS!*" As I drop my hard hat and ball my hands into fists along my sides, Virgil's expression turns to astonishment. He turns and looks at Shay, then at Mule. They, too, appear stunned. Suddenly all three of them burst out laughing. Shay shoves Virgil's shoulder, knocking him sideways a step.

"LOOKS LIKE HE HAS HEARD UH 'AT PLACE, DUMB-ASS." Shay puts his arm around my neck. "DON'T PAY NO AT-TENTION TO HIS FAT ASS. HE'S JUST TRYIN' TO JERK YA AROUND CUZ YER NEW. C'MON, I'LL GET HIM TO SHOW YA AROUND THE RIG."

Å Å Å

"This here's the doghouse." Virgil waves his arm around the narrow boxlike room. The walls, roof, and floor are all made of steel. There are two doors; one opens onto the rig floor under the derrick, the other onto a landing near the engines at the top of the stairs. Along one wall is a steel bench and a row of tall locker compartments. Like the walls, ceiling, and most of the equipment in the doghouse, they're painted bright Luskey red. However, unlike the equipment and walls, which are clean and freshly painted, the lockers are covered with vulgar graffiti. *Shit-bird, Big Faggot, I Like Pussy,* and *Virgil Sucks* are just a few of the messages etched into the paint, along with dozens of foul drawings. Virgil looks around the room. "This is where ya change yer clothes, eatchur food, and take yer ass time."

"What's ass time?"

He lowers his brow and stares at me with his bloodshot eyes.

" 'At's when ya ain't gotta work." He takes a puff from his cigarette and motions out the door toward the derrick. "When yer drillin' off a joint, or yer on the bank waitin' on a log, ya sit down and get some ass time. Ass time is good."

I nod and follow Virgil out of the relatively muffled rumbling doghouse to the diesel-engine roaring windswept floor beneath the derrick. Centered directly under the derrick, a wheel-like segment of the floor turns with a rhythmic clank. There's a square hole in the middle of this turning wheel segment, and coming down through the derrick, a length of square-shaped pipe goes through this square hole and down into the earth. Driven by the turning wheel segment of the floor, the square-shaped pipe turns as well. Virgil explains that these are the *rotary table* and the *kelly*, which, together, are responsible for turning the drill string and drill bit, which make the hole.

"YER ENGINES TURN THE TABLE, AND THE TABLE TURNS THE KELLY, AND THE KELLY TURNS YER DRILL STRAYNG. SO YER BIT'S DOWN ON BOTTOM, TURNIN' AND DRILLIN' WITH THE WEIGHT UH THE DRILL STRAYNG SITTIN' ON IT."

I point down through the rig's steel floor.

"HOW LONG IS THE DRILL STRING?"

"AW, I THANK WE'RE ABOUT SIXTY-SIX HUNERD RIGHT NOW."

As Virgil points out other components of the rig, a theme emerges. For some reason animals figure prominently in the mind of the roughneck. For example, in addition to the *doghouse*, there is the *rat hole*—a cased twelve-inches-in-diameter hole drilled at a slight angle from the rig floor down some forty feet into the earth—where you store the kelly when not drilling. And the *mouse hole*—a smaller cased hole that goes through the rig floor into the ground—where you store the next joint of drill pipe to be added to the drill string. The *monkey board* is a platform high up in the derrick on which the derrickman stands and manipulates the upper end of the drill pipe when you pull it out of the hole. The giant flat hook on the traveling block, from which the drill string is suspended in the derrick, is the *cow's cock*, and when you hoist a joint of drill pipe up from the racks where they're stored on the ground beside the rig, you use the *cat head*, a spinning drum, to raise and lower the *cat line*, and drag the pipe up the *catwalk*, a narrow iron platform sloping from the rig floor to the ground.

After Virgil expounds on the power and function of the rig's three engines, we step to the back rail of the elevated rig floor and look down upon a series of trenches and diked pits which have been dug in the ground near the rig, each full of a slimy brown substance. From the creeping whorls on the slime's surface, I gather that it's moving.

"WHAT'S THAT?"

"MUD."

"MUD?"

Virgil takes a handless puff from his cigarette hanging in the corner of his mouth and stares at me with his buggy eyes.

"CAIN'T DRILL WITHOUT MUD."

"WHY?"

Virgil frowns, as though only a total idiot would fail to comprehend the role of mud in drilling.

"FER ONE THAYNG, IT KEEPS YER BIT COOL. WHEN YA GET DOWN IN THE GROUND A WAYS, IT GETS HOTTER'N A DOLLAR WHORE. AND THEN YA ADD YER FRICTION FROM YER BIT ON TOP UH THAT, AND YA GOT A HOT-ASS SITCHEEATION DOWN 'ERE. SO YA PUMP YER MUD DOWN AROUND YER BIT AND IT KEEPS HER COOL.

"ALSO, YER MUD BAILS YER HOLE OUT. YA PUMP YER MUD DOWN YER DRILL STRAYNG AND IT COMES OUT DOWN AROUND YER BIT, THEN IT CARRIES YER CUTTIN'S BACK TO THE SURFACE AROUND THE OUT-

SIDE UH YER DRILL STRAYNG." He points down off the rig to a metal screen propped at an angle on the ground at the edge of a mud trench. A pipe gushes mud onto the screen. The mud itself filters through the screen and runs into the trench. Separated from the mud by the screen, tiny gray rock pieces sluff into a pile.

"SO THOSE ARE THE ROCKS COMING UP FROM THE EARTH?"

He looks at me.

"HELL YEAH. WHERE'D YA THANK THEY'S COMIN' FROM, SANNY CLAUS?" He laughs a hacking chain-smoker laugh and takes another handless drag from his cigarette.

"AND ANOTHER THAYNG," he says, "YER MUD KEEPS YER HOLE FROM BLOWIN' OUT."

"BLOWING OUT?"

"YEAH. WHEN YA GET DOWN INTO THE GROUND EVER'THAYNG'S PRESSURED UP, 'SPECIALLY OIL AND GAS. THE DEEPER YA GO, WORSE IT GETS. IF YA CUT A GOOD OIL OR GAS ZONE DOWN AROUND EIGHT, NINE THOUSAND FOOT, YA BETTER HAVE YER GODDAM MUD IN SHAPE, ELSEWISE SHE COULD COME SEE YA."

"WHAT DO YOU MEAN EXACTLY, COME SEE YA?"

He opens wide his bleary eyes and stares at me.

"WHEN THE DAMN DRILL STRAYNG BLOWS OUT THE TOP UH THE DERRICK AND SCATTERS EVER'WHERE LIKE A PLATE UH SPAGHETTI, AND YA GOT A GODDAM BALL UH FIRE FIVE HUNERD FEET IN THE AIR MELTIN' EVER' DAMN THAYNG WITHIN A QUARTER MILE, YOU'LL FIGGER OUT WHAT I MEAN."

RAAAWWW . . .

Suddenly the rig engines right behind us accelerate and blast even louder. Black smoke pours from their flapper-lidded exhaust pipes and blows sideways in the wind over our heads. I look up and see the traveling block and the kelly going up into the derrick. I plug my fingers in my ears and look at Virgil.

"WHAT'S HAPPENING?"

"KELLY DOWN. C'MON."

I follow Virgil around the *draw-works*, or the huge drum of cable that feeds up and around the *crown block* and down through the derrick where it connects to the traveling block. Under the derrick is the *brake*, a large lever, about four feet long, that sticks diagonally from the rig floor and acts as a brake on the draw-works. Wearing his hard hat and gloves, Shay stands at the brake and looks up into the derrick. With his mud-caked work boot, he works a control pedal on the rig floor, called the *foot-feed*, which, like in a car, is a foot-operated throttle for the three rig engines. As he presses down on the foot-feed, the engines roar and the draw-works turns, slowly pulling the drill string up out of the earth into the derrick.

Mule is down off the rig rolling a joint of drill pipe across the racks to the sloping iron catwalk.

Virgil takes a drag from his cigarette, then flicks it over the rail and puts on his gloves.

"GETCHUR GLOVES ON, WORM," he yells.

I put on my gloves.

When Shay has raised the entire kelly, which is about forty-five feet long, out of the hole and up into the derrick, a joint of drill pipe, connected to the kelly, rises up through the rotary table. Shay eases off the foot-feed and pushes down on the brake.

REEET.

The draw-works locks. Now the drill string hangs in suspension in the derrick. Mud oozes down the four flat sides of the kelly and spills off the rotary table across the rig floor.

"GRAB THESE SLIPS," Virgil yells. He points to three large pieces of wedge-shaped steel, connected together with hinges, sitting on the rig floor by the rotary table. There are two thick rope handles by which to lift them. Virgil and I each take a handle. We heave the slips and stumble and slide across the mud-slick steel floor.

CLANK.

We drop the slips in the hole around the round joint of drill pipe protruding from the rotary table. The slips are designed so that they wrap around the joint of pipe and wedge between it and the hole in the rotary table. When Virgil and I have the slips in place, Shay releases the brake lever. The entire sixty-six-hundred-feet-long drill string settles into the wedged slips, hanging from the massively braced rig floor.

Virgil grabs a large armlike device, about four feet long, suspended from the derrick by cables. He swings it over and locks it around the kelly, just above where it is connected to the drill pipe. He grabs the arm with both his gloved hands and pulls against it, holding it in place. He nods to another similar armlike device suspended from cables behind me.

"GETCHUR BACKUP TONGS AND MAKE 'EM UP RIGHT HERE." He slaps the mud-slick joint of drill pipe protruding from the rotary table. I'm apprehensive, being thrown into my job without any training. I look at Shay. He nods and indicates for me to go ahead. I grab the large red armlike device. It has jaws and teeth on one end and a fifteen-feet-long piece of chain attached to the other. I swing it over and, according to Virgil's instructions, set the jaws around the joint of drill pipe below the kelly. Virgil nods to a thick scarred pipe sticking up like a post from the rig floor about six feet behind me near one of the enormous legs of the derrick.

"NOW RUN YER RAT'S ASS BACK AND WRAP IT AROUND THE DEAD MAN."

I grab the length of chain attached to the backup tongs.

"THIS?"

"YEAH. 'AT'S YER RAT'S ASS. LOOP IT AROUND THE DEAD MAN OVER 'ERE."

I look back at the scarred metal post and the big diagonal derrick leg.

"I DON'T UNDERSTAND."

Virgil frowns with exasperation.

"THROW YER RAT'S ASS AROUND THE DEAD MAN! LET'S *GO!*"

"I DON'T SEE A FUCKING DEAD MAN!"

Shay laughs.

Thweeet!

He whistles and gestures for Mule to come up to the floor. Mule runs up the steps and takes Shay's place at the brake. Annoyed, Virgil releases the huge armlike device and lights another cigarette. Shay walks over and points to the thick metal post.

"TAKE YER CHAIN AND WRAP IT AROUND THIS POST. IT'S CALLED THE DEAD MAN. THE CHAIN WILL HOLD THE BACKUP TONGS SO VIRGIL CAN BREAK OFF THE KELLY WITH HIS BREAKIN' TONGS."

With Shay's guidance, I wrap the chain several times over the top of the post.

"NOW HOLD IT LIKE THIS." Shay shows me to hold the chain with one hand in front of the dead man, and to press the palm of my other hand against the wrapped chain, holding it against the post. "YA GOTTA KEEP IT LAYIN' AGAINST THE DEAD MAN LIKE THIS SO IT'LL BITE WHEN VIRGIL PUTS A BIND ON IT."

I nod.

"WHEN YER ALL SET," he says, "HOLLER 'RAT'S ASS.' 'AT'S SO VIRGIL KNOWS YER READY FER HIM TO CRANK UP THE BREAKIN' TONGS. GOT IT?"

I nod and Shay returns to his place at the driller's controls.

Now that he's helped me set the rat's ass, it's obvious what I'm supposed to do. What we're doing is unscrewing the kelly from the joint of drill pipe. So while Virgil applies the hydraulic tongs to the kelly, I'm supposed to man the backup tongs, which are affixed to the drill pipe by their jaws and to the sturdy dead man by the chain, or rat's ass. In effect I'm holding the drill pipe in place and keeping it from turning along with the kelly, so that Virgil can *break* their connection and unscrew the kelly from the drill pipe.

More comfortable now with my role, I take my palm off the wrapped chain, and instead I hold it in place by pulling on the extra chain behind the dead man. This seems an easier way to hold the chain in place.

With Shay back in his place at the brake, Virgil takes hold of his breakin' tongs.

CLANK.

He latches them around the Kelly and looks at me.

"READY, WORM?"

I clear my throat and yell my ready call.

"RAT'S ASS!"

Virgil spreads his feet, secures his hold on the hydraulic tongs, and lays his finger on the power switch.

Thweeet!

"HO! HO!"

Virgil stops and we all turn. Mule stands in the doghouse doorway pointing at me. Shay looks at me and shakes his head. He motions for Mule to again take his place, then shaking his head, he walks up and slaps my hand which I have repositioned on the chain behind the dead-man post.

"DON'T *EVER* PUTCHUR HAND BEHIND THE DEAD MAN LIKE 'AT. ALWAYS HOLD THE RAT'S ASS *AGAINST* THE DEAD MAN LIKE THIS." He places the palm of my hand against the chain like he showed me before.

"WHY?"

He points at a long-handled sledgehammer propped against the wall of the doghouse.

"GIMME 'AT SLEDGE."

I get the huge heavy-headed hammer and give it to Shay. He

pulls tight the extra chain hanging from the series of loops around the dead man, then places the big, baseball-bat–sized wooden hammer handle between this extra chain and the dead man, which is exactly where I was holding the chain.

"AR-IGHT, VIRJ," Shay yells, "RAT'S ASS!"

VRRRRRRT.

Virgil engages the hydraulic tongs. The kelly and drill pipe spin with tremendous force, jerking the arm of the backup tongs and snapping tight the rat's ass. Because the chain is not being held properly against the dead man, it slips and pinches the sledgehammer handle.

Crack.

The handle snaps like a toothpick.

"*HO!*" Shay yells.

Virgil stops the tongs. Shay holds up the crushed, two-inch-thick handle.

"SEE? 'AT WOULDA BEEN YER HAND. AND YA MIGHT WANNA HANG ON TO YER HAND. MIGHT WANNA PET SOME OL' GAL'S ASS WITH IT SOME DAY, DON'CHA RECKON?"

I wiggle my fingers, stare at the splintered wood, and nod.

Å Å Å

After *makin' connection* and adding a new joint to the drill string, we enjoy several hours of ass time. The engines thunder; the rotary table turns—*clank, clank, clank*; the kelly slowly drills down; and we sit in the doghouse listening to Virgil tell jokes. Thrilled to have fresh ears, he sits beside me, chain-smoking and regaling me with a stream of stupid jokes. Obviously Shay and Mule already know all of Virgil's jokes, but they hang on every word and laugh hysterically at his punch lines; then they ask him to tell one of their particular favorites, like "the one about the nun with VD," or "the trucker with two dicks." At the punch line of each joke, while laughing themselves, I notice that all three of my colleagues monitor my reaction. So in order to suck up, I pretend that Virgil is absolutely the funniest comedian I've ever heard. When he tells the one about the boy born with no eyelids, and the boy's doctors, in a fit of confusion, decide to graft the foreskin from his circumcision onto his eyes, and all turns out well except the boy is slightly *cockeyed*, I throw back my head, howl like a hyena, hold my sides, and beg for mercy from this *tour de force*. Although this ass-kissing tactic has the drawback of encouraging Virgil to continue his performance for at least an hour, by the end, when he has dredged up every pitiful joke in the annals of redneck lore, I seem to have been officially accepted as a member of the day-tour crew.

But nothing can prepare me for what is next.

When the kelly is drilled down and the massive yellow traveling block hangs just above the rig floor, we put on our gloves and step out beneath the derrick. At first I think we're about to repeat the quick violent task of connecting a new joint of drill pipe, but as Mule fastens a large safety belt around his waist and shimmies up the girders into the derrick, I start to wonder.

"WHAT ARE WE DOIN'?"

"GONNA TRIP FER A BIT," Virgil yells.

"WHAT'S THAT?"

"GONNA TRIP OUT THE DRILL STRAYNG AND CHANGE BITS."

"OH. HOW DO WE DO THAT?"

Virgil looks at me with his buggy bloodshot eyes and bursts out laughing.

"*AH-HA-HA.*"

RAAAWWW . . .

The engines roar; the draw-works spins; and the traveling block rises into the derrick, hoisting the muddy kelly up from the rotary table. Working the foot-feed, Shay raises the kelly until the joint of drill pipe below it comes up through the floor.

REEET.

He sets the brake, hanging the drill string in the derrick.

CLANK.

Virgil and I toss in the slips.

We break off the kelly from the drill string, and as Shay lowers the kelly back down, we store it in the rat hole away from the rotary table.

Then begins the task of *tripping for a bit.*

After Shay hoists the drill string up into the derrick for a distance of three joints, or ninety-three feet, Virgil and I drop the slips, and, using the hydraulic tongs, rat's ass, and dead man, we break the connection at the bottom of the third joint. Shay then raises this three-joint *stand* of drill pipe a little higher, allowing it to *crap* itself of mud. The warm brown slime gushes out, splattering everything and everyone on the floor. Then Virgil and I, slip-sliding on the muddy floor, push the lower end of this ninety-three-feet-long, eighteen-hundred-pound stand of drill pipe from under the derrick and position it above the *whore board*, a wooden platform of railroad ties on the rig floor. As we strain and hold it in position, Shay eases off the draw-works brake, drops the stand down, and *stabs* it in place on the *whore board*. Mule, high up in the derrick on the *monkey board*, maneuvers the upper end of the stand into the *finger board* and racks it. Thus, the three-joint *stand* literally stands racked in the derrick.

Now, one instance of this sequence—with all its roaring, screeching, chain-snapping, mud-slipping, eighteen-hundred-pound muscle-burning exertion—is a wild harrowing event in itself, but in order to bring up the bit from sixty-six hundred feet, we have to do this not one, not two, not ten, but *seventy-one* times. Seventy-one times without pause I flail about in the mud and dangling steel, terrified of losing a hand to the rat's ass or a foot to a falling stand of pipe.

What's more, upon pulling up the entire sixty-six-hundred-foot drill string, disconnecting the giant 250-pound tricone drilling bit from the bottom stand, and replacing it with a new sharp-toothed model, do we stop to rest or celebrate our accomplishment? Hell no. We immediately begin tripping back *in* the hole, which, essentially, is the same sequence done in reverse.

As we go back in the hole with our fourth stand, as my shoulders and legs quiver and ache and I'm afraid I'm going to fall on my butt from exhaustion, the evening-tour crew appears at the top of the rig stairs. Smoking cigarettes and carrying lunch pails and big two-liter bottles of pop, they're a ragtag foursome of fat muscular tattoo-armed men ranging in age from twenty to fifty. They go into the doghouse, then come out moments later wearing red Luskey work overalls, hard hats, and gloves. With a loud exchange of vulgar but good-natured banter between us, they step right in and take over our positions, and Luskey Drilling, Inc.'s business of tripping back to bottom continues without pause.

I'M DOZING ON THE DIVAN WHEN THE PHONE RINGS. I DON'T know if I should answer it or not, so I just let it ring. Then I realize it might be Merle himself trying to call me. I run to the study and get it.

"Hello."

"Merle?"

"Uh . . . no, Merle's not here."

"Who's this?"

"This is Erwin Vandeveer. I work for Merle."

"Where's Merle?"

"He went out of town."

"Out uh town, huh?"

"Yeah."

"Got any idea when he'll be back?"

"Tonight, maybe. Or tomorrow. He didn't know exactly."

"Tonight or tomorrow. Ar-ighty. Well, I sure do appreciate it."

"Uh, may I tell him who called?"

"Naw. Hell, I'll just shout at him later. You have a good day now. Drive careful."

Click.

I hang up. *Drive careful?* Why in the hell would someone say that on the phone? Then it occurs to me that the voice on the phone sounded like that sheriff yesterday, sort of nasal with a twangy drawl. Then again, everyone around here sounds like that. Who knows, maybe *Drive careful* is just something they say down here.

I go upstairs and take a shower in Merle's bathroom. I turn the water up hot and stay in for a long time. My shoulders and arms ache like hell from tripping pipe.

I put on some clean clothes and get ready to go into Abilene. I'm starving. Thank God Merle advanced me fifty bucks this morning.

As I walk out of the garage and across the driveway to Ol' Blue, I hear tires crunching along the rocky ranch road. I look around the house. It's a cop car. I duck back in the garage and peek out. It's a white-and-gold Taylor County Sheriff's Department patrol car, exactly like the ones that chased us yesterday. It creeps by, tires popping on the rocky road. I look, but the side windows are tinted green and I can't see who, or how many people, are in the car.

I watch it drive back about a half a mile or so along the road through the tall dry grass to the back of the ranch, then I decide it's safe to go. I run out and hop in Ol' Blue. I find the two wires under the dash and touch them together like Merle showed me this morning.

Rar-uh-rar-uh.

The starter turns the engine, but nothing happens. I try again.

Rar-uh-rar-uh.

Dammit. I look out across the grass. The sheriff car is still way down at the back of the ranch. I pump the accelerator and try again. Finally.

Rar-uh-tut-tut-tut-tut-tut . . .

The engine coughs and starts. A cloud of white exhaust blows sideways in the wind from behind Ol' Blue. Engine stuttering, white exhaust blowing, I back around and pull out for the road.

Tut-tut-tut—

Ol' Blue dies in the driveway about ten yards from the road. I shove the transmission in park, find the two ignition wires under the dash, and try again.

Rar-uh-rar-uh.

Rar-uh-rar-uh.

Sonofabitch. I look up. Here comes the sheriff car, headed back toward the highway.

Rar-uh-rar-uh.

Fuck. I start to hop out and run for the house, but I'm afraid that would look too suspicious, so I just step out and stand by Ol' Blue.

The sheriff car comes cruising back up along the road. Through the front window I recognize the driver. It's the sheriff, Jack Nall. He stops and rolls down his window.

"Heidi," he says. He wears a straw cowboy hat and dark sunglasses and has a brown cigar stub stuck in his mouth.

"Hello," I say. I walk out to the road. Sheriff Nall's cigar is all frazzled and wet, and a brown juice stain trails down his double chin onto the collar of his uniform. He pushes up the front brim of his hat, smiles, and holds his hand out the window.

"How ya doin'? Jack Nall."

I shake his hand.

"Yes. I'm Erwin Vandeveer. I met you yesterday. With Merle."

" 'At's right. Hell. How ya doin'?"

"Fine. Is there some kind of problem?"

"Naw. Ain't no problem. We's just out drivin' around." He motions to the person beside him. "This is Don Brock." I lean down and look in the car. It's the bald gray-eyed banker from yesterday. He's wearing a gray-and-ivory pinstriped suit.

"Of course," I say. "Hello."

He nods and pats his forehead with a folded white handkerchief. Sheriff Nall leans out and spits a glob of brown cigar juice on the white-rock road.

"And this ol' boy back here," Sheriff Nall points over his shoulder to the backseat, "is Weldon Barnes."

I lean in and acknowledge an old white-haired, white-mustached guy in the backseat.

"Weldon's in real estate," Sheriff Nall says.

Don Brock scowls and elbows Sheriff Nall.

"Oh," Sheriff Nall says. "Yeah, well, uh, Weldon does a lil bit uh ever'thayng." He gnaws his soggy cigar and smiles. "Perty day, ain't it?"

"Yes. It certainly is."

"Where'd ya say you's from?"

"I don't know that I did. I'm from Boston."

"*Boston?*"

"Yes."

"Goddam." Sheriff Nall licks his cigar stub. "What in the world are—"

Don Brock elbows him again.

"Let's go, Jack." He glances up the road and pats his bald head with his handkerchief. *"C'mon."*

Sheriff Nall turns back into the car and mumbles.

"Ease up, Don. I toldja, he's out uh town. Won't be back till tonight or tomorrow. Sure ya don't wanna go back and look around 'at creek bottom again? May not get another chance."

"*No*, dammit. Let's *go*."

"Just hang on, Don." Sheriff Nall looks back at me, lolls his cigar, and smiles. "You wouldn' happen to know exactly how many acres Merle's got out here, would ya?"

"Goddammit, Jack!" Don Brock says. "Just shut up and drive the fucking car."

Sheriff Nall frowns.

"Gee whiz, Don." He pulls the transmission into gear and looks at me. "Well, reckon we better run. Drive careful, Boston." He rolls up the window and they drive away.

I get back in Ol' Blue and try to start it.

Rar-uh-rar-uh.

Rar-uh—

WHAM.

A crash jolts the air, followed by a roar. I look up the road toward the highway. Sheriff Nall's car, rolling in reverse at high speed, comes winding in wild S's back up the road. Like an angry bull, Merle's huge red truck bears down on it, charging and smashing the front of it. As the two vehicles pass the driveway, Sheriff Nall whips back into Merle's yard. Merle swings his truck in.

WHAM.

Merle rams the patrol car, crumpling its hood. Sheriff Nall jumps out and raises his pistol in the air.

POP.

POP.

He fires two rounds into the sky.

Sonofabitch. I open the door, dive out of Ol' Blue, and crawl behind its front tire.

"Back off, Merle!" Sheriff Nall yells.

"Fuck you, Jack! Get off my land!"

Merle's diesel engine roars.

RAAAWWW-RAAAWWW.

I peek over Ol' Blue's hood. Smoke rises from the crumpled grille of the patrol car. Sheriff Nall, hat spilled to the ground, kneels his fat body behind the opened door of his car and aims his gun through the V between the door of his car. I don't see Don Brock or Weldon Barnes. I guess the gunfire sent them, like me, scuttling for cover. Merle, however, sits in his truck, looking at Sheriff Nall through the windshield. Sheriff Nall wraps his other hand on the gun and braces his aim.

"Merle! I don't wanna have to shootchoo!"

Merle, cowboy hat tilted up off his face, revs his engine and points to his forehead.

"Well, Jack! If ya do shoot, ya better hit me right here 'tween the eyes, cuz if ya miss, I'm gonna run yer ass over dead, I guarantee."

"Aw c'mon, Merle!" Sheriff Nall yells. "Get out uh the truck and let's talk. I don't wanna shoot."

Merle keeps pointing at his forehead.

"Go ahead, Jack! Here I am. Butcha better shoot straight or I guarantee, yer a dead man." Merle guns the engine again.

RAAAWWW.

The hood of his red truck bristles and black diesel exhaust pours from his tailpipe.

Both hands braced on his gun, licking his cigar, Sheriff Nall stares at the chrome grille guard of Merle's truck.

"Ar-ight, Merle! I'm gonna holster my gun, then if you'll back out, I'll just drive right on out uh here. 'At way nobody gets hurt."

Merle nods and eases off the accelerator.

"Ar-ight, Jack. I'll back off. but 'fore I do, by God, I got somethin' to say." He steps out of the truck. "Don! I know yer in 'ere. Raise up and look at me, goddammit."

Slowly, Don Brock raises his bald head from the floorboard of the patrol car.

"Don!" Merle says. "I know I owe ya a lot uh money, but by God, I'm gonna figger a way to pay ya. Ya hear me? Ya ain't gettin' one damn piece uh iron off my rigs, and ya ain't gettin' this land or this house. And if I catch ya out here again, I'll hurtchur ass. 'At goes fer you, too, Jack! Keep yer fat ass off my property. ya hear me?"

There is a long wind-gusting silence.

"Ya hear me?"

"Yeah, Merle," Sheriff Nall says, "I hear ya."

Merle gets in his truck and backs away. Sheriff Nall puts his gun in his holster, picks up his hat and puts it back on, then gets in his car and slowly drives away.

Somehow, I guess in that last blow Merle delivered to the front of the patrol car, either the axle or one of the front wheels was bent out of line. As the patrol car drives away, the wheels scrape and the front of the car bobs up and down.

Screek, screek, screek . . .

Smoke pouring from under the hood, the patrol car hobbles away.

Merle pulls around Ol' Blue and parks by the garage. I walk across up the driveway and meet him.

"Are you all right, Merle?"

"Hell yeah." He props his hands on his hips and stares out toward the highway as the patrol car turns from the ranch and limps toward town. "Crooked no-good sumbitches."

"How was your trip?"

"Not worth a damn."

"You didn't get a loan?"

"Hell naw. Minute ya mention the word drillin' rig, 'em bankers start laughin'. Ain't nobody gonna give me a dime against a rig." He shakes his head. "I never shoulda bought them two new rigs last year. But goddam, who could uh known the bottom was gonna drop out like this?"

The wind gusts and wobbles the brim of his hat. He stares out over the prairie.

"Harvard."

"Yeah?"

"Looks like I'm gonna have to figger a way to get my ass out uh the fire. And uh course ya ain't obligated to me or nothin'. You can roughneck day tour however many days ya want, then shag ass on home to Boston like we agreed." He sighs. "But I been thankin' and, well, I ain't no Bible-thumper, but I stand good with the Lord and I figger there must be a reason why you all uh sudden turned up in town when ya did. And . . . well, I don't know, hell, I's hopin' ya might stick around here awhile and help me out."

"Help you out? How?"

"I ain't sure exactly. But 'tween yer book smarts and my horse smarts, we'll figger somethin' out. Course I'll pay ya—a hunerd dollars a day. I'd just like to know I can count on ya to stick around till I get this sumbitch straightened out."

"I don't understand, Merle. How could *I* help?"

"Whadda ya mean? Hell, yer sharper'n a snake's ass. You can be my rat killer—ya know, run do this or that. Help me do paperwork if I have to. Listen, son, I know I can count on you to do somethin' right. My other hands, hell, they cain't even read." He sighs again. "Goduhmighty, Harvard, I got less'n thirty days 'fore they shoot my ass off. I gotta do somethin', boy. I ain't gonna lose these rigs. They're my lifelong dream and I ain't givin' 'em back. Ya hear me? I just ain't."

I look out to the west. The sun, red and round, floats over the horizon. Although I feel sorry for Merle and his problem, frankly I don't see how in the world I could help him. Then again, if he's willing to pay me a hundred dollars a day . . . assuming I stick around for thirty days, that's three thousand dollars, which is way the hell more than I've ever made. What the hell. Why not? I look at him.

"Okay, Merle. I'll hang around for a month and help you out, but . . . I mean . . . you *are* going to pay me, right? You said a hundred dollars a day."

He nods.

"Damn straight." He holds out his hand and we shake. "By God, I appreciate this, Harvard. I really do."

"You're welcome, Merle. I hope I can help. I don't know what I can do, but I'll do my best."

"I know ya will, son. I know ya will. Aw hell, I nearly fergot. I gotcha somethin'." He opens the big mounted chrome toolbox in the bed of his truck and brings out a large square plain cardboard box. "Here ya go, boy."

I open the box.

Boots!

Beautiful dark brown cowboy boots. I throw down the box lid and take them out. The bottoms, or horizontal foot parts, are made of strips of polished grainy dark brown hide sewn together. The tops, or vertical ankle parts, are dark brown as well, but they're made of a plainer less grainy hide decorated with rows and rows of swirling gold and ivory stitching.

"Goddam, Merle." I hold them up. The heels are tall, about three inches, and the toes very long and pointed. And they smell. They have this excellent new leathery smell.

"They're chocolate lizards," Merle says.

"What?"

"They call 'em chocolate lizards. Cuz they're brown like chocolate and they're made out uh lizard skin."

I run my finger along the strips of polished hide across their toes.

"This is lizard skin?"

"Yep. They're damn nice boots. I saw 'em on sale in Fort Worth. I just eyeballed yer size. They're nines. Zat about right?"

"Hell yeah." Actually I'm an eight or eight and a half, but sometimes I wear a nine.

Merle nods toward the house.

"Well c'mon, let's go inside. You can try 'em on."

"To hell with that. I'll try them on right now." I kick off my loafers and sit down in the driveway. I pull on the right boot, then the left. I leave my jeans wadded in their tops and stand up. They are fucking beautiful! Shiny dark brown, sharp toes, huge heels. Merle waves his arm.

"Well, walk around. See if they bite."

Smiling like an idiot, I clomp back and forth across the driveway. They may be just a shade too big, but who cares? The heels are so tall, they sort of force my feet forward anyway.

"They feel ar-ight?"

I look down at them.

"Hell yes. Absolutely."

"Good. They look good on ya." He points to my loafers lying on the driveway. "Ya need to throw them chickenlicker sumbitches 'ere in the trash."

I laugh and clomp past Merle. I clomp in and around the garage, then back out. I smile.

"Merle, these are fucking excellent. They're perfect, man."

He nods.

"Well, good. Gladja like 'em."

"I don't know how I can ever repay you."

He grabs his front brim and pulls his hat down on his head.

"Well, boy, I don't rightly know, either. But by God, we're fixin' to find out."

THE MIDDLE

MERLE SCREECHES TO THE CURB AND FLASHES HIS BRIGHTS across the building. Painted on the front window:

ABILENE

ASSOCIATION OF

PETROLEUM

GEOLOGISTS

He turns off his engine and his lights. The traffic light at the end of the block blinks yellow and sways in the wind.

"What are we doing?"

He pulls his silver flask out of his boot and unscrews its tiny cap.

"We're gonna learn about exploration."

"Exploration?"

"Yep."

"Exploration for what?"

"Oil, boy." He reaches back over the seat and brings up a sloshing half-full bottle of Jack Daniel's. He uncaps the bottle and pours a tiny stream into his flask until it is brim full. He caps the flask and slips it back in his boot, then takes a swig from the bottle. He grimaces and sucks air through his teeth. "Aw yeah."

He returns the bottle to the backseat and opens his door. "C'mon. Grab 'at coffee."

I get the paper sack containing two plastic foam cups of coffee that he bought at the convenience store and step from the truck. My chocolate lizard boots, now several hours on my feet, have rubbed both my little toes raw. Merle says this is normal, that I'll have to break them in. What happens with cowboy boots is the heel is so tall your foot is forced forward down the slope of the boot into the wedge of the pointed toe, which pinches your toes together. Then they rub when you walk. But even though my feet hurt a little, I don't care. I can't stop staring at my boots. They are gorgeous. They're *huge*.

Merle steps from the truck, opens his chrome toolbox, and brings out a crowbar and a flashlight. He nods for me to follow. We walk around the side of the building to a dark paved alley in the rear.

Along the back of the building, between an air-conditioning unit and a trash Dumpster, a dull yellow light shines over a metal door. Merle looks up and down the alley.

Ptt.

He spits on his fingers, reaches up, and unscrews the light until it goes off. He tries the doorknob. It's locked. He shoves the end of the crowbar between the door and the building.

"Merle," I whisper, "what are you doing?"

"Openin' this door."

"Why?"

"Cuz we got work to do."

"*Work?* For Christ's sake, Merle, this is illegal."

He tilts his hat up off his forehead and looks back at me.

"Well, son, if yer gonna get from here to there, sometimes, by God, ya gotta step on a few toes." He jerks the crowbar.

WHAM.

The door swings open and my heart starts pounding.

We step into the dark building. Merle closes the door behind us, flicks on his flashlight, and shines it down a pukish green linoleum floor hallway. We walk down past a tall artificial potted plant and a water fountain to a door marked:

LIBRARY

AAPG MEMBERS ONLY

Merle tries this door. It, too, is locked. He tucks the flashlight under his arm, slips the crowbar into position, and spreads his stance to jerk.

"*Merle.*"

WHAM.

He steps into the room and waves the flashlight beam across the floor, prompting me to follow.

"C'mon, boy. Get in here."

I look up and down the dark hallway, then step into the room. He closes the door, shines his flashlight along the wall, and walks around the room. I follow him, whispering over his shoulder.

"Merle, would you please tell me what the hell's going on?"

His flashlight beam falls across a bookshelf marked Monthly/Annual Production Reports. Apparently uninterested in this information, he moves on.

"Do what?" he asks. He seems to think it's fine to talk in a normal full tone of voice.

"What are we doing here?"

"Aw, hell, I ain't too sure."

"*What?* Are you fucking kidding me?"

His flashlight beam slides across the bookshelf to a stack of magazines. He leans up and carefully examines their spines.

"Here we go. These look good." They are entitled *Wildcat: Journal of Petroleum Exploration in West and North Central Texas.* He scoops up the entire stack of magazines and holds them out to me. "Here ya go."

I refuse to take them.

"Listen, Merle, I have a right to know. What the hell is going on?"

He sighs.

"Hang on, dammit. I don't wanna wear out my batteries standin' around jawin'." He sets the magazines on a study table and turns off his flashlight, leaving us in complete blackness. "Ar-ight, Harvard. If I cain't get no loan, then by God, only way I know to prove up a bunch uh money fast is find some oil. So what we're doin' here is tryin' to get our teeth into somethin' and figger a way to find some oil."

"But why do you have to break in like this?"

"Cuz. This is a private outfit. They don't let just any jackleg come in and look at their dope. Ya gotta be a member."

"Well, for God's sake, can't you come back tomorrow and join?"

"Naw, I checked on 'at. If ya wanna get in, ya gotta give 'em a letter and some money, then get approved by the board at their next monthly meetin'. And guess what?"

"What?"

"Next time these sumbitches get around to meetin', I'm liable to be shinin' boots out 'ere on the fuckin' sidewalk."

"Well, what about the public library? Can't we just go there?"

"Hell, son. The public library ain't got this kind uh dope. This is a geology library. Now here's whatchur gonna do. Yer gonna read these here magazines, along with anythayng else we can find in here tonight, then yer gonna tell me what's the best way to start goin' about lookin' fer oil."

"*Me?*"

"Yep."

"Jesus shit, Merle, are you *nuts?* I'm a drama student from Boston, Massachusetts. I don't know the first thing about prospecting for oil."

"Harvard."

"What?"

"Lemme tell ya somethin'."

In the pitch darkness I hear the tiny scraping noise of his flask cap being unscrewed.

Gulp.

He takes a swallow and a blast of whiskey breath hits my nose.

"It's clear as day yer a smart sumbitch, butchoo got a bad habit."

"Oh yeah? What?"

"Ya like to sell yerself short."

"Aw, c'mon, Merle. Get real. You've been in this business for years. How in the hell can I help you?"

Gulp.

Another swallow.

"I'm gonna tell ya one more time, boy. I'm a roughneck. They call me up and say, 'Merle, we got a location staked out 'ere a half mile south uh the road, go drill the mutherfucker down to seven thousand feet.' And 'at's what I do. Rig up and drill it. Now why the hell they decided to put 'at stake 'ere, I ain't go no idea. Understand? Hell, I cain't even hardly write my own goddam name, let alone read a bunch uh fuckin' books."

"Okay. Fine. But that doesn't change the fact that I'm—"

"Hey!"

He pauses and swigs his flask.

Gulp.

"You listen here, boy. 'Ere's a reason you showed up in town when ya did. The Lord sentchoo to me. Yer my savin' angel. Ya got 'at Harvard education and ya turned up right when they're fixin' to kick my teeth in. And yer gonna help me."

I roll my eyes in the dark. The guy's brain is fried on Jack Daniel's.

"Merle."

"Yep."

"I'm not an angel. I promise. I'm just a mortal guy. A mortal Yankee guy stranded in town."

Gulp.

I hear the cap being screwed back on his flask, then suddenly his hand gropes out of the darkness and grabs the top of my head. He squeezes my head as though palming a basketball.

"Hey, boy. I worked my whole life to get my rigs, and I got less'n thirty days 'fore they jerk the rug out from under me." He squeezes my head harder. "*Thirty* days. Now I know this don't make sense to ya, but by God, 'at's all I got left, is what don't make sense. Now let's cut the bullshit and get to work. I ain't payin' ya a hunerd dollars a day to stand 'ere and bellyache." He flicks on the flashlight and lays it on the table by the magazines. "I wancha to read through these damn thayngs and tell me whatcha thank."

I look at the flashlight and stack of journals. I want to run out the door, down the alley, and keep running. Merle's a fucking lunatic. I mean this is just great. I can just see getting busted for breaking and entering in Abilene, Texas. And even if we aren't caught, what the hell does he want me to do? I know zip about geology and oil. Jesus. My toes burn inside my boots. I wiggle them and tap my heels on the floor, trying to jog my feet back up out of the narrow toes. I sigh and shake my head. Well, shit, what can I do? I can't just run out into the night. And hell, at least I'm being paid a hundred bucks a day. I pick up the flashlight.

"All right, Merle. I can't see what good it will do. But I'll read for you."

He pats my back.

"Attaboy."

🐾 🐾 🐾

Snoring, mumbling, sipping his flask, and farting, Merle lies on the floor in the darkness to my right, while I drink coffee and, using the flashlight, grind through twelve issues of *Wildcat: Jour-*

nal of Petroleum Exploration in West and North Central Texas.
The articles are pretty technical. At first I have no idea what the
hell they're about. But I poke around the library and find a shelf
of textbooks, including *Basic Petroleum Geology and Typical
Hydrocarbon-Bearing Structures of the Permian Basin.* Using the
glossaries of these books, as well as the books themselves—
especially the chapters on geophysics and seismic surveys—I start
to get at least a rough feel for the articles. As I keep reading, one
idea pops up over and over again. In fact, it's the subject of almost
every article—3-D.

You see, what happens is, oil is found down in the earth in
porous rock formations (usually sandstone or limestone) that are
covered by nonporous formations (usually shale). The nonporous
rock acts like a lid and traps the oil in the porous rock. These
buried oil-bearing formations are not just flat and uniform. They
have ridges and peaks and valleys and sometimes they're fractured
and thrust up or down along faults. Generally, deep in the earth,
if a rock formation is porous it contains some type of gas or fluid.
If fluid, it's usually either oil or saltwater or a combination of the
two. Because oil is lighter than water, over millions of years it has
migrated up as high as it can rise in these porous structures. So
essentially, when you explore for oil what you're looking for is the
high points of porous formations where the oil has floated up and
been trapped.

Apparently, back in the old days wildcatters explored for these
highs by just drilling holes and comparing the data they got from
drilling. They measured the depths at which various holes en-
countered a formation, then created a structural map of this formation based on this drilling data.

But since the 1970s the key tool of the wildcatter has been
seismic data. You get seismic data by creating energy waves at the
earth's surface (either by shooting off dynamite or dropping huge
weights on the ground). This energy, as it travels down into the
earth, reflects back up from the various rock formations (or

strata). You record this reflected energy with sophisticated instruments strung out along the ground called *geophones*. In turn, you process this recorded data with a computer, which gives you an image of the earth's layers and internal structures.

Throughout the seventies and eighties seismic data was mostly two-dimensional. That is, geophones were arranged in a straight line along the ground and the energy source was applied along this line as well. Thus, the energy bouncing back up provided a two-dimensional or planar image of the earth under this line, a sort of earth slice that revealed the *highs* in the buried rocks along this plane.

However, with the development of more powerful computers in the early nineties, exploration has turned to three-dimensional (3-D) seismic, which entails laying out huge grids of geophones and energy sources. After processing the raw data with computers, you can create a 3-D image of any particular formation under this grid and pinpoint its highs. The samples of 3-D seismic in the journals and *Basic Petroleum Geology* look like colorful topographic maps, where various shades of bright color represent corresponding elevations of a buried rock formation.

Drilling on a 3-D high does not guarantee that you will find oil, because even if your data is exactly accurate, you can still run into two kinds of pitfalls—(1) your target formation, though high and porous, can be *wet*, or full of saltwater with no oil or gas, or (2) your target formation can be high but *tite*, i.e., lacking porosity so that no oil or gas (or water, for that matter) occupies it.

Nonetheless, according to the journals, with the advent of this 3-D seismic data, wildcatters' success ratios have soared. One article says that since '91, for exploration companies using 3-D in West Texas, the overall ratio of successful producing discoveries to dry holes has gone from 1:9 to 1:3.

As I read along through these statistics I start to think maybe Merle is not doomed. Maybe he has at least a one-in-three chance to hit oil. But then I come across a journal article entitled "History of a 3-D Seismic Survey," and I read that not only is 3-D expensive—the author says to get good-quality data, at least two sections of land (640 acres per section) must be covered, and the average cost per 640-acre section runs about sixty-one thousand dollars—but 3-D also requires a great deal of another commodity that Merle definitely lacks.

Time.

Once you determine the area you want to survey, you must (1) lease the right from land/mineral owners to conduct your exploratory operations, (2) contract and coordinate a surveyor, a bulldozer company, and a seismic acquisition company to lay out and conduct the survey, then, finally, (3) hire a specialized computer processing firm to interpret the raw data of your survey. In other words (depending on the size of your project, of course), from the moment of conception to the time when the actual hard data is available requires at least six months, and typically a year or more. Therefore, as far as 3-D seismic goes, Merle, under the gun of less than thirty days, is a dead duck.

I lean back in my chair and rub my eyes. I feel sorry for Merle, but at least I did my job. I yawn and wiggle my toes in my boots. My feet feel better since I've just been sitting here all night.

I yawn again, then grab the flashlight and shine it at Merle. He lies on his back on the puke green linoleum floor with his hands behind his head for a pillow. Beside him on the floor are his hat and flask. I aim the flashlight beam at his face. His mouth is open and he snores lightly.

Vurrrt.

"*Ohhhh.*" He farts and moans, then rolls his head away from the light and licks his lips. Poor bastard. I get up and move away for a minute while his fart fades, then I walk back and nudge his arm with the toe of my boot.

"Merle."

"Huh? Goddam sumbitch, yeah, what?" He sits up and looks around, blinking his eyes.

"We better leave. It's four-thirty."

He puts on his hat.

"Ar-ighty." He uncaps his flask, pours the last few drops onto his tongue, then tucks it in his boot. He stands up. "Well, boy, joo figger anythayng out?"

"*Shhhhh.* Yeah, I think so."

"Well, whadja figger out?"

"To have the best chance at hitting a well, you have to have three-D seismic."

"Three-D seismic."

"Yeah."

He stares at me.

"Zat it? 'At's all ya learned?"

"Yeah. For God's sake, what did you expect? That I'd become a doctoral geologist in six hours?"

He snatches the flashlight from me and grumbles.

"Well, ar-ight. By God, 'at's the way we'll go, then. Three-D seismic." He starts toward the door.

"Merle. It takes six months to a year to do a three-D survey."

He turns around.

"Six months?"

"Yes. At least."

"I ain't got six months."

"I know."

"What all ya gotta do?"

"There are several steps. First, you have to use subsurface geology to determine a good prospective area to survey, then you have to lease the right to conduct your operations from the land and mineral owners, then you have to hire a surveyor, bulldozers, and the seismic crew to lay out and record the survey, then you have to process and interpret the raw field data with computers."

"Goddam."

"I know. I'm sorry, Merle."

"Sorry's ass. By God, we'll just have to skip over some uh them sumbitches. C'mon." He turns and clomps toward the door.

Mom and Dad,

I hope you're not too concerned that I'm not home yet. I'm in Texas. It's a long story, but I ran into some difficulty on the bus and was forced to get off here. Don't worry. I'm okay. I'm staying on a ranch outside Abilene. It's windy and flat—just like *Giant!*—and the people are some real characters—very generous and colorful. Their dialect is hilarious. I have a good job roughnecking on an oil-drilling rig, as well as helping the owner with various clerical duties; or, as he puts, I'm his "rat killer." I'm paid $100 a day. Please don't be alarmed. This is only temporary. In about a month, when I've saved up some money ($3,000!), I plan to continue on home, whereupon I will repay you, Dad, and begin looking for a real job as we agreed.

I hope all is well with you both. I'll write again when I know more precisely when I'll be coming home.

Love,

Erwin

P.S. I have a pair of chocolate lizards, i.e., authentic dark brown cowboy boots made of lizard hide. Yeehaw, pardner!

I smile. It's perfect. Maverick nonchalance to needle Dad, but assurance of my well-being for Mom. I fold it, tuck it in the envelope, and seal it.

I intentionally left out specifics such as Merle's name or phone number, or his company's name, because I don't want Dad calling and raising hell. He's going to be livid. His four-hundred-dollar wire to the Hollywood Western Union so I could pay off Ahkman at the Viva Sol, get my stuff, and catch a bus home was completely out of character, and now I pull this stunt. Oh well, if I show up at home with almost three grand in my pocket and pay his four hundred dollars back, maybe he'll forgive my little sojourn here in the badlands. I doubt it, though.

As I address the envelope to Cambridge, I decide it would be too cowardly to keep them from at least being able to write. So in the corner I include a return address of Merle's route and box number, Abilene, Texas, and the zip code. I lick a stamp and stick it on.

I know I could wait until tomorrow morning to put it in the mailbox, but I'm eager to break in my boots some more. Last night Merle was still in Dallas or Fort Worth researching a way to get some 3-D seismic, so I went to town and walked around inside the mall, and today both of my little toes are sore and red. When I got home from the rig this afternoon, I wrapped them in Band-Aids.

It's beautiful outside. A bright glowing orange sun sits perched on the western horizon, casting an orange veil up into the sky and out over the windswept grass. My shadow stretches long and skinny into the field like a Giacometti sculpture as I crunch along the white crushed-rock road in my boots.

Out along the highway I see a bright red truck gliding along. As it nears the ranch entrance, it slows. His telltale diesel engine rattles and clatters. It's Merle. He turns in on the ranch road and, white dust trailing up behind him, rumbles toward me. Elbow propped out his open window, he slows to a stop. He pushes back his hat.

"Hey, boy. What the hell ya doin'?"

I hold up my letter.

"I'm going to put this in the mailbox."

"What's uh matter? Ol' Blue die on ya?"

"No. I just wanted to walk."

"Aw hell, get in. I'll give ya a ride."

I go around and get in the truck. He guns the engine, swings around into the dry grass field, and, slinging rocks under his double back tires, launches back out toward the highway.

"Well?" I say. "Did you find anything?"

"Yeah, I poked around till I thank I found some uh that three-D seismic."

"And?"

"Well, I couldn' get close enough to it without spookin' the ol' boy who's got it." He skids to a halt by the mailbox. White dust blows back over the truck across the highway. "But I ain't done yet. I'm gonna sic yer ass on him."

"*My* ass?"

"Yep. I called around and found this ol' boy named Wild Bill. He runs a pawnshop outfit in Fort Worth, and he specializes in cameras. I went by and saw him this afternoon. I got us some spyin' equipment lined up."

"*Spying* equipment?"

"Yep. Yer gonna make one hell of a spy, son."

I stare at him. He points out to the mailbox.

"Go on. Mail yer letter."

"SUMBITCH, 'ERE IT IS." MERLE SWERVES THROUGH THREE
lanes of traffic and skids to a halt on the right shoulder of the
freeway. Ahead of us, against a bright blue sky, stands downtown
Fort Worth, its small cluster of buildings gleaming in the morning
sun. To our right, above a steep grassy embankment along the
freeway, a store—Wild Bill's Camera and Pawn. "Dammit,"
Merle says, " 'ere's Wild Bill's outfit right 'ere. I missed my get-
off."

"So what?" I point up the freeway. "Just go on up. There'll
be another exit, then you can just loop back around to the frontage road up there."

Merle looks up the grass embankment.

"Aw hell, the sumbitch is right 'ere. I ain't gonna drive from
here to tomorrow just to get right 'ere. Hang on, lemme get
wound-up good." He turns his wheels toward the embankment
and revs the engine. I look at the embankment, then the three
streaming lanes of rush-hour traffic immediately to our left.

"Merle, I don't know about this. It's got to be illegal, and for
God's sake, there's hundreds of witnesses."

"Aw hell, they don't care about us. They got their own rats
to kill. Hang on." He pops the clutch and guns the engine. With
a diesel roar we lurch up onto the embankment. Digging for trac-
tion and slinging dirt down onto the freeway, the truck bucks,

bounces, and climbs. Our momentum shoots us over the crest of the hill, over the curb, and into the frontage road.

URRRRRR.

A blue compact screeches to a halt as we shoot out and stop in its path.

BEEP-BEEEEEEP.

The driver, a heavyset bald guy, honks and shoots Merle the bird. Merle points at him.

"Settle down, fat boy." Merle looks both directions, then slowly continues across the road, into the parking lot of Wild Bill's Camera and Pawn.

Ⱥ Ⱥ Ⱥ

"Mornin', Wild Bill." Merle nods and shakes Wild Bill's hand over a glass case of cameras, watches, and pistols.

Wild Bill is about forty and, except for his gold wire-rim glasses, looks like a biker—thick salt-and-pepper beard, long salt-and-pepper hair pulled back into a ponytail, black leather vest and black T-shirt with a picture of a motorcycle shooting yellow flames from its exhaust, and faded blue jeans. Behind him, arranged along the wall, are dozens and dozens of shotguns, rifles, and hunting bows.

"Morning, Mr. Luskey," Wild Bill says.

Merle hitches up his pants. He is dressed a notch above his normal attire. He wears his gray cowboy boots (which, I've learned, are made of bull's hide), a hideous gray western suit with wide lapels, a white shirt, a thin black tie, and his straw cowboy hat. He gestures to me.

"Wild Bill, this here's Harvard."

Wild Bill holds out his hand and I shake with him.

"I'm sorry," he says. "What's your name?"

"Er—"

"Harvard," Merle says. " 'At's where the lil sumbitch went to school. Harvard University."

Wild Bill raises his eyebrows, apparently impressed, then lifts a board between two glass cases and motions for us to come behind the counter.

"Okay. I believe I have everything ready. Mr. Luskey, Harvard, if y'all will step back here."

Wild Bill leads us into the back room, past shelves full of used cameras, guns, stereo components, TVs, and VCRs, to a wooden workbench. On the bench, under a bright jeweler's lamp, sits a small black box about the size of a pack of cigarettes. Sticking out from the center of the box, about a half inch in diameter and one inch in length, is a silver metallic cylinder with a glass lens. From the bottom of the box runs a tiny black cord about three feet long, at the end of which is a metallic buttonlike device. Wild Bill strokes his beard and gestures to the box.

"Harvard, meet Little Ivan."

"What *is* that?"

Merle smiles.

"It's a goddam lil ol' camera. Tell him about it, Wild Bill."

"Yes sir. This is a Kavorsky Nine Hundred. Designed and manufactured by the Russians back in sixty-four for the KGB." Wild Bill picks it up and turns it slowly under the lamp. "He's my pride and joy. Bought him last year in Amsterdam."

"Tell him how it works."

"He's very simple, really. That's his beauty. We'll strap him to your chest here with gauze tape." Wild Bill pats the center of my chest. "Then you'll put your shirt on over him. The lens will extend between the buttoned seam in your shirt, then we can either cut a hole in your tie here, or I have a particular tie I recommend, with a hole already in it and a pattern that disguises the lens."

I start to feel queasy. I look at Merle. He smiles.

"Can ya believe 'at lil ol' thayng takes color pictures?"

"Uh, excuse us, Wild Bill." I take Merle by the elbow and lead him across the room behind a shelf of dusty TV components. Although he told me spying was to be involved in our business in Fort Worth, I didn't expect anything quite this involved. "All right, Merle, what the hell's going on now?"

"We're gonna try to get some pictures uh some three-D seismic. Wild Bill said 'at camera'll do it. Ya cain't hear it click or nothin'." He smiles. "Nobody'll ever know yer takin' pictures." He points over his shoulder with his thumb. "And ol' Wild Bill's got some kind uh gadget back 'ere 'at'll blow up the pictures real big so we can see ever' lil ol' thayng."

I sigh.

"And, of course, you want *me* to wear the camera."

"Damn straight."

I nod.

"Damn straight. That's what I thought." Although I want to scream, I whisper. "Look, Merle, I'm just an innocent party to all this. I lost some goddam money playing poker on a bus, and now I'm here. Okay? This is *your* thing, *your* dream that you're trying to save. So Merle, *you* need to wear the camera. Not me."

He pushes up his hat brim and scowls.

"Listen here, ya lil sumbitch. I'm a driller from Abilene, Texas. My backyard's where this company man does his work. He ain't gonna lemme get near his seismic map. But *you*—" He gestures to me. I'm wearing my garb for cold-calling agents—navy pinstriped suit, cream shirt, gold-and-maroon paisley tie, and black loafers (Merle refused to let me wear my chocolate lizards). "Yer from Boston, New Anglin'. Yer a damn Yankee with 'at stick-up-yer-ass way uh talkin'. He ain't gonna worry aboutchoo. You can get right up 'ere behind his desk and get some good pictures."

"Whatever, Merle. This is probably corporate espionage. What if I end up in a federal penitentiary because of this?"

He scoffs.

"Bullshit." He waves out toward Fort Worth. "We're a skeeter on a bull's ass compared to these ol' boys. They ain't gonna do nothin' to us."

I shake my head.

"C'mon, Merle. Isn't there some other way to get three-D seismic?"

"Yeah. I looked into it. You can shootchur own, but like ya said, 'at takes months. And ever' few months they have auctions where people sell it, but the next auction's not till summertime. And goddammit, I ain't got time fer 'at. This is *it*, son." He leans down into my face. I feel nauseous. Spying? Stealing?

"I don't know, Merle. I just don't see why I—"

"Look here, ya lil sumbitch. I give ya a job and a place to stay when ya's flat on yer ass. And 'em chocolate lizards I give ya, they ain't no jackleg boots, boy. They cost me damn near five hunerd dollars. Now if yer ever gonna be worth the damn thayngs, yer gonna—"

I hold up my hands.

"Okay, okay." I turn and look at a shelf of rusty TV guts.

What the hell. He's right. I won't know anybody at the oil company—I don't live anywhere near here. And I'm sick of him calling me a loser. I sigh and look back at him.

"I'll wear the fucking camera, Merle." I point my finger in his face. "But if we get caught, you better stand up for me and tell the truth. I'm just a hired ignorant flunky following orders. I don't want to go to jail over this."

"Hey." He opens his eyes wide in a deadly earnest expression. "You go to jail, and I guarantee I'll sprayng yer ass 'fore ya can whistle 'Dixie,' son."

I pat his arm.

"Thanks, Merle. Thanks."

"HANG ON. ONE MORE THAYNG 'FORE WE GO IN." AS MERLE
fumbles with his keys and unlocks the chrome toolbox in the
bed of his truck, I step up to the side-view mirror and study
my guise. It's true. The tie Wild Bill rigged me with is perfect
camouflage. In its pattern of tiny silver-rimmed gray bubbles
Little Ivan's lens is undetectable. Even out here in the bright
sunshine I have to look for several seconds before I find the
one tiny bubble slightly duller than the rest. The problem is,
the tie doesn't go with my suit. It's gray and dark green and
my suit is navy with powder blue pinstripes. I'm afraid someone, clued by this fashion clash, will stare at my tie and see
Little Ivan.

"Fuck, Merle, this tie does *not* match this suit."

"Aw hell, these are oil-field people we're gonna see. They
wouldn't know the difference if ya went in 'ere with yer jockstrap
hangin' around yer neck." He throws open his toolbox and brings
out a paper sack. "Com'ere. I need ya to do somethin'." He pulls
a football from the sack and tosses it to me.

"What the hell's this?"

"It's a football."

"*Duh.* What am I doing with it?"

"Yer autographin' it."

"*Autographing* it?"

"Yeah, here." He takes a black felt marker from the sack and gives it to me.

"Uh, Merle, why would anybody want a football with my autograph on it?"

"Goddam, son, yer not gonna autograph *yer* name."

"Oh, of course. Not *my* name."

"Hell no. Here." From the sack he brings out a long scroll of paper. He unrolls it. It's a poster of Troy Aikman, number 8, the Dallas Cowboys' quarterback. Legs spread wide, ball cocked behind his helmet, Troy is set to fire a bomb down the field. Merle points down to the bottom of the poster to Troy's autograph reprinted against the green AstroTurf. "I figgered ya could use this as a guide. But I wancha to personalize the sumbitch. I wannit to say, 'Max, Best Wishes, Troy Aikman.' And be careful. Make all the letters look like ol' Troy's writin' here."

I offer the ball back to him.

"Merle, why don't you do it? You can—"

"Goddammit, I write like a monkey. Now c'mon, ya didn' get 'at Harvard education fer nothin'. Sign the fuckin' ball."

Ä Ä Ä

Sun-Pride Oil and Gas headquarters is in a modestly sized but very beautiful building in downtown Fort Worth. Its main feature is a vast open-air atrium that rises up some twelve floors to a green translucent skylight. Two transparent glass elevators shuttle up and down the west side of the atrium, and each floor has a balcony all the way around the inside, so you can look down at the moss green granite floors, brass chandeliers, and planter boxes of green and red caladium.

While Merle, drawing curious looks from cigarette smokers in the lobby, beelines for the men's room with his football tucked under his arm, I wait by the planter boxes and look over a display case of information about the company.

Beginning in 1928 as a two-man venture in Wichita Falls, Texas, Sun-Pride O & G's first well, the Lilly Burton #2, "came in" at a mere fourteen barrels per day. And yet, from such humble origins, today Sun-Pride owns oil and gas production in over twelve countries, including Bolivia, Canada, Nigeria, the Philippines, and Venezuela. Moreover, the most exciting discovery of the company's entire history came last year, when, in the Cordillera mountains of southwest Colombia, its wildcat well, the Padre Rico #1-E, struck 380 feet of oil-pay and tested at over seventeen thousand barrels per day. This Colombian discovery has boosted Sun-Pride's worldwide reserves to over 1.5 billion barrels of oil and 1 trillion cubic feet of gas.

God Almighty, one point five bill—

"Ar-ight, which wall ya gonna shoot pictures of?"

I turn to find Merle fondling his football.

"Stage right, behind the guy's desk. There should be a three-D seismic map there."

"Ar-ight. Whatever ya do, don't fuck up and take pictures uh the wrong stuff. Got it?"

"Got it."

"And tell me one more time, whadda you do?"

"I'm a graduate student in English Literature at Harvard. I received my undergraduate degree in Dramatic Arts last year from Harvard, and now I'm a graduate fellow working on my master's degree in English."

(I thought "graduate fellow" would sound impressive, but Harvard doesn't have a graduate program in drama, so I'm going with English Lit.)

"Graduate fellow," Merle says. "English Literature. Ar-ight." He points at my groin. "How's yer waynger trigger?"

Held in place against my skin by a strip of gray duct tape, Little Ivan's shutter-control cable runs from the camera itself— which is strapped to my chest under my shirt and tie—down my stomach, to the right of my dick, and through a small hole in the lining of my pocket. I reach into my pocket. The shutter control is securely in place.

"Waynger trigger, check."

"Ar-ight, by God, let's go find some oil."

We board the elevator and whisk up into the atrium's expanse.

At the top floor we step out into a receiving area with several sofas and chairs and a small desk manned by an old guy in a gray security uniform. Behind him on the wall, in shiny brass letters: Exploration and Development—North America/South America.

"Good morning, gentlemen," he says. "Who were you to see?"

Merle steps up to the desk, palming his football down along his side.

"Max Dugan. Exploration manager fer West Texas. I ain't got no appointment. I's in here yesterday and uh—" He points to me with his thumb. "I had to stick around town till this mornin' and pick up my nephew over at DFW. We're on our way back to Abilene. I just thought I'd drop by real quick and see Max."

"Your name and company?"

"Merle Luskey. Luskey Drillin'. Out uh Abilene."

The security man scribbles this down, then makes a phone call.

"Mr. Merle Luskey with Luskey Drilling from Abilene is here to see you . . . yes sir." He hangs up. "I'm sorry, Mr. Luskey, but Mr. Dugan is tied up this morning."

"Ar-ight . . . well." Merle holds up the football. "Ya might wanna call him back real quick and tell him I got Troy to sign him a ball." The security man stares at the football.

"Troy Aikman?"

Merle smiles.

"Yep." Merle turns the ball and points to my bogus inscription.

"You know Troy?" the security man asks.

"Hell yeah. I used to work with his daddy up in Oklahoma pullin' wells. I knowed Troy since he was crawlin' around in a shitty diaper."

The security man stares at the ball and picks up the phone.

"Uh, yes, Mr. Luskey has a football for you, autographed by Troy Aikman . . . okay." He hangs up and points down along the wall. "Mr. Dugan will see you."

"Thanks," Merle says. "C'mon, Harvard."

We walk down along the atrium balcony. A tall stoop-shouldered guy wearing a forest green golf shirt, khaki slacks, and loafers, steps from a doorway. About fifty years old, he has thinning brownish gray hair, tired-looking puppy-dog brown eyes, a big nose, and deep wrinkles like parentheses around his mouth. He smiles and nods.

"Merle, good to see you again."

"Max. How the hell are ya?" Merle steps up and shakes his hand. "Max, this is my nephew from Boston. Harvard. 'At's what I call him cuz 'at's where the sumbitch goes to school. Harvard University. He's a goddam graduate degree. Shake ol' Max's hand, Harvard."

I step up and offer my hand.

"Erwin Vandeveer."

"Pleasure to meet you, Erwin," Max says. He nods and shakes my hand. Merle holds up the football.

"I hope I ain't tormentin' ya, Max. I had to stick around town and pick Harvard up at the airport this mornin,' so I went over to Dallas last night and saw Troy. Got him to sign ya a ball." He gives Max the football. Max smiles and reads the inscription on the ball. He raises his eyebrows as though quite impressed.

"Gosh, Merle. Thanks."

"Hell yeah, Max. Glad to do it. Ya said ya was a big fan. Normally I don't like to lean on Troy fer stuff like 'at, but now and then I meet somebody I figger deserves it."

Max smiles.

"Like somebody who might drill some wells with you?"

"*Ah-ha-ha.*" Merle laughs and grabs Max's arm. "You wudn' born in the barn, was ya, Max?"

Max chuckles and motions to the door.

"Y'all come in. Please." We follow him into a large room. The walls are lined with computer terminals, filing cabinets, and racks of long white scrolls of paper, which I guess are maps. Over each rack are plaques on the wall with names of geographical areas like South Texas, West Texas, Louisiana, Arkansas, New Mexico, Wyoming. A dozen or so small offices branch off from this large room. Some of their doors are open, revealing men and women working at drafting tables. They glance at us as we walk across to a doorway with a big plastic plaque over it: Director, West Texas Exploration.

We step into Max's office, and he gestures to two chairs arranged in front of his desk.

"Y'all sit down."

I take a seat and glance at the wall to my left behind his desk. Sure enough, up on the wall, held in place by large magnets at its corners, is a large colorful map. Just like in the books and articles I saw the other night, it looks like a thermographic image—a long diagonal mass of bright colors ranging from blue to purple to red to orange to yellow to white. Max sets the football on his desk and sits down.

"So, how's Troy's elbow?"

"Do what?" Merle says.

"Troy's elbow. I read in this morning's paper he had orthoscopic surgery on his elbow yesterday. From that riding accident he had up in Oklahoma last week."

Merle stares stupidly.

"Oh, yeah, hell, Troy's *elbow.*" He scoffs. "Aw, hell, it's fine. He's just got a lil ol' bandage on it."

Max nods.

"Yeah, the paper said he should be able to throw the ball in less than a week."

"Hell yeah. He could throw tomorrow if he wanted. You know Troy. Sumbitch is tougher'n a keg uh nails."

Max smiles and nods. He turns to me.

"So, you're from Boston?"

"Yes sir, I am," I say, exaggerating my accent.

"What brings you down here?"

"Oh, just visiting. It's spring break and I haven't seen Uncle Merle in . . . gosh . . . six years, so I decided to get out of the slush and come down to warmer territory for a bit." I glance at Merle. "See how the old redneck sonofabitch is doing."

Merle laughs awkwardly.

"Look out, Yankee boy."

"Merle said you're a student at Harvard? Is that right?"

"Yes."

"Wow. *Harvard.* What do you study?"

"I'm a graduate fellow in English Literature."

Max whistles, apparently impressed.

"Forgive me for being so dumb, but what does that mean exactly, a graduate *fellow*?"

"Well, essentially it means the university underwrites my expenses—tuition, stipend, et cetera—and in turn, I assist by teaching undergraduates."

"Really? At Harvard?"

"Yes."

"What classes do you teach?"

"Oh . . . uh . . . primarily just basic surveys of literature. You know, English between the wolves, Beo to Virginia." I smile, hoping Max will like my old English professor's joke, but both he and Merle stare at me and nod seriously.

"That's impressive," Max says.

"Oh, not really. So, I guess you are what? A geologist?"

Max looks down and fidgets with a paper clip on his desk.

"Well, not officially. My degree is in Petroleum Engineering. I went to Lamar University. It's a small school down in Beaumont. You've probably never heard of it."

I shake my head.

"No, I can't say I have."

He smiles.

"Well, it's no Harvard, that's for sure."

"Yeah," Merle says, "but I betcha 'ere's a bunch uh good-lookin' split-tail runnin' around down 'ere, huh?"

Max smiles.

"A few."

Merle slaps my shoulder.

"Listen to 'at, would ya. A *few*. Hell, I bet ol' Max had to beat 'em back with a two-headed hammer."

Max smiles, picks up the football from his desk, and turns it in his hands. He looks at me.

"Anyway, to answer your question, I've worked in the oil business for twenty-five years nearly, and done a little bit of everything, so even though I'm only degreed as an engineer, I fancy myself somewhat of a geologist, too."

I look around the walls at the maps and photographs of drilling rigs and pumping jacks.

"What a fascinating business. It must be exciting to search for something hidden in the earth."

Max glances around his office.

"Yeah, I enjoy it. Being with a company like Sun-Pride allows me to be a part of some exciting, fairly big projects."

"Big is right," Merle says. He looks at me. "Ol' Maxy-boy's gonna drill fifteen or twenty wells out in my neighborhood this year. And I'm gonna drill ever' damn one of 'em, ain't 'at right, Max?"

Max smiles.

"We'll see, Merle. We'll see."

"Aw, I'm just tormentin' ya, Max. But I really would like to drill fer y'all."

"I appreciate that, Merle. I can't make any promises, but I'll do my best."

"Ar-ight. Hey, Max, mind if I use yer phone real quick? My goddam mother broke her hip, and while I'm in town I'm supposed to pick up some kind uh orthopedic thayng to help her sit up straight. I wanna make sure the place is gonna be open durin' lunch."

"Sure," Max says. He turns his phone around for Merle. "I'm sorry to hear that about your mother."

"Aw, thank ya, Max. I tell ya what, gettin' old's a rough-ass bizness. When I get up 'ere perty good, I'm gonna get me a case uh Jack Daniel's and a couple uh whores, and hole up in a motel room somewhere and see if I cain't finish myself off." He laughs, picks up the phone, and dials a number. Max leans back and looks at me.

"So, English Literature. What do you plan to do with that? Or do you mind me asking?"

"Uh . . . no, of course not." I cross my legs and lean back in my chair. "Actually, drama is my area of specialty, particularly . . . uh . . . the expressionist movement. You know, O'Neill, Rice, Strindberg. And . . . uh . . . ultimately I would like to direct, to stage some of O'Neill's lesser-known works. You know, the sea dramas. *In the Zone, The Long Voyage Home, The Moon of the Caribbees.*"

Max raises his eyebrows and nods.

"Wow."

I hold up my hands.

"Please. Academia is overrated, I assure you. The real world is far more interesting. In fact, I'm curious about what you do, exactly."

"Oh, sure. Well, let me show you."

As Merle talks into the phone, pretending to inquire about

the status of an orthopedic device for his mother, Max invites me around his desk, shows me a map of West Texas, and gives a fascinating overview of the Permian Basin. Going back three million years, he describes the prehistoric environment and the depositional events which led to hydrocarbons being formed and trapped below the earth's surface.

"My God," I say, "that is amazing. I had no idea these processes were so *ancient.*"

"Oh yes, it took Mother Nature millions of years to work her magic."

"Incredible. Utterly incredible. And what in the world is *that?*" I point to the colorful map on the other wall. "Some type of satellite photograph?"

Max smiles.

"No, that's a three-dimensional seismic survey." He glances at Merle.

"Goduhmighty," Merle says into the phone, "whadda ya mean ya cain't find it. Lemme talk to yer boss. I'm gonna get me a piece uh somebody's ass."

"Com'ere," Max says, "I'll show you."

We step across to the 3-D seismic map. In the lower right-hand corner, the legend reads:

SUN-PRIDE OIL AND GAS

WEST BOOMERANG 3-D SURVEY

KENT COUNTY, TEXAS

CANYON REEF

As Max explains the geological origin of buried limestone reefs and their prolific nature as hydrocarbon producers, with my right hand harmlessly in my pocket, I *ooh* and *ahh* at his fascinating presentation.

WILD BILL WORKS HIS TONGS IN THE EERIE LIGHT. ONE BY ONE he dips photographs into the solution bin, then hangs them with clothespins on a string along the wall. Merle follows immediately behind him, leaning his face within inches of the dripping images.

"Goddam, Wild Bill, they're all the same thayng."

"Mr. Luskey, please." Wild Bill washes a picture in the ammonia solution and coaxes the image to life. "Like I told you yesterday, given the highly detailed nature of what you're looking for, we're going to need some optical enhancement."

"Well, hell, let's enhance one uh the sumbitches."

Wild Bill sighs and sets down his tongs. He wipes his hands with a rag and looks at the drying photos.

"All right, since we do have some duplication, I don't suppose it would hurt to jump the gun and have a look at one on the CAOE." He plucks down the first photo and leads us through a curtain and out the darkroom door to the back of his shop. As we pass into normal lighting, the photo in his hand changes from a blend of grays to a sharp image of bright colors, exactly like the seismic map on Max Dugan's wall, though, of course, on a much smaller scale.

Wild Bill closes his office door and boots up his computer. He tapes the photo onto a white glass plate beside his computer, then carefully places a rectangular box over it. The box, he explains, is a CAOE, or computer-assisted optical enhancer. Using a lens and high-intensity light in the box, together with computer software, it inflates the scale of the photo and produces this inflated image on the computer monitor.

Wild Bill sits at his computer. With Merle leaning over his shoulder, he adjusts the rubber-band cinch on his salt-and-pepper ponytail, lights a cigarette, and, using keystrokes to manipulate the image on his monitor, starts our high-res analysis.

The resolution is amazing. At a scale at least twice that of the original map on Max Dugan's wall, Wild Bill scans the photo piecemeal on his monitor and sends commands to his printer. One by one, 8½-by-11 color reproductions roll from his laser printer.

Merle and I piece the overlapping images together on Wild Bill's desk, and soon we have a perfect reproduction of the seismic survey's legend and keys, including the structural values represented by the various colors. Based on what Max Dugan told me about the Permian Basin in West Texas and the particular formation represented on this map, called the Canyon Reef, combined with what I learned the other night at the geology library, I try to explain to Merle and Wild Bill, as best I can, more or less what we're looking at.

In the Pennsylvanian period, or about 320 million years ago, what is currently known as West Texas was a huge oceanic basin. This basin sloped down from east to west and the ocean encroached from the west, filling the entire basin to depths of up to several miles.

However, through a process lasting millions of years, a vast mountain range in modern-day Arkansas and Missouri was eroded by weather and carried down to this basin by rivers. Thus, gradually the basin filled with sediment from the east, causing the ocean to retreat westward and eventually disappear altogether.

In its heyday, though, before it was overcome by sedimentary deposition, this West Texas ocean teemed with animal life. Among the creatures in this primordial marine world were microscopic algae. Sort of like barnacles, these algae clumped together in colonies, or reefs, in the warm, sunny water near the ocean's surface. Over time, as the water level rose in the basin, these creatures built their colonies upward, following the surface of warm, sunlit water. Thus, in the course of the Pennsylvanian period, enormous mountain-range-like reefs developed in the oceans and warm bays of Texas.

Later, as deposition from the east gained the upper hand, these reefs were covered by layers and layers of various fine-grained silts. Through a slow metamorphic process of heat and pressure, resulting from more and more sediment being piled on them, these reefs turned to limestone, a soft porous rock (made essentially of the skeletons of the algae). Because they're organic in origin, these buried limestone reefs often contain hydrocarbons, sometimes in mind-boggling quantities. For instance, Scurry County Reef, near the West Texas town of Snyder, has produced over two billion barrels of oil.

After sixty years of drilling and 2-D seismic exploration, most of the major structures like Scurry County Reef have been discovered and produced. However, scattered under West Texas, usually on the flanks of known large reef bodies, there remain isolated pinnacle reefs, or tall, spindly reef bodies that tower like skyscrapers under the ground. Because of their shape—tall and narrow—many pinnacle reefs eluded 2-D seismic exploration, for unless the 2-D line lay right over the top of them, they didn't appear on the data. But with the advent of 3-D seismic, these gangly structures, if they lie somewhere under the grid of the survey, are revealed.

According to Max Dugan, pinnacle reefs are the prize game of the modern West Texas wildcatter. If penetrated at their exact tops where the oil accumulates, they come in at a high rate—sometimes over five hundred barrels per day—returning one's investment fairly soon. Also they typically hold up for years, producing hundreds of thousands, even millions, of barrels per well.

Thus, our seismic map is a three-dimensional image of approximately twenty-six square miles of the Canyon Reef under Kent County, Texas, which is about one hundred miles northwest of Abilene. And though what is represented lies well over a mile underground, again, it looks like a topographic map of a mountain range on the earth's surface, where various colors correspond to various elevations. From the legend I discover that the elevations are determined relative to sea level and have negative values. In other words, the base of the Canyon Reef is about 10,000 feet underground in Kent County, but the ground elevation is roughly 2,000 feet above sea level, therefore the base of the reef is about 8,000 feet below sea level, or −8,000. But from this base—or the areas of the reef body with the least buildup—the reef rises over 1,200 feet in places to a subsea elevation of −6,800. Again, it is these high areas of the reef where oil and gas accumulate.

As I relate everything I can remember from Max Dugan's presentation, as well as my own personal crash course, Merle paces anxiously around Wild Bill's desk with his hands on his hips and his hat tilted back up off his forehead.

"Ar-ight, ar-ight," he says, "enough uh this Mickey Mouse crap. What's 'at damn map say? Is 'ere somewhere I can drill?"

"Just hang on, Merle. We have to understand the legend before we can understand the map."

Although the general scheme is obvious—dark colors represent the lower areas of the reef, light colors the higher—I look over the legend's color scale again to familiarize myself with its values. Starting with black, which represents the areas with a sea-level elevation of −8,000 to −7,950, the scale moves through about twenty-five color values—dark blues, royal blues, purples, reds, oranges, yellows, and finally white, which represents the very highest value of −6,800 or higher.

Satisfied that we have at least a working idea of our legend,

I pull up a chair beside Wild Bill and we begin to scan the map on his computer monitor. Merle paces back and forth behind us, looking over our shoulders.

Long and narrow, the overall reef body is oriented diagonally, southwest to northeast. Wild Bill begins scanning from the southwest.

Almost immediately he moves across a spot where the reef builds to a dull yellow, indicating a high peak in the structure with an elevation value of $-7,000$ to $-6,950$. And yet, drawn on the map with a red pen, no doubt by Max Dugan's own hand, a box surrounds this yellow high. Beside the box: a scribbled note that says *Three-Year Lease Secure*, followed by a date, which we decide must be the day the lease was purchased.

We scan further up and again find another yellow high, only to see that it, too, is boxed in red and noted, *Three-Year Lease Secure.*

Again and again Wild Bill scans to a yellow high on the reef, only to reveal a surrounding red box and somewhere in close proximity, Max Dugan's red-penned note—*Three-Year Lease Secure.* With each of these boxed-in yellow highs, Merle, leaning down over our shoulders, curses and grumbles. It's like torture. Right there under the ground could be his financial salvation, except Sun-Pride Oil and Gas already has leased the land over the reef high, giving them sole right to drill and exploit the appropriate acreage.

After an hour or so, having scanned the entire main reef body, we reach its far northeast extent.

"Goddammit!" Merle jerks off his hat and throws it on the floor. "What the hell was I thankin'? These boys ain't jacklegs. Ain't no damn way they're gonna go out 'ere and spend all 'at money shootin' seismic, then walk off and leave a hickey unleased. I arta have my ass kicked." He jerks his wallet out of his back pocket. "Whaddo I owe ya, Wild Bill? I'm gettin' the hell out uh here. C'mon, Harvard. This is makin' me sick."

I get up from my chair and pick up his hat. Merle grits his teeth and prepares to shell out Wild Bill's fee.

"C'mon, dammit. Whaddo I owe ya? Fer the spy camera, makin' the pictures, this computer work, the whole shootin' match. How much?"

Wild Bill strokes his beard and studies the monitor.

"Hey, Harvard. Com'ere."

"What is it?"

"I don't know. You tell me."

Merle and I both step back up behind Wild Bill. There on the monitor, out by itself, about a mile west of the northeast end of the main reef body, surrounded by black and rising up through rings of the entire spectrum—blue, purple, red, and yellow—to the highest level on the legend, white, stands an enormous isolated pinnacle. It's fairly broad across the top—it looks about one-third of a mile in diameter at its peak—and the white color of its apex indicates that, from the black base surrounding it, it rises at least twelve hundred feet high. But most interesting of all, Max Dugan has penned a red box around the feature and, above it, in red letters, written, *240 Acres. Owner Will Not Lease!*

His black oiled Elvis-like hair drooping across his forehead, Merle leans down between Wild Bill and me and stares at the monitor.

"Sweet Mary's ass. What the hell's 'at thayng, Harvard?"

"I guess it's a pinnacle reef. It's obviously very high. It's white on top. That's as high as it gets. Minus sixty-eight hundred or higher."

"And the sumbitch ain't leased?"

"I guess not. At least that's what it says."

Merle grabs his hat from me. Still gawking at the monitor, he pulls his hat down on his head and runs his hands along the brim.

"Goduhmighty, look at that thayng, boys. She's just sittin' out 'ere waitin' fer some jackleg like me to come along and drill her. Wild Bill, ya long-haired sumbitch! I love ya!"

"RECKON IT'S ABOUT TIME FER A TASTE UH WHISKEY,
don'choo?" Hurtling down a narrow two-lane highway, diesel engine roaring, Merle reaches back and brings up his ever-handy backseat half-gallon bottle of Jack Daniel's. He takes a swig, then offers the bottle to me. I just ignore him and keep staring up the road. I don't want to be a jerk, but it's the middle of the day and we're driving, for God's sake. He looks at me. "What's uh matter?"

"It's barely after lunchtime, Merle. We're *driving*. Haven't you ever heard of this thing called a DWI?"

He frowns.

"Well goduhmighty, I ain't never seen nobody turn up their nose at a taste uh good whiskey like you."

"Whatever."

In the side-view mirror I can still see downtown Fort Worth behind us. Before us, about 250 miles to the west is the town of Jayton, Texas, county seat of Kent County. There, in the county courthouse, Wild Bill said, there should be a record of who owns the minerals under the north half of Section 255 in the H&TC Railroad Company Survey, which, after further analyzing our stolen seismic map, we determined to be the land situated directly over the pinnacle reef which Merle calls the *big hickey*. And before that courthouse in Jayton closes today at five o'clock, Merle intends to learn who this mineral owner is. But, in his typical hardheaded fashion, he doesn't seem to understand that there's no way we can get there by five o'clock.

As I stew over his stubbornness, I stare out at the rolling golden-grass prairie and the fence posts flicking by along the road.

"Let me put it this way, Merle. To get there by five you're going to have to drive over ninety miles an hour the whole way. Do you understand that?" I turn and look at him. He swigs his bottle.

"Hell, we're gonna have to do better'n 'at." He nods up the road. "We gotta go through a bunch uh lil ol' towns. 'At's gonna cut our time perty good." He looks down at his speedometer. "I figger I hold on here just over a hunerd, we arta make it."

"A *hundred*?" I lean over and check the speedometer.

105.

"Jesus, Merle." I tighten my seat belt and suddenly I get mad as hell. Why can't the dumb sonofabitch do anything normal? I mean duh, no wonder he's about to go bankrupt. Who can run a business swigging whiskey all day and driving around like the Indy 500?

I take deep breaths and try to just chill, but I can't. We're practically flying and Merle's getting tanked and I'm about to die in a flame-ball crash out here in the middle of nowhere. I look at Merle.

"Sometimes you piss me off, you know it?" I snatch the bottle from him and take a burning swig. He looks at me and nods.

" 'Ere ya go, son."

Å Å Å

We roll into Throckmorton and stop at its one traffic light: to our left, a Dairy Queen, to our right, a John Deere tractor dealership. Another big four-door cab pickup truck pulls up alongside us. It's navy blue and occupied by three girls, all sitting in the front seat and all wearing cowboy hats.

Urrr-Urrr.

They honk. I look at them. The driver, a chubby-faced girl about eighteen years old with long blond hair flowing out under her hat, smiles and motions for me to roll down my window. I do.

"Heidi," she says.

I nod.

"Hi."

"You sure are good-lookin'," she says.

"Oh? You think so?"

"Hell, yes."

Her friends laugh and duck their faces behind their hats. After more than a few encounters with Jack Daniel's to lube my fear of a high-speed death crash, I'm pretty lit. I prop my elbow up on the door, lean out, and give her a big glamour smile.

"Well, you're looking rather righteous yourself, sugar cake."

Her friends giggle.

"*Righteous?*" she says.

"Uh-huh."

"What's 'at mean?"

"It means . . . *delicious.*"

Her friends burst into hysterics. She smiles.

"You talk funny. Where ya from?"

"Cambridge."

"*Cambridge?* Where's 'at?"

I point back over the bed of her truck toward the John Deere tractor yard.

"It's back up that way."

"You ain't from Oklahoma, are ya?"

"Hell no."

"Well honey, you just need to get over here in this truck. We'll show ya how we party in Throckmorton."

Her friends laugh again. Merle grumbles behind me.

"Goduhmighty," he says.

The light turns green. Merle pops the clutch and guns the accelerator full speed out of town, but the girls race up beside us.

"*Hey, good-lookin'!*" the blond driver yells, her hair flapping in the wind. "*Don't go! I think I love you!*"

Laughing, her friends pull her hat off. She slows and veers off the road. I roll my window up.

Apparently shaken by my exchange with the cowgirls, Merle clutches the bottle and stares gravely up the road. I try to grab the bottle from him, but he won't let go. He swigs it and scowls.

"What the hell's wrong with you?" I ask.

Holding the bottle by its neck, he points his finger at me.

"I'm tellin' ya, boy. Watch out fer women. Ya let 'at ol' pecker do yer thankin' and you'll wind up in a world uh hurt. Ya hear me?"

I laugh and grab the bottle from him.

"Chill out. I was just talking to them."

He scowls.

"I don't care. 'Em gals are crooked sumbitches. They start off lovin' on ya like 'ere's no tomorrow, but 'fore ya can turn around and spit, yer just a goddam money sack to 'em."

I raise the bottle to my lips.

"Hell," he says, "all five uh my wives were just alike."

Pppppppp.

Midswig from the bottle, I burst out laughing and spray Jack Daniel's across the dash.

"You've been married *five* times?"

He snatches the bottle away.

"It ain't funny, son."

"I know. I'm sorry. What were their names? Your wives?"

Staring out at the road as we thunder along at a hundred plus, he sighs and reaches down and scratches his nuts.

"Aw hell, let's see. First 'ere was Jaylene. We got married way too young. We was both eighteen. She was a good-lookin' lil sumbitch, but *goddam*, she turned mean."

I crack up laughing. He pushes up his hat and frowns.

"It ain't funny, goddammit. I'm tryin' to give ya some good advice, son."

I crack up again.

"BY GOD, THIS ARTA BE IT. SEE 'AT WORKIN' PEN?" MERLE points to an old gray wooden corral across the barbed-wire fence. He looks at a photocopy of an aerial photograph from the court-house. "Yep, 'ere's Comanche Peak right over 'ere." He points to a low hill on the north horizon. "Scheermeyer's three-twenty starts right here." As Merle lets the truck roll slowly down the dirt road, we look across the barbed wire at the 320 acres owned by, according to the deed records in the Kent County Courthouse, Mr. Alton Scheermeyer. The sun hangs low on the horizon, bath-ing with orange the west side of fence posts, the gray sagging-board corral, gold grass, dark scrubby cedar bushes, and clumps of cactus. From across the land, heads bobbing and eyes wide with eagerness, a herd of black cows trots toward us.

"Hey, look at the cows."

"Uh-huh," Merle says. He stops the truck. As though we're the pied piper, the whole herd of about five hundred trots up and congregates across the fence from us. Most are black with white heads, though some are entirely black. They twitch their ears, swish their tails, and stare with big curious eyes.

"What are they doing, Merle? They seem like they're in-trigued by us."

"Hell, they're hungry. Look at 'em. Rangy-lookin' sum-bitches."

"So they think we have food?"

"I reckon. Ol' Scheermeyer prob'ly throws 'em cake out uh his truck." He studies our computer-generated copy of Sun-Pride's seismic survey. "Where's 'at big hickey at?"

We compare the seismic map and the aerial photograph from the county courthouse.

"I guess it would be under the ground right out there about, what, two thousand feet?" I point northwest, to the middle of Alton Scheermeyer's land. Merle nods.

"Yep." He lays the papers on the seat between us and stares out over the herd of curious cows. "By God, Harvard, we gotta get this lease." He starts again up the road.

MAAAAAA.

One of the cows raises its nose, rolls back its eyes, and bellows.

MAAAAAA.

Others join in, then, in one galloping, shoulder-to-shoulder troop, they turn and follow along beside us.

A few hundred yards down, at a dented white mailbox, a dirt road leads over a raised bridgelike structure made of rusty pipes lying parallel across a gap in the fence. Down this road, about a half of a mile back, sits a long white trailer house. Merle turns and eases onto the bridge of pipes.

"What are these pipes for?"

"Cattle guard."

"Oh."

The cows, dust swirling and blowing over their backs, ramble up and gather on the road before us, blocking our path.

MAAAAAA.

"Look out, ya starvin' bastards!" Merle pushes the accelerator and launches the truck forward.

"Jesus, Merle!" I think he's going to run them over, but the cows jerk their heads up and whirl away, clearing the road for us.

We break free of their ranks and drive down the road, but they follow us, trotting right behind us, heads bobbing up and down.

Alarmed, I guess, by our clattering diesel engine, not to mention the bellows and trouncing hooves of our reception committee, as we approach the trailer house a fat white-haired guy steps out carrying a shotgun. He's barefoot and his hair is tousled and shaggy as though he just woke from a nap. He wears a sleeveless white T-shirt and faded blue jeans with suspenders dangling from his hips. Glaring down at us from the top step of a cement stoop in front of his trailer house, he holds the shotgun horizontally before him, propped on top of his big round stomach.

"Goduhmighty," Merle says, "ol' boy's a lil touchy, ain't he?" Merle stops the truck back about twenty yards from the trailer house and kills the engine. The cows swarm around us. Merle tries to open his door, but the herd is jammed up against the truck.

MAAAAAA.

"Goddam heifers." Merle shoves his door, pushing back the herd, and steps out among them.

"Who the hell are ya!" the man yells.

"I'm Merle Luskey! From Abilene. You Alton Scheermeyer?"

"Yeah, 'at be me. What the hell ya want?"

"Like to talk some bizness with ya."

"What kind uh bizness? Ya ain't another goddam oil man, are ya? I ain't signin' no drillin' lease. If 'at's whatchur after, you can just turn around and get the hell out uh here."

Merle chews his lip.

"No sir," he yells, "I ain't no oil man."

"Then what the hell ya want?"

"I'm in cattle. like you. I's thankin' about pickin' up a few hunerd acres a lil ways back toward Jayton. I heard you knew more about runnin' cattle around here than any other sumbitch in the whole county. I wanted to talk to ya."

Alton Scheermeyer takes one hand off the shotgun and scratches his armpit.

"Ar-ight, goddammit. Come on in." He aims the shotgun in the air.

BOOM.

He fires the gun.

"Get on, heifers!" he yells.

The cows bolt and scramble away.

Å Å Å

Alton Scheermeyer frowns and waves to his door.

"Y'all come on in, dammit."

Merle and I follow him into his trailer house. He props his shotgun by the door and points to an old tattered green sofa.

"Sit over 'ere."

Merle and I sit. To our left: a dark kitchen separated from this long narrow living area by a counter covered with rope, spools of wire, wire cutters, pliers, leather gloves, aerosol cans labeled Hoof Treater, and a heap of sweat-stained hats and caps. Across from us: a beige Naugahyde recliner, a small table, and a floor lamp. A *Penthouse* magazine lies on the table, a smiling blonde on its cover, her cleavage bulging from a red V-necked sweater. Along the opposite wall: an entire *bank* of magazines, hundreds of them, neatly stacked some five feet high against the wall. I can't see any covers, but each has that certain thickness—about three-quarters of an inch—like porno mags such as *Penthouse* and *Playboy*. To our right: perched up on a stack of plastic milk crates, an old black-and-white TV with a large V-shaped antenna on it. The picture is on—it's *Wheel of Fortune*—but the volume is down.

Scheermeyer groans and lowers himself into the recliner across from us. He looks like he's about sixty, though it's hard to tell because he's obviously spent a lot of time in the wind and sun. Under his messy cotton-white hair and around his clear blue eyes, his face and forehead are splotched with red streaks and lined with tiny spiderweblike wrinkles. His stomach bulges under his white T-shirt and drapes over his lap. His bare feet are snowy white and his toenails are hideously thick and yellow.

"So what the hell you boys want? Say yer thankin' about buyin' some land?"

Merle nods.

"Yes sir, I'm lookin' at a couple hunerd acres back east uh here about twenny miles. Fact, we were at the bank today lookin' into financin'." He gestures to us. " 'At's why we're all gussied up."

Scheermeyer nods.

"Say ya wanna run cattle on this land?"

"Yes sir, I been kickin' the idea around."

"Got any water on it?"

"Yes sir, it's got a tank or two."

"Rain fed, or ya got steady water?"

"It's got some irrigation on it."

"Any good grazin'?"

"Yes sir, it's mostly in cultivation. I—"

"Goddam, son, sounds like a damn good piece uh dirt. Whadda they askin' fer it?"

"Hunerd and twenny an acre."

Scheermeyer scowls.

"*Goddam*, they're proud of it, ain't they."

Merle nods.

"Too proud. Hey, we got a bottle uh Jack Daniel's out'n the truck. You interested in a lil taste?"

Scheermeyer's face softens. He scratches his armpit.

"Hell yeah, I'll have a faynger uh good whiskey."

Merle goes out to the truck and I sit with Scheermeyer. He turns his scowl to me.

"He yer daddy?"

I smile.

"No."

"Brother?"

"No. I work for him."

He nods.

"What kinda cattle y'all run?"

"Uh . . . big . . . black ones, like you have."

"Blackface baldies?"

"Uh . . . yeah." I point to the magazine on the table beside him. "You like *Penthouse*?"

"Huh?" He looks at the magazine. "Aw, hell yeah. 'Ere's some perty good-lookin' puss in this'n."

"And actually, sometimes *Penthouse* has some pretty good articles."

"Say what?"

I point to the magazine.

"The writing, the articles, they're not bad."

He frowns.

"Hell, boy, I don't *read* the damn thayngs. I just look at the puss. Tell ya what, one lil ol' gal in this'n got an ass on her like a two-hunerd-dollar yearlin'." He picks up the magazine and flips through it. He turns out the centerfold and shows it to me—a naked bronze-butted blonde on her hands and knees, smiling back over her shoulder. "How about 'at lil ol' thayng, huh? Reckon you'd know what to do if she was to wave 'at thayng atcha?"

I smile.

"By God I would," he says. He turns the centerfold and looks at it. "*Goddam*, son, 'at lil ol' monkey winks atcha, don't it?"

Merle steps back in, the half-gallon of Jack Daniel's swinging by his side. Scheermeyer gets up with a groan, goes into the dark kitchen, and returns with three small glasses. Merle fills each half full, then proposes a toast.

"Here's to good rain and dollar cows."

"Hear, hear."

We sip our whiskey.

"So," Merle says, "ya say ya got a bunch uh oil men beatin' yer door down?"

Scheermeyer scowls.

"Hell yeah."

"Well, maybe ya got some oil under ya."

"Bullshit. Ain't no oil out here."

"Then how come they're after ya?"

"Beats hell out uh me. About a year ago some big outfit out uh Fort Worth come by and offered me five dollars an acre to make some kinda map or somethin'. I didn' pay much nevermind. I just said ar-ight as long ya don't tear up my roads or spook my cows. They said, 'Oh no, we ain't gonna bother nothin', Mr. Scheermeyer. You won't even know we're out here.' So hell, I said ar-ight and signed the paper, and they gimme a check fer sixteen hunerd dollars. Hell, I thought I'd done me a perty good deal, ya know?"

Merle nods. Scheermeyer sips his whiskey and continues.

"Well, 'fore I could turn around and spit, 'em sumbitches was out here strayngin' wire ever'where. I mean back and forth, this way, 'at way, ya never seen so much goddam wire in yer whole life.

"Then one mornin' about nine o'clock they set off a bunch uh fuckin' dynamite. I mean ya never heard such a racket. Like goddam France in forty-four. And not one uh 'em sumbitches come by and told me what was goin' on. Hell, 'fore I could pull on my britches and get out the door, my goddam cows took off on a scalded-ass stampede over my north fence. Took me all day to round 'em up, and another to mend my damn fence."

"So you were a lil upset with this Fort Worth bunch?"

Scheermeyer scowls and drinks the rest of his whiskey.

"Damn right, son. But by the time I run my cows back across, the bastards was gone. I mean, just like the damn circus, they packed up and shaggy-bootled. I called Fort Worth wantin' to chew somebody's head off over 'ere, but they just kept connectin' me with somebody else. Never would talk to me. Then lo and behold, here about two months ago, the sumbitches come back with their hats in their hands wantin' to buy a damn drillin' lease. Hell, I got my gun and run 'em off. I don't care how much money they throw at me, I ain't havin' nothin' to do with no more oil people. Crookeder'n a barrel uh snakes, ever' damn one of 'em."

"So this same company out of Fort Worth, they're the ones tryin' to get a drillin' lease from ya?"

"Hell yeah. Bunch uh damn bandits."

"So you haven't leased to anyone?"

"Hell no. And I ain't gonna."

Merle finishes his glass of whiskey, then refills his and Scheermeyer's glasses.

"Well, by God, I don't blame ya, Alton. 'At sounds awful. Anyhow, I's wonderin' if ya might tell me a lil about ranchin' in this area."

"Aw, good goduhmighty," Scheermeyer says. He scratches his armpit and launches into a two-hour dissertation about raising cattle.

Fascinated by his scowling demeanor and his real-life cowboy dialect, I sit and listen to the old fart for about an hour, but when he starts droning on and on about NAFTA and his theory that the Department of Agriculture is conspiring with "the Mescans" to break the domestic cattle market, I get up and look at his magazine collection stacked along the wall.

Merle, of course, continues to feign fascination for Scheermeyer's theory.

I was right. Scheermeyer's magazines are all pornos, mostly *Playboy* and *Penthouse*, with an occasional *Hustler* mixed in. Hundreds and hundreds of them. I flip down through the stack and find issues dating back to 1966 with big-hipped women wearing beehive hairstyles.

I discover that, in spite of its vast size, Scheermeyer has an incredible familiarity with his collection. As I randomly pull out various issues and flip through them, he pauses his diatribe against the federal government and comments on whatever particular edition I have in hand.

"Hey, look at the big-titted Mescan gal toward the back in 'at one. She is somethin' else, boy."

"Oh, hey, 'at one 'ere's got a bunch uh college gals from Californee in it. One of 'em's got the sweetest lil ol' ass on her ya nearly ever saw."

"Oh yeah, look at the redhead toward the front in 'at one. She's got her monkey shaved up real perty."

Regardless of what sector of his collection I pull a magazine from, Scheermeyer, just by glancing at its cover, directs me in it to some model or photograph that he finds particularly worthy. And when Merle stands up and announces that we'd better be going, it takes us at least fifteen minutes to get to the door, because Scheermeyer, touched by my interest, jerks out various editions and shows me further highlights of his trove, most of which involve freakishly large breasts.

"Look 'ere," he says, pointing to a blonde with tits as big as basketballs. "If we could fill 'em sumbitches with 'at Jack Daniel's, by God we'd sure enough have somethin', don'cha reckon?"

Merle laughs and pats his back.

"Damn straight, Alton. Damn straight."

Ã Ã Ã

Rumbling shadows in the moonlight, Scheermeyer's cows escort us from his trailer house out to his cattle-guard gate. Merle points out into darkness as we bounce along the dirt road.

"Yes sir, Harvard, we're gonna drill out 'ere over 'at big hickey, and ol' Merle's gonna jerk his ass right out uh the fire."

"What do you mean? You heard the old guy. He said he wouldn't lease the right to drill for anything in the world."

"Yeah, well, I thank I know how to snuggle up to ol' Scheermeyer."

"Snuggle up to him? I don't get it."

"You just leave 'at to me. Here's what I wanchoo to do. I'm gonna drop ya off at the house this evenin', and tomorrow I don't wancha goin' to the rig. You go into town first thayng tomorrow mornin' and talk to a lawyer, or go to the courthouse, or the library, or wherever the hell ya gotta go, but I wancha to write me up an oil and gas lease fer 'at ol' boy. Got it? Find out whatever it is he's gotta sign and get it ready to go by sundown tomorrow."

Oh boy, here we go again.

"Now wait a minute, Merle, I don't know anything about—"

"Dammit, don't start bellyachin.' I know damn well ya can handle this lawyer rat-killin'. Yer sharper'n a—"

"Okay, okay. I know. I'm a snake's ass. I'll do my best to handle it, but where are you going?"

"Dallas."

"*Dallas?* Tonight?"

"Yep."

"What for?"

"Gonna hire me a hand."

"A hand? What kind of hand?"

"Hell, you seen all 'em girly books in 'ere."

"Yeah. So?"

"So. We're gonna ambush 'at sumbitch."

"*Ambush* him? How?"

He pushes back his hat and stares out in the green glow of the dash light.

"With pussy."

I CLOMP OUT TO THE DRIVEWAY AND CRUNCH ACROSS THE
crushed rocks. Oh yeah. Much better. This afternoon when I got
back from the courthouse I tore the loose skin off my blisters and
put on new Band-Aids and fresh socks. It helped. My toes aren't
burning nearly so badly.

It's nice out. The wind has eased to a breeze. I hop up on ol'
Blue's tailgate, swing my chocolate lizards back and forth, and
look out toward the highway. I'm sort of worried about Merle.
He dropped me by the house last night, then left straight for
Dallas, and I haven't heard from him since. I wonder where he
is. He said to be ready by sundown, and with the sun sitting fat
and pink right over the horizon, I'd say it's officially sundown.

I decide to proof my work one more time. I pull the lease
from my shirt pocket and read through it.

I started this morning at the Abilene Public Library with a
book called *Baron's Guide to Oil and Gas Law*. I read the section
on leasing mineral rights to get a basic swing of the concept. In
order that an operator—the company who drills and operates an
oil/gas well—be able to drill for oil/gas, it must lease the right to
do so from the party (or parties) who own the minerals under
said land. In exchange for this right, the operator gives the mineral
owner (1) a royalty interest in any oil/gas that may be produced

from the land, and sometimes (2) a signing bonus, or a per-acre sum paid when the lease is signed.

After reading that all oil and gas leases must be filed for record with the county in which they're located, I went to the Taylor County Courthouse in Abilene and looked through dozens of actual leases. Almost all of the newer leases were on the same legal form, something called an API Producer's 88 form. On this form all the nitty-gritty details of the lease agreement are already spelled out. You just have to insert the parties' (Lessor's and Lessee's) names, the date of the lease, the legal description of the land subject to the lease, the term (either one, two, or three years), and the amount of royalty that Operator (Lessee) must pay Mineral Owner (Lessor). When I asked the clerk at the courthouse if she knew a business supply store that might stock these lease forms, she reached under the counter and gave me a tablet of them. She said somebody had left them there, and I could have them.

Wahlah.

However, I had read in the legal manual at the library that before he takes a lease, a duly diligent operator will *run title*, or check back through the deed records and ensure that the party from whom he is leasing actually owns the minerals. Since it wasn't even noon yet, I drove Ol' Blue up to the Kent County Courthouse in Jayton. Working through a shelf full of dusty tomes, I chained back through the official records:

a 1956 *Conveyance of Deed* from Karl Scheermeyer Jr. to Alton Scheermeyer;

a 1922 *Conveyance of Deed* from Karl Scheermeyer Sr. to Karl Scheermeyer Jr;

and a fascinating original handwritten 1893 *Land Grant* from the governor of Texas, J. S. Hogg, to Karl Scheermeyer. Therefore, according to the state of Texas, the mineral and surface owner of 320 acres of land, being the north half of Section 255 of the H&TC Railroad Company Survey, is indeed Mr. Alton Scheermeyer.

As I sit on Ol' Blue's tailgate proofing my work, I hear a rumble. I look up. Here comes Merle, kicking up a trail of white dust behind his truck on the ranch road.

Urrr-Urrr.

He honks and swings into the driveway. As he clatters toward me, the sunset's glow fills the cab, and I see he is accompanied by a large-maned silhouette.

Merle turns off the engine and steps out. Holding a big white plastic foam cup in one hand, he pulls down the front brim of his hat with the other and grins.

"Hey there, boy." He walks to the front of the truck and shakes my hand. It's obvious from his hazy eyes and silly grin that he's bombed out of his mind. "Ja get 'at lease ready?"

I hold it up.

"Right here. I'm no lawyer, Merle, so I can't vouch for—"

"Aw bullshit. By God, if you done it, I know it's right." He slaps my back. "Yer a star hand, son. Com'ere. I got somebody I wancha to meet."

I follow him around the truck. He opens the door and offers a hand to his passenger. Out steps a tall woman with long glittering earrings and white blond hair starched into a tall monumental coif. Merle closes the door, revealing her stunning figure— from bright red high-heel shoes, her tanned legs run thin and shapely up to a black leather miniskirt that hugs her hips and barely covers her butt and crotch. Along the top of her skirt, accentuating her narrow waist, a glimmering silver-sequined belt. Tucked into this sparkling band, a knit ivory sweater that clings up her thin stomach and *out* at her impossibly humongous breasts. They're as big as basketballs. Her sweater plunges from her shoulders and runs diagonally down across the equators of her boobs, framing their sensationally hoisted cleavage. Just above this fleshy crevice, on a gold chain, she wears a large red pendant in the shape of a heart. Her thick mask of makeup—bright red lipstick, red rouge, blue eye shadow, and thick false eyelashes—makes it hard to guess her age, but based on the wrinkles around her mouth and the folds of loose skin beneath her chin, I'd say she's pushing forty-five. In her hand of long red fingernails, she holds a white plastic foam cup, its rim stained with red lipstick. Merle puts his hand at the small of her back.

"Harvard, this is Miss Tex-Ann Big-Love, from Dallas. Tex-Ann, this is my star hand, Harvard. And we don't call him Harvard fer nothin'. 'At's where the lil sonofagun went to school. Harvard University. He's a damn actor. Gonna be in the movies one day."

Tex-Ann Big-Love smiles.

"My gracious," she says, "just look atchoo." Her speech startles me, for although she looks the epitome of femininity, her voice is gruff and ragged, as though she's smoked cigarettes for years. "It's such a pleasure to meetchoo . . . *Harvard?* Is that right?"

"Actually, my name is Erwin."

She tilts her head and stares at me.

"My God, Erwin, you *do* need to be in the movies. Has anybody ever toldja, honey? Yer the spittin' image uh Montgomery Clift."

I roll my eyes and nod.

"My God," she says. She grabs my chin with her red-fingernailed hand and turns my face right, then left. "I swear on my granny's grave, you might as well be him." She laughs and steps beside me, then puts her arm around me and pulls me to her. My shoulder sinks into the heft of her right breast. "I tell ya what, darlin', they come and they go, but there's only been *one* Montgomery Clift. Big Merle, you better ferget the oil bizness, honey, and get this kid out to Hollywood."

Merle sips from his plastic foam cup.

"Heck, 'at's where he just come from."

Tex-Ann looks at me.

"Really?"

I nod.

"Yeah. I bombed out."

She turns to me. Her breath reeks of whiskey.

"Well," she says, "siss on Hollywood. You need to come to Dallas with me. We'll throw together a lil show. I'll wear a black wig and we'll do a lil Liz and Monty number. Folks love that nostalgia stuff. Whadda ya say?" She squeezes my arm. "Shoot, you've even got the muscles fer a dancer."

I laugh.

"Yeah, right. I'm afraid I'm not equipped in a manner which I'm sure is required of male dancers."

Tex-Ann laughs.

"Oh, I betchoo are too, Erwin." She winks at me. "Besides, you'd be surprised what those boys do with a pair uh athletic socks and a rubber band."

"Aw, goduhmighty," Merle says, "y'all cut it out." He steps up and gently lifts Tex-Ann's arm off my shoulders. "Harvard ain't goin' nowhere. He's my rat killer. And if we can just get this ol' boy to sign this lease tonight, we're gonna be back in the saddle, by God."

"Big Merle," Tex-Ann says, "you just relax, darlin'. By the time I'm through with Mr. Alton Scheermeyer, you'll be able to squeeze him through a keyhole, honey." She winks at Merle. He blinks and stares at her with a confused expression. "Well," she says, "idn' that whatchoo want? Or do my eyes tell me big Merle Luskey's turnin' jealous?"

Merle frowns. She kisses him on the cheek and leans up to his ear under his hat brim.

"Don't ferget, doll. Bizness is bizness. And the other thayng is the other thayng."

"Aw hell," Merle says. He swigs his drink. "So 'at lease is all ready to roll, Harvard?"

I give it to him.

"Yeah. You just have to negotiate the term, or how many years the lease will be in effect, and the amount of royalty you'll pay him if you sell oil. Then once you fill those items in where I've marked, have him sign it. You may be obligated to pay a signing bonus, as well. But I'm not sure about that. It's not part of the actual lease, *per se*."

Blinking his eyes, trying to focus on the page, Merle looks over the lease for about five seconds.

"Ar-ight, by God, 'at's what we'll do." He folds it in thirds and stuffs it in his shirt pocket.

"Honey," Tex-Ann says. "Let's don't get sloppy." She plucks the lease from his pocket and gives it back to me. "Here, Erwin, you hang on to it."

"What're ya doin', baby?" Merle asks. "Harvard ain't goin' with us."

She kisses his cheek again.

"Big Merle, somebody's gotta drive the truck. You were gettin' a little weavy on the way in."

Merle stares at her and blinks. Suddenly he smiles.

"Ar-ight. You and me can sit in back."

She kisses him again.

"There ya go, Big Merle. Now yer thankin' straight."

"Ar-ight, Harvard," Merle says, "yer drivin'. Ya ready?"

I shrug.

"I guess."

"Ar-ight, hang on. Lemme run in and rob my cookie jar. We're gonna need money fer whiskey. Damn sure don't wanna get up 'ere and not have enough to drank." Merle starts toward the garage, then wheels around. "Sweetheart, ya need to use the ladies' room or anythayng?"

Tex-Ann smiles.

"No, honey. I'm fine. Butchur a gentleman fer askin'. Thank you."

"How aboutchur drank? Ya ready fer a splash?"

"Well," she says. She takes a long draining drink from her cup, then rattles the ice cubes in it. "Okeydokey, I guess ya might freshen me up a lil."

Merle opens the door and brings out a bottle of Jack Daniel's, which is nearly empty, and pours a long gurgling dose into Tex-Ann's cup.

"Thank ya, Big Merle," Tex-Ann says. She swirls the ice and whiskey in her cup.

"You bet, darlin'," Merle says. He pours the rest of the bottle into his own cup. Drink in one hand, empty bottle in the other, he walks into the garage, whistling.

Tex-Ann brings out a long cigarette and a lighter from her purse in the truck. She flicks the lighter, but can't make it light in the breeze. I cup my hands around the end of her cigarette. She lights it and takes a deep puff.

"Thank ya, Erwin. I betchoo don't starve fer girlfriends, do ya?"

I shrug.

"Oh, I don't know. I'm not much of a dater, really."

She takes a sip from her drink, another deep drag from her cigarette.

"Sure yer not."

"No, really. I'm always too busy. Acting, school, you know."

"Sure."

"I'm serious."

"*Mm-hm.*"

I smile.

"So, you guys had a nice drive from Dallas?"

She has another sip, another drag.

"Yeah. Big Merle started pourin' Jack Daniel's in my drive-way, and we were both half-tooted by Fort Worth, best friends by Ranger, and pulled over screwin' in Cisco." She laughs a grav-elly lung-congested laugh, then turns and flounces the back of her hair. "How's my hair holdin' up?"

"It looks great."

"Good. It's a lil breezy out here. But I do love West Texas."
Cigarette between her fingers, about eight silver bangles jangling
on her wrist, she waves her hand at the orange and pink horizon.
"Look at those colors in that sky. And all this beautiful space.
Here, hold this, will ya, doll?" She hands me her drink and props
her cigarette in her mouth. She reaches under her boobs and
hoists them up. "This bra is a killer, honey. I knew I shouldn' uh
wore a new one." She slides her hand in her bra and rearranges
her right breast. "I don't know who designed this damn thayng,
but somebody oughta strangle 'em with it."

I laugh.

"Thank ya, doll," she says. She takes back her drink and nods
down at my boots.

"I like yer chocolate lizards."

"Thanks. I just got them a few days ago. They're not quite
broken in yet. Merle gave them to me."

She puffs her cigarette.

"Idn' he an angel?"

"Yeah. He's very generous."

"And *lonesome*. My God, that man is lonesome."

Å å å

The motor rumbles and our headlights, the only light for miles
across the prairie, glide over the road. A half-moon lies on its
back, orangey yellow in the east. The dash control-panel lights
glow green before me, but the backseat is dark. In the rearview
mirror I can only see the dim silhouette of Merle's cowboy hat
leaning in close to Tex-Ann's big-hair coif. I hear the sloshing
rattle of someone sipping their Jack Daniel's on ice, then Merle's
voice in a low indecipherable murmur. Tex-Ann snickers.

"No *sir*."

"Aw, baby."

"*No*, Big Merle, not now. Big Merle . . . Big Merle. *Merle*, put that thayng away."

Merle chuckles lewdly. I look in the mirror and see their silhouettes merge in a kiss, then over the rumble of the diesel engine, I hear the rustle of some major shifting around going on back there.

Then Tex-Ann says, "Big Merle . . . Big Merle . . . *wait*."

I get a sick queasy feeling. I don't know exactly what's going on back there, and I don't *want* to. I turn on the radio and tune it to a slow syrupy country song. I crank the volume up loud, aim my rearview mirror down into the front seat, and just keep driving.

Ä Ä Ä

"Yep, he's 'ere."

Across the dark prairie a square of soft light shines at the window of Alton Scheermeyer's trailer house. I drive down the dirt road along his fence and turn across the iron pipe cattle-guard gate.

MAAAAAA.

Black cows swarm us. I slam the brakes and stop. To our left and right, they're big shadows in the moonlight. In front of us, they stand ten deep in the glare of our headlights, staring at us. Their eyes glow bright orange in the headlights like they're demonically lit from inside. They raise their noses and open their big pink-tongued mouths.

MAAAAAA.

"Oh my God," Tex-Ann says, "look at 'em, y'all. They're precious."

"What're ya doin', Harvard?" Merle says. "Goddam, let's go."

"I can't. They're right in front of us."

"Hell, they'll move. Just go on."

"Erwin, don't hurt the poor thayngs."

"Bullshit, he ain't gonna hurt 'em. Give it the juice, boy."

I ease off the clutch and roll forward. The cows don't move. I stomp the brake. Merle leans over the seat.

"Dammit, let's go! 'Fore the ol' fart thanks we're out here stealin' his cows and starts shootin'."

I close my eyes, release the clutch, and push the accelerator. We lurch forward. To my surprise, we don't hit anything. I open my eyes. Parting like the Red Sea, the cows whirl away and fall in alongside us.

I pull up to the trailer house and stop. Hooves rumbling, the cows gambol up and gather around us.

MAAAAAA.

Our headlights shine over the cows' heads across the front of the trailer house. The door flies open and out steps Alton Scheermeyer with his shotgun. He looks exactly as he did last night—barefoot, faded blue jeans with his suspenders dangling from his hips, sleeveless white T-shirt, and white hair sticking up as though he were just jarred from a nap. Squinting and scowling at our headlights, he wields the long shotgun diagonally before him.

"Cutchur lights, Harvard," Merle says. I turn off the lights and kill the engine. The cows rustle against one another and bellow.

MAAAAAA.

"Who the hell are ya!" Scheermeyer yells.

"Goduhmighty." Merle grumbles and pushes at his door, trying to open it against the huddled cows.

"*No,*" Tex-Ann says. "Now Big Merle, you hired me fer this, so just lemme handle it. Y'all stay right here in this truck till I wave." Tex-Ann cracks open her door and pushes against a cow. "Shoo. Shoo. Get back, cow. *Pssss. Pssss.*"

The cows lower their heads and back away from Tex-Ann's hissing sound. She steps out and closes the door.

"Roll down the winduhs," Merle says. I turn on the ignition

and roll all four windows down. A cool breeze, reeking of cows and cow manure, blows through the cab.

"Yoohoo!" Tex-Ann calls. "Alton! I'm a friend, ar-ight darlin'?" White plastic foam cup in her left hand, silver bracelets on her right wrist, Tex-Ann holds her arms up above the cows and wades through the herd toward the trailer house. Scheermeyer squints into the darkness.

"Who is 'at?"

"It's Tex-Ann! How ya doin', honey?"

"Who?"

"Tex-Ann! Don'choo worry, I don't mean no harm."

Scheermeyer takes the shotgun in one hand, reaches back through the door, and brings out a flashlight. He turns it on. The light beam swings across the tops of the cows and falls on Tex-Ann.

"Yoohoo! Hi, Alton!" She waves toward the light. Face glowing in the halo of the flashlight, Scheermeyer leans down and stares at her. His brow folds and his jaw drops.

"Uh . . . uh . . . hang on 'ere, ma'am. Lemme get them damn heifers back." He puts the flashlight down and points the shotgun in the air.

BOOM.

Hooves rumbling like thunder, the cows bolt away, leaving Tex-Ann standing alone between the front of the truck and Scheermeyer's stoop. The cows run about fifty yards away, then turn, stand in a long line in the moonlight, and watch us.

Scheermeyer props his gun by the door, grabs up his flashlight, and shines it down on Tex-Ann. He points the beam at her face and wide blond hair, then he moves it down to her chest, then down to her hips and black miniskirt, then slowly down her legs to her red high heels standing on the dusty ground. He raises the flashlight beam back up to her chest, then finally to her face again.

"Alton," she yells, "yer not gonna shoot me if I come up there and say heidi-doo, are ya?"

"Uh, no ma'am. I sure ain't."

"Ar-ighty, here I come." She sashays toward the stoop. Scheermeyer turns off the flashlight and sets it down by the shotgun. Backlit by the rectangle of dim door light, he tucks his T-shirt into his pants, pulls his suspenders up over his shoulders, and smoothes down his hair. Tex-Ann walks up the steps. "Heidi-doo. I'm Tex-Ann."

He nods and hangs his thumbs in his pockets.

"Heidi. I'm Alton Scheermeyer."

"It's a pleasure to meetchoo, Alton." She puts her arms around him, hugs him, and kisses his cheek. He stares wide-eyed.

"Uh . . . how can I help ya, ma'am?"

"Oh, call me Tex-Ann, please. That ma'am stuff just knocks the starch right out of a girl."

"Aw . . . uh . . . how can I help ya, Tex-Ann?"

"Oh shoot, I don't know. How about havin' a sip uh Jack Daniel's with us? Maybe we can have a lil fay-do-do out here." She hooks her arm around his and turns him so they're looking out toward us. "It is so beautiful out here. Look at that ol' yelluh moon. And my gracious, the stars. I never *dreamed* there were so many stars. Oh my word—" Shoving her boobs in his face, she reaches across in front of him with her drink-holding hand and points into the sky. "Are those the Seven Sisters?"

He doesn't look at the sky. He just stares into her cleavage.

"Uh . . . if you say so."

She clucks her tongue and looks at him.

"*Alton.* Yer not even lookin'."

He looks up in the sky.

"By God, yes, 'em are the Seven Sisters. Ever' damn one of 'em."

She smiles and kisses his forehead.

"You are such a doll."

In the backseat Merle shifts and grumbles and gulps his drink.

"Goddammit," he says.

"Well," Tex-Ann says, "wouldjoo like to have a lil cocktail with us? I got some friends out there in the truck. I thank you know 'em. Merle Luskey and Erwin Vandeveer. They're from Abilene. They're just good ol' boys like us. We just been out drivin' around, seein' what kind uh havoc we can create."

He looks out toward the truck.

"Aw yeah. I knew I seen 'at truck somewheres. They's out here yesterday evenin'."

"That's right. They mentioned that. They said it was beautiful out here and by golly they weren't lyin'. Well, whadda ya say? Ya wanna party with us?" She sips her drink, shakes her boobs, throws back her head, and lets out a piercing yell.

"*Yee-yee-yee-yee-aw-haw!*"

He stares at her.

"Uh . . . sure. Heck yeah." He nods toward the door. "I hope ya ain't offended. My place ain't real clean or nothin'. And uh, 'ere may be a few . . . magazines layin' around. And they ain't exactly church readin', ya know. But they ain't mine. My brother brayngs the dadgum thayngs over here."

Tex-Ann takes her arm from around Scheermeyer and props her hand on her hip.

"Alton Scheermeyer, are you tryin' to tell me you have dirty picture magazines in there?"

"They ain't mine, I swear. My—"

She pats his stomach.

"Oh, I'm pullin' yer leg. I don't care aboutchur silly ol' magazines. Heck, if I lived way out here like this, I'd have me some magazines, too. Besides, ya never know, I might be in one of 'em." She smiles and throws back her shoulders, hoisting her boobs up. He stares and nods.

"By God, ya arta be."

"Oh, you angel. Thank ya fer sayin' so." She kisses his forehead again.

Merle grumbles in the backseat.

"Well I be goddam," he says. "She ain't gotta kiss the ol' sumbitch ever' time he turns around, does she?"

I look back at him. A block of moonlight shines across him from the open window. Head-wobbling drunk, he stares out from under his hat brim with a pitiful pouting expression. He takes a loud throat-gulping drink from his cup.

"Hey, Merle," I say, "you better slow down on the booze. You look like you're about to go down."

Ignoring me, he takes another drink and points over the seat. "Just look at her up 'ere lovey-doveyin' all over 'at ol' fat goat-ropin' sumbitch."

I sigh, roll my eyes, and turn back around.

"Okeydokey," Tex-Ann says, "you go freshen up, and I'll go yoohoo and tell my friends to come on in."

Scheermeyer goes in the trailer house, and Tex-Ann comes down the steps and back out to Merle's truck. She gets in the backseat.

"Ar-ight, boys, I thank we're on track." She lights a cigarette and rattles the ice in her cup. "Big Merle, ya mind fortifyin' my toddy? And make it a double. Alton smells a whole lot like his little black friends out here." She puffs her cigarette and blows the smoke through the cab.

MAAAAAA.

A cow bellows in the distance. Crickets chirp. I hear the cap being unscrewed from the bottle and Jack Daniel's gurgling into a cup.

"What's uh matter, Big Merle?" Tex-Ann says.

"I don't know, darlin'. God dog, do ya gotta kiss on the ol'—"

"Now wait a minute. Let's have a lil time-out here. Now honey, ya hired me to come out here and help ya get that oil lease signed. Is that still whatchoo want?"

"Hell yeah. I gotta have 'at."

"Okeydokey then, yer just gonna have to toughen up. Cuz I promise ya, honey, you ain't seen nothin' yet. You *do* know how the cow ate the cabbage, don'cha?"

"Ar-ight, ar-ight. I'm sorry. I just feel a lil upset about it, 'at's all. I didn' know I's gonna take such a big likin' to ya."

"Oh, you precious thayng."

I hear weight shifting in the back, then kissing noises, then Tex-Ann's voice in a low whisper.

"Now you just listen. 'Member what I said. Bizness is just bizness. Now whatchoo and me have, darlin', is different. You know that. This afternoon back here in the truck was wonderful. And this evenin', too. I *want* to be with you, Big Merle, and that makes all the difference."

More kissing noises.

"Okeydokey?"

"Ar-ight. I'm sorry, sweetheart. I won't be upset no more."

"Well you shouldn' be, cuz there's no reason to. But now ya are gonna pay me the other thousand if he signs, right?"

"Why hell yeah."

"Ar-ight then. Erwin, sugar, let's have that paperwork."

I take the lease from my shirt pocket and give it to Tex-Ann. She folds it, puts it in her purse, and drags her cigarette.

"Ar-ighty, boys, let's get to work."

Ã Ã Ã

One long bare leg crossed over the other, Tex-Ann sits on the coffee table, bobbing her red high heel. Merle and I sit on the divan. Scheermeyer's trailer house looks the same as last night. Across from us in this narrow living area: his beige Naugahyde recliner, side table, and floor lamp. To our right: a small black-and-white TV with a V antenna on top (an episode of *Cops* is on). To our left: a kitchen separated by a counter covered with heaps of rope and tools and cattle-care supplies. However, apparently in an attempt to cloak his perversion, Scheermeyer has spread a dark green army blanket over his bank of porno mags along the wall.

From the back, through the kitchen, Scheermeyer appears. Although white beard stubble covers his cheeks and throat, he has oiled and combed his white hair into a neat part down the center of his scalp. He has put on a party shirt as well, a hideous loud yellow number with red western stitching across the front and down the sleeves. He wears black cowboy boots with his jeans tucked into their tops and, holding his jeans across his big round belly, red suspenders.

"Woo-woo!" Tex-Ann yells. "There he is."

Scheermeyer smiles and mumbles bashfully and walks into the room. She hops up and puts her arm around him.

"Y'all remember Alton, don'cha?"

Scheermeyer reaches over the coffee table. Merle and I shake his hand and say hello.

"C'mon, boys. It's my night to get drunk!" Tex-Ann says. She helps Scheermeyer get glasses and ice from the kitchen and brings them out to the coffee table. She dumps her and Merle's plastic foam cup drinks into the glasses, then she pours Scheermeyer and me a glassful each of Jack Daniel's on ice.

We sit—Scheermeyer in his recliner, Tex-Ann on the coffee table, and Merle and I on the divan—and visit. Tex-Ann and Scheermeyer do most of the talking. They talk about cows and what it's like living out in the country, et cetera.

I'm worried about Merle. He's obliterated. His eyes are blurry and unfocused, and his face is frozen in a stern blank expression. Other than shaking Scheermeyer's hand and mumbling "Howdy," he hasn't said a word. As Tex-Ann and Scheermeyer talk, I try to steal the glass of Jack Daniel's in his hand. He whacks my arm and grumbles.

"Goddam, boy. Don'choo ever." He gulps his drink and resumes his catatonic stare.

Suddenly Tex-Ann stands up, finishes her drink in several consecutive gulps, holds her arms in the air, and whirls around. Laughing and slinging ice from her glass, she stumbles and catches herself against the wall. I can't tell how much is character and how much real (after all, like Merle, she's been drinking since this afternoon), but in either case she's convincingly drunk. She stares at her empty glass, then at the ice pieces scattered on the floor.

"Oh God, I'm sorry. I'm sorry, Alton. That was stupid. I got ice on yer floor." She kneels down on all fours, heaves her tits out, and crawls around picking up the ice.

"Aw goddam, don't worry about 'at," Scheermeyer says. "Hell, it's just water."

She looks up and stares at him.

"It *is* just water, idn' it?"

"Why heck yeah."

Ah-ha-ha-ha.

She bursts out laughing.

"I love it!" she yells. "It's just water." She stands up, pours several more inches of Jack Daniel's into her empty glass, and downs it. She slams her glass down on the coffee table. "God, boys, I just feel so good and drunk. Y'all ain't gonna get mad at me if I dance, are ya?" She bites her lower lip and rubs her thighs with her red-fingernailed hands. "*Oh*, I swear, y'all, I feel like dancin'." She steps over the coffee table, straddles Merle on the sofa beside me, rubs her tits in his face under the brim of his hat, and throws her head back. "Can I dance, big Merle? *Please*, can I dance?"

Merle just stares into her cleavage with a pained look on his face. She puts her hands on his shoulders and shakes him.

"Oh please, Merley, please. Can I dance? Can I dance?"

"*Goddam*," Scheermeyer says, "yes, you can dance."

She looks at Scheermeyer and smiles.

"Thank you, Alty." She climbs off Merle and looks around the room. "Where's the music? Don'choo have a stereo, Alty?"

Scheermeyer guzzles his drink and smacks his lips.

"Naw, I ain't got no radio." He leans over and pours himself another drink. "But hell, we'll sang fer ya." He looks at Merle and me. "Whadda we know, boys? How about 'Dixie'? We can sang 'at. C'mon." Staring at Merle and me, he stomps his boot rhythmically on the floor and wags his finger back and forth, then he nods his head and starts.

"*I wish I was in the land uh cotton. Ol' times 'ere are not forgotten. Look away, look away, look away, Dixieland.*" He frowns at us. "Goddam, ain'chall gonna sang? The lady wants to dance. C'mon."

"No, no, no," Tex-Ann says. She steps over and kisses the top of Scheermeyer's head. "Yer precious fer tryin', Alty, but that ain't gonna do. When I dance, honey, I *dance*. Erwin, go pull the truck up right outside the door, and in my purse there's a tape. Put in side A and turn it up loud so we can hear it good."

I step outside. The cows are back. They're herded in a mass around the stoop, hundreds of them. They stare at me and swish their tails.

MAAAAAA.

I step down off the stoop among them. Pushing through their wet warm-breath–blowing noses and hard bristly flanks, I walk out to the truck. I start it up. Jerking forward in short bursts, I drive through the herd and park alongside the stoop. I turn off the engine, put Tex-Ann's tape in the cassette player, and turn up the volume full blast.

Sssss . . .

BOOM-CH-BOOM-BOOM-CH-BOOM-BOOM . . .

A fast disco song blasts from the speakers out the truck windows. The cows bolt and rumble out into a moonlit cactus-dotted field. In the distance, they stop in a wide rank, turn, and watch.

As the disco music thumps across the prairie, up to the Milky Way, and into the trailer door, I walk back in.

Tex-Ann stands atop the coffee table in her red high heels, wagging her hips back and forth and bouncing her tits up and down. I stand by the door. Hands in his lap, one clutching his drink, Merle stares up at her with a foggy expression of amazement and pain. Scheermeyer, on the other hand, leers with lurid excitement. Still dancing, Tex-Ann picks up the big bottle of Jack Daniel's and swigs it. She sets the bottle down, closes her eyes, chews on her lower lip, and runs her palms up and down herself. She grabs at her sweater along her stomach and pulls.

"God, y'all," she says, "I'm sorry, but I just feel so . . ."

"What, darlin'?" Scheermeyer says. "Goddam. Whadda ya feel?"

Eyes closed, chewing her lip, she smiles.

"*Nasty.*"

"Well hell, get nasty," Scheermeyer says. "Ya sure ain't gonna hurt my feelin's none." He throws back his drink and pours himself another. Tex-Ann pulls at her sweater.

"Okay, y'all," she says. "I'm gonna do it. I swear to God I'm gonna do it."

"Do it!" Scheermeyer yells. "By God, do it!"

Slowly, she pulls her sweater out of her skirt and up over her head, revealing her huge tits hoisted up in a black bra. She turns and pitches Merle the sweater. He stares at it mournfully, then carefully folds it and lays it on the divan beside him. Tex-Ann keeps dancing. Her bra-hoisted tits, red heart-shaped necklace above her cleavage, and hair all bounce in sync to the music. She pulls her arms out of the shoulder straps of her bra and turns toward Scheermeyer. She reaches back and unsnaps it.

Zing.

Her bra flies out and hits Scheermeyer in the face.

My God, her breasts! They have to be fake. They're way too round and firm and gravity-defying to be that big and real. Especially for a woman her age. Her thick brown nipples point up toward the ceiling. Her arms and the rest of her torso are obviously middle-aged, a little loose-skinned and wrinkled from time and too much sun or tanning booths, but her tits, my God, they look like they belong to Shewonga, Amazon princess.

Scheermeyer pulls the bra off his face, sniffs it, and stares in wonder at Tex-Ann.

"*Yeeeeee-haw!*" he yells. He raises his glass and looks up at the ceiling. "Good goduhmighty, Lord, I don't know what I done to deserve this. But thank ya, sweet Jesus! *Yeeeeee-haw!*" He stomps his boot and whirls the black bra over his head.

Tex-Ann unfastens her sequined belt and throws it to Merle, then unzips her black leather skirt and slides it down, revealing tight silky black underwear. Merle continues to stare with a pained dumbstruck expression. She winks at him and, with the toe of one shoe, holds out her skirt. He frowns and takes it.

Tex-Ann's lower body looks pretty good. She has some cellulite around the tops of her thighs and squiggly stretch marks below her navel and along her hips, but her legs are long and strong.

Bouncing her tits to the beat, she hops down off the coffee table and skips across the room to me. With her back to Scheermeyer and Merle, dancing in only her red shoes, black panties, and red heart pendant, she holds out her hands and wiggles her fingers, gesturing for me to join her. I don't understand why she's hitting on me. I guess I'm supposed to say no, so then she can go ask Scheermeyer. I smile and shake my head.

"No, thanks."

Scheermeyer is turned in his chair, watching us. He scowls at me.

"Goddam, boy, what's uh matter? You a chickenlicker? Dance with her."

Tex-Ann leans down, presses her warm tits against my chin and throat, and speaks into my ear.

"C'mon, Erwin. I don't wanna go to him too fast. I gotta warm him up. Merle has gone apeshit. I *need* you."

"Okay," I say. Smiling at the insanity of it all, I gulp my drink, set it on the counter by a spray can marked Hoof Treater, and take the floor. Bobbing my head and snapping my fingers, I hop around with the almost naked Tex-Ann.

"*Yeeeeee-hai!*" Scheermeyer yells. "Attaboy!"

My blistered toes burn in my chocolate lizards, but who cares? As Tex-Ann moves in close and presses her bouncing tits against me, I laugh and try to mirror her hip-wiggling ass-shaking dance.

"*Yeehaw, hot damn!*" I yell.

Then I notice Merle. He's sitting on the sofa glaring at me with a murderous look. I keep dancing, but I tone it down and back off Tex-Ann.

Scheermeyer sits on the edge of his chair, throwing back shots of Jack Daniel's, stomping his boot to the beat, and staring with a lewd grin at either Tex-Ann's tits or her butt, depending on her orientation.

After several minutes of dancing, Tex-Ann backs me to the wall of army-blanket-covered porn magazines. She puts her hands on either side of my head, her legs on either side of my legs, and leans down to my ear.

"Now you listen to me, ar-ight?"

I nod.

"Merle has lost his fuckin' marbles, so you and me are gonna have to pull this off. Putchur hands on my ass."

I laugh.

"Yes, ma'am."

I reach around behind her and put my palms on her silky underwear buns.

"*Yeeeeee-hai!*" Scheermeyer yells. "Attaboy!"

She continues to talk into my ear.

"Go sit by Merle and don't let him do nothin' stupid. I'm gonna start workin' the ol' guy. When I look atchoo and play with my heart necklace, you get Merle and take him outside. Y'all just wait for me out there in the truck. Got it?"

I nod. She leans back, smiles, kisses my forehead, then whirls around, hops up onto the coffee table, and starts dancing. I walk around and sit by Merle on the divan. Glassy-eyed and wobble-headed, he looks at me with a deranged, vicious expression.

Tex-Ann hops down off the coffee table and holds out her hands to Scheermeyer, inviting him to join her. He grins like a maniac, slams back his drink, and stands up.

"Goddam, darlin'!" he yells.

As she sways and bounces and swings her arms gracefully to the beat, he hops around and does a potbellied, hand-clapping, boot-stomping jig.

For several minutes they dance around the tiny space between the TV, the coffee table, and the wall of blanket-covered magazines. Tex-Ann alternates. For a while she dances facing him, thrusting her bouncing tits at his grinning face, then she turns away from him, bends over, and wags her round black-pantied butt at him. This sends Scheermeyer into a howling, stomping, clapping frenzy. Playing the support Tex-Ann seems to want, I smile and stomp and clap along with the beat. Merle just sits beside me, slump-shouldered and snarling.

Suddenly the music stops. The TV is still on at low volume. The local weather forecaster points to a map of Texas and discusses the high and low temperatures for the day. An idiotic grin glued on his face, Scheermeyer coughs and wheezes.

"*Goddam*, darlin'," he says. "You got the pertiest lil ol' ass I ever seed."

Tex-Ann ignores him. Apparently greatly frustrated that the music is over, she stomps her foot.

"Aw, shit," she says. She pouts.

"What's uh matter, darlin'?" Scheermeyer asks.

Tex-Ann sighs and wrings her hands. Brow furrowed, she looks around, grabs the bottle of Jack Daniel's, and takes a long gurgling swig. She puts the bottle down, stomps her foot, and flaps her hands as though flustered.

"What's uh matter, sugar?" Scheermeyer asks.

"I don't know," she says. She sighs again, then reaches down with her right hand and slips her long red fingernails just under the top hem of her black panties. She rubs her stomach up and down. "I'm such a bad girl. But I just . . . I just . . ."

Scheermeyer starts to tremble.

"Ya just what, honey? Ya just what?"

"I feel so worked up, I guess I just need one uh you men. I just don't know who." Slipping her hand a little further into her panties, she moans and chews her lip and looks at me. "Erwin, yer so young and handsome." She looks at Merle. "And Merle, yer so big and tall."

"Goddam, darlin'," Merle says. He starts to stand up. "Ya ain't gonna do this. I'll figger—"

"Shutup, Merle!" I yell. "She needs it."

Tex-Ann turns and looks at Scheermeyer. His hands are quivering. He drops to his knees, puts his palms together like he's praying, and looks up at her.

"Please, darlin'. Let it be me. Please. Goduhmighty, please."

She steps up to him and rubs his white beard-stubble cheek.

"You are kinda cute, ain'cha."

He leans up and kisses her stomach.

Pp-pp-pp-pp-pp.

"Please, darlin'. Goduhmighty, please."

"Okay, it's you, Alty. It's you."

Scheermeyer bursts out with joy.

"Oh, God bless ya, honey. God bless ya."

"Bullshit!" Merle says. "Ya ain't—"

"Shutup, Merle!"

Tex-Ann looks at me and fondles her red heart necklace.

My signal.

I jump up, take Merle's drink from his hand, and put it on the table, then I grab him under the armpit with both hands and jerk him onto his feet. He tries to pull away, but he's off-balance and wobbly.

"No, Tex-Ann," he says. "Honey, I—"

"Cut it out, Merle! Don't be a bad sport." I pull him stumbling out onto the stoop, then I slam the trailer door closed. "C'mon, Merle, let's go for a walk."

"Bullshit! I ain't walkin' nowhere." He hiccups.

"Okay. Let's sit in the truck."

He scowls.

"*No!* I ain't doin' 'at, either."

"Okay, let's sit right here then." I guide him down to a sitting position on the stoop steps. I sit beside him. The breeze is cooler, almost cold, and the half-moon is higher overhead and white. Cricket chirps pulse all around. The dance music now over for several minutes, the cows have returned and gathered around Merle's truck at the foot of the stoop.

MAAAAAA.

Behind us, through the closed door, we hear Tex-Ann's and Scheermeyer's muffled voices. Merle hiccups.

"By God, *no!*" he says. He tries to stand up, but I grab his arm with both hands and pull. He spins around and falls back to a sitting position beside me. I squeeze his arm and stare in his face.

"Merle, what the hell's wrong with you? You hired her to do this."

He scowls.

"So. I love 'at gal, goddammit." His breath is nearly toxic with alcohol fumes.

"Oh c'mon, Merle. She's a prostitute, for Christ's sake."

He slaps his hand on my chin, clutches my jaw, and glares at me.

"Ya better watchur goddam mouth, boy. She's an exotic dancer."

The door swings open and Tex-Ann steps out in her red high

heels, black panties, and red heart necklace. She closes the door behind her and holds up the lease.

"Ar-ight, I got it all worked out. He'll sign for a one-year lease at one-fifth royalty."

"Goduhmighty, honey," Merle says. He hiccups, stands up, takes off his hat, and tries to cover her tits with it. "Ya art not to run around like 'at." He leans down and kisses her neck. She gently pushes him away.

"Not now, darlin'. We're right in the middle uh bizness. Is that ar-ight with you? One year, one-fifth royalty?"

"Aw, baby." He tries to kiss her neck again.

"Yes," I say. "That's fine, Tex-Ann. Just do it."

"Ar-ight, y'all wait here. I shouldn' be too long." She kisses Merle on the cheek, then opens the door, goes back in the trailer, and slams the door. The doorknob rattles and clicks. Crickets chirp and the cows push closer around the stoop as Merle stands, slump-shouldered, staring at the closed door. Tex-Ann's muffled voice comes from inside.

"Okey-dokey, Alty. No, wait, honey. Alty, hang on. Alty . . . Alty . . . I hate to hurtchur feelin's, sweetie, butchur not ready. Here, lemme help . . . Gracious me, the Lord didn' leave any dough in the bowl when he putchoo together, did he?"

"No, goddammit!" Merle yells. He grabs the doorknob and pulls, but the door is locked. He steps back and kicks at it with the heel of his boot. I jump up and try to stop him, but he shoves me away. Scheermeyer's long-barreled shotgun stands propped against the trailer house by the door. "Here I come, darlin'," Merle says. He picks up the shotgun.

"No, Merle!" I try to grab the gun away. He jabs me in the chest with the butt of the gun.

"Get back, goddammit." He cocks the hammer, aims the long black barrel at the doorknob, and pulls the trigger.

Click.

Nothing happens. He frowns.

"Sumbitch. Here." He gives me the shotgun, grabs the door-knob, and starts pulling again.

"Thanks," I say. I raise the iron gun barrel up high and slam it down across the crown of his cowboy hat.

Å Å Å

"Harvard. Harvard."

"*Huh?*" I sit up. Out the back windows, over the patio, the sky is gray with dawn. The wind is up, nudging and whistling at the windows. Merle stands by the sofa in his black socks and white boxer shorts. A shock of black hair dangles across his forehead.

"Did we get the lease?" he whispers.

"What do you mean?"

"Last night. Did Scheermeyer sign the lease?"

"You don't remember?"

"Naw. I 'member ya drivin' us up 'ere, but I don't 'member gettin' 'ere or nothin'."

"Yes, Merle, you got the lease. Scheermeyer signed."

"Good. Where the hell is it?"

"What?"

"Goddam, the lease. Ever'thayng I got's ridin' on 'at thayng."

Well, you lunatic sonofabitch, I think, why'd you get so hammered you nearly ruined everything? I throw the blanket off me and rub my eyes.

"It's in the kitchen, Merle."

I get up and follow him to the kitchen. He flicks on the light. On the counter is the lease—at the bottom, across the line designated *Lessor,* in childlike printed letters, is Alton Scheermeyer's signature.

"It's for one year and one-fifth royalty," I say. I point where Tex-Ann filled in the terms on the form. Merle claps his hands and rubs them together.

"Hot damn, son. I'm gonna save my rigs." He opens the refrigerator, brings out a can of Coors beer, and cracks it open. I blink my eyes and stare in disbelief. "Sweet Mary's ass," he says, "I'm glad we got 'at deal done." He raises the beer to drink.

"*Merle*. What the hell are you doing?"

He stops and holds the can of beer just inches from his mouth.

"Whadda ya mean?"

"My God, you were so drunk last night you can't remember anything, and now you're at it *again?*"

"Good Lord, son, it's just a beer." He nods toward the refrigerator. "Ya want one?"

I sigh and shake my head.

"No, Merle. I don't want one."

"Sure? They're good and cold."

"Yes, I'm sure."

He shrugs, takes a gulping swig from the beer, and sets the can down by the lease. He shakes his head, grimaces, and rubs the top of his head.

"Sumbitch, I thank somebody cowcocked me last night."

I glare at him.

"Somebody did." I point to myself. "Me."

"*You?* What happened? Joo and me get sideways?"

"Actually, Merle, I saved your ass. You were so drunk you turned into a moron and got jealous about Tex-Ann and what she had to do to Scheermeyer. You were going to keep her from doing it, so I had to knock you out and stop you."

He looks at me and blinks.

"Goddam, boy, wha'd ja hit me with?"

"A shotgun."

He winces and rubs his head.

"Sumbitch, ya really laid one on me, didn' ya."

I stare at him, trying to be mad, but the absurdity of it hits me and I crack up laughing. And I can't stop. I go into hysterics. I laugh so hard tears roll from my eyes and my stomach muscles ache. I slide down along the wall and sit on the floor. Merle sips his beer and watches me with hungover deadpan seriousness. He rubs his head.

"Well," he says, "I reckon I appreciate it."

"No problem," I say. I roll onto the floor laughing and kicking my feet.

KKKKKKKK.

The CB explodes with static crackle and Merle's voice blares through the cab.

"*BREAK ONE-FOUR. HARVARD, YA GOTCHUR EARS ON?*"

I slow Ol' Blue and grab the hand mike lying on the floor-board.

"Ten-four. My ears are definitely on. This is Harvard."

KKKKKKKK.

"*TEN-FOUR. THIS IS MERLE. WHAT'S YER TWENNY?*"

"Just north of town. I'm on my way out to the yard. I'm glad you—"

KKKKKKKK.

"*TEN-FOUR. JOO GET THE LEASE SQUARED AWAY?*"

"Ten-four. I went up to Jayton this morning and filed the lease in the courthouse. Then I came back down to the Railroad Commission office in Abilene. I have some forms I have to complete for your drilling permit. I need—"

KKKKKKKK.

"*TEN-FOUR. MIGHTY FINE. YER A STAR RAT KILLER, BOY.*" At five thousand decibels he goes on to explain that Rig Two, which he has slated to drill the Scheermeyer #1, has finished its job in Stonewall County and is now at the equipment yard receiving a few minor repairs, and that he intends to move the rig to Scheermeyer's land and start drilling in two days. "*'AT'S OUR PLAN, BOY.*"

Up ahead I can see the rig itself, lying crosswise in the yard between its five idle cohorts and the office trailer house.

"Okay. Ten-four. What is your twenty? I need—"

KKKKKKKK.

"*I'M SORRY. COME AGAIN.*"

"Your twenty. Where are—"

RAAAAAAWWWWWW.

Merle and Tex-Ann roar past me at well over a hundred miles an hour. The wind sweep of his big dual-rear-tire truck rocks Ol' Blue and sends me swerving off the road into the dirt.

"Shit!"

KKKKKKKK.

"*AH-HA-HA-HA. I JUST BLEW AROUND YER ASS. 'AT'S MY TWENNY. THIS IS MERLE. WE GONE, BYE-BYE.*"

"Ten-four, asshole."

By the time I get back on the road and down to the yard, Merle and Tex-Ann are driving out of the gate. I park by the trailer-house office, gather up my Railroad Commission forms, seismic surveys, and land surface maps, and step out. Merle pulls up and Tex-Ann rolls down her window. She has her makeup on, including bright red lipstick and long fake eyelashes. Her hair is puffed into a big blond do, and she wears a tight pink sweater and her red heart pendant. She reaches her arm, adorned with silver bangles, out the window.

"Oh, gracious, I'm so glad we ran into you. I was heartbroke when I woke up and Big Merle said you'd ar-eady gone." She smiles. "I swear to God, yer just the best-lookin' thayng I ever saw." Jangling her bracelets, she motions with her red-fingernailed hand for me to step closer. "Com'ere and lemme hug yer neck."

Papers and maps rattling in the wind, I step up to the truck window. She wraps her arm around my neck, pulls my head into the window, and smashes my face into her shoulder and tit.

"It was just an absolute pleasure to meetchoo, Erwin. You take care, now, ya hear? And if ya come to Dallas, you look me up. We'll burn down the town, you and me." She winks and kisses my cheek.

"It was nice meeting you, too, Tex-Ann. Take care."

"Ar-ight, son," Merle says, "get 'at drillin' permit knocked out. I'm gonna run her back to Dallas, and I'll see ya back at the house this evenin'."

"Wait, Merle, there's a problem."

He raises the brim of his cowboy hat.

"What?"

I hold up the papers and maps.

"In order to get your drilling permit, you have to specify the exact location on Scheermeyer's land where you're going to drill."

"Yeah, so?"

"*So?* For God's sake, where do you want to drill it?"

"Whadda ya mean? Hell, set me smack dab on top uh 'at big-ass hickey."

"Shit, Merle, I don't know how to correlate all these maps. Listen, you need to hire—"

"Aw, bullshit. Yer my savin' angel, son. You just set me right on 'at dude, and I'll drill her down." He winks at me. "See ya this evenin'."

"*Merle, I—*"

RAAAAWWWW.

He guns the accelerator, fishtails out onto the paved highway, and screeches away.

"Dumb sonofabitch."

I walk out back into the rig yard. Behind the office, Rig Two's huge derrick lies horizontally across a trailer and a massive iron rack. The day-tour crew—Shay, Virgil, and Mule—dressed in their sleeveless red overalls, stand at the crown of the derrick. Virgil and

Mule smoke cigarettes and watch as Shay, a gray mask and helmet over his head, directs a bright white welding torch at a rolling pulley wheel in the crown. Several small red hoses run from Shay's welding torch along the ground to a small trailer stocked with tall thin gas tanks and a roaring, exhaust-spewing diesel generator. Virgil and Mule, hands in their pockets, cigarettes in their mouths, stare at me as I approach. I smile and wave. Virgil nudges Shay, who raises up from his work and flips up his welding helmet.

"WHAT?" Shay says, yelling above the generator.

Virgil drags his cigarette and nods toward me.

"LOOKEE WHO FINALLY SHOWED UP FER WORK."

Welding torch hissing in his hand, Shay turns around. He smiles.

"HARVARD. WHAT'S GOIN ON, MAN?"

"NOT MUCH." I hold up the maps and Railroad Commission forms. "I HAVE SOME PAPERWORK TO DO FOR MERLE. I NEED TO USE THE TYPEWRITER IN THE OFFICE."

Shay nods.

"YEAH, MERLE SAID YA BEEN DOIN' A GOOD JOB RAT-KILLIN' FOR HIM. BUT WE WANCHA BACK ON THE RIG. FAT-ASS HERE NEEDS HELP." Shay swings the blazing white welding torch across Virgil's forearm. Virgil jumps back and flicks his cigarette at Shay. It bounces off Shay's chin and rolls across the ground. Virgil looks down at my boots with his buggy bloodshot eyes.

"I'LL BE DAMN. THE WORM GOT HIM SOME BOOTS. THEM'RE NICE. WHAT ARE THEY, LIZARD?"

I nod.

"YEAH, CHOCOLATE LIZARDS." I pull up the leg of my jeans so they can see the stitching along the top. Virgil whistles, leans down, and runs his fat fingers along the strips of lizard hide. He raises up and slaps my shoulder.

"GODDAM, NOW YER JUST YANKEE FROM THE KNEES UP."

I SIT IN A BOOTH SIPPING ICED TEA AND WAITING FOR MY
Chicken-fried Steak Deluxe plate. I tried it yesterday on Tammy
the afternoon waitress's recommendation, and man oh man. It's
unquestionably the Wildcat Cafe's premier fare—two battered
and deep-fried steaks and a heap of real homemade mashed potatoes, all drowned in cream gravy; a mountain of crispy fried
okra; and two giant butter-plastered fresh-baked rolls. I smell the
steaks frying in the kitchen and go into a stomach-growling frenzy.
I haven't eaten all day. Merle's paperwork turned out to be more
of a pain in the ass than I expected, but I finally finished it all,
including the Public Notice of Intent to Drill, which I submitted
to the local newspaper, and the W-1, or Permit to Drill, which
was approved by the secretary at the Railroad Commission.

I just hope I didn't screw up picking the location of the well.
I'd like to kick Merle's butt. I mean where does he get off leaving
such a crucial call to me, a frigging actor from New England? I've
decided either the guy's brain is fried from constant alcohol abuse,
or he's some kind of redneck Gatsby, so ridiculously optimistic
about his dream and saving his rigs that he has no concept of
reality whatsoever. But what can I do? He just dumps this stuff
on me. So I just do my best. Every way I could think of, I compared the seismic map with the Kent County land-ownership map,
the topographic contour map, and the aerial photograph, and fi-

nally I decided to put the well at 1,340 feet from Scheermeyer's north line and 2,265 feet from his west, which should be right over the middle of the egg-shaped summit of the reef structure on the seismic map. But what if the seismic or the surface maps are wrong? Or what if there's some other factor that I don't even know about? But hell, if Merle wants to be that hardheaded and stupid, what can I do? It's his ass, not mine.

I sip my iced tea and look out the window. The wind has really kicked up this afternoon. Sheets of dust swirl by and Ol' Blue, parked just outside, rocks back and forth on its shocks. Big round tumbleweeds and pieces of litter roll down the street as though the town were tilted on its side.

"Here ya go, darlin'," Tammy says. She slides the platter in front of me. Steam rises from the thick white gravy smothering the steaks and mashed potatoes. The okra pieces are crispy brown, and yellow butter drips down the sides of the rolls. "Need anythayng else, handsome?"

"No, ma'am." Saliva glands gushing, I salt and pepper the gravy and cut into one of the steaks.

Mmm. God. Unbelievable. As I take a butter-dripping bite from a roll, the front door swings open and Sheriff Nall, accompanied by one of his deputies, walks in. Although they are dressed alike—black cowboy boots, dark brown pants, wide black belts with holstered guns, khaki shirts, and straw cowboy hats—they're as different as night and day. The deputy is young, tall, and handsome, with broad shoulders, square jaw, dimpled chin, and blue eyes. Sheriff Nall is short and dumpy with a pink face and several extra chins hanging over his collar. They glance around. The deputy points at me.

"Zat him?"

Sheriff Nall, gut slung over his belt, hands on his hips, looks at me and lolls the cigar propped in his mouth.

"Yep. 'Ere he is."

The deputy walks to my booth. His last name, I see by the

plastic tag under his badge, is Buck. He reaches back along his belt, pops open a pouch, and brings out a clinking set of hand-cuffs. My heart starts pounding.

"What's going on?"

"Yer under arrest."

"Under *arrest?* What are you talking about?"

"C'mon." He jingles the handcuffs and motions for me to slide out of the booth.

"Look, you must have the wrong guy. I haven't done anything wrong."

"C'mon," he says.

I glance around the café. Two old men sit at the big round table near the door; Tammy stands behind the counter; and the cook stands in the kitchen service window. They all stare at me.

"C'mon." Deputy Buck reaches down and grabs my arm.

"I don't understand. What's going on?" I slide out of the booth. He clamps one of the handcuffs around my right wrist, then tries to turn me around. I jerk away.

"Wait a minute, dammit. *Why* are you arresting me?"

"Shutup, Yank."

"No. You can't just arrest me without telling me why. I'm an American citizen. I have rights. What am I being charged with? What have I done?"

Deputy Buck frowns and looks at Sheriff Nall.

"Hey, Sheriff!"

Sheriff Nall is busy hitching up his pants and staring at Tammy.

"Yeah, Buck."

"You better com'ere."

Sheriff Nall smiles at Tammy, then frowns at Deputy Buck and ambles back along the booths.

"What's the problem, Buck?"

"Sir, the Yank here says we gotta tell him why we're arrestin' him."

"Goddam, Buck, I didn' tell ya to visit with him. I said arrest him."

"Sorry, Sheriff." Deputy Buck whirls me around and slaps the other cuff on me. Hands locked behind my back, I jerk away and look at Sheriff Nall.

"What's going on here, Sheriff? What have I done wrong?"

Sheriff Nall looks down at my plate. He plucks his cigar from his mouth, reaches down, grabs one of my rolls, smears it in gravy, and takes a bite.

"*Mm-mm.*"

"Sheriff, what's going on here? What have I done?"

He smears the roll in my gravy again and crams the whole thing in his mouth.

"Huh?"

"You can't *do* this. It's against the law. Why are you arresting me?"

He chews and swallows the roll.

"Ar-ight, boy. Yer bein' detained for questionin'."

"Questioning? Regarding what?"

"On account uh . . . suspected communism."

"*Suspected communism?* What the hell are you talking about?"

He licks the gravy off his finger.

"I'm talkin' about the fact thatchoo come from up 'ere in Yankeeland, boy."

"What are you saying? Because I'm from Boston I'm a Communist? How can you draw—"

"Hey, smart boy! Don'choo tell me what I can draw." He lays his hand on his gun. "I'll draw my damn gun. How'd ja like 'at? Huh?" He puts the cigar stub back in his mouth. "C'mon, Buck. Quit playin' with him. Let's go."

Deputy Buck grabs me and pushes me toward the door.

"Hey! What the fuck is going on? You can't do this!"

Walking along beside us, Sheriff Nall turns and tips his hat to the people in the café.

"Y'all have a good evenin'. Drive careful." He holds the door open and Deputy Buck shoves me out into the wind.

Â Â Â

"*Ow.* Hey, you sonofabitch, you're hurting my shoulder."

"Shutup and walk, Yank." Deputy Buck pushes my handcuffs and sends me stumbling down the corridor of steel-barred cells.

"I demand to know what's going on!"

"Here we are." He grabs my handcuffs and snaps me to a halt. "Hotel suite number five." He pulls open the cell door, removes my handcuffs, and shoves me in. I stumble and fall to the cold cement floor.

Clang.

He slams the door and locks it.

"Wait, what about my phone call? I want to call a lawyer."

"Go ahead," he says. He cups his hands around his mouth. "Hey, lawyer!" He laughs and points through the bars. " 'Ere's a pilluh and a blanket on the cot, and if ya gotta piss or take a shit, do it in 'at drain hole." He points beside me to a hole, about three inches in diameter, in the floor. I look at the hole, then at him.

"Listen here, goddammit. I demand to use the phone. Federal law provides me the right to an attorney."

He grins and scratches his crotch.

"Zat right?"

"Yes. It's the law."

"Well, sorry, Yank, butchur in Taylor County, Texas. The law ain't shit around here." He winks and walks away.

I stand up, lean at the bars, and try to see down the dim gray cinder-block corridor.

"Hey! Where are you going?"

Footsteps fade and a metal door clangs shut.

DEPUTY BUCK SHOVES ME INTO THE ROOM. SHERIFF NALL SITS
behind his desk with his back to us playing *Pac-Man* on a computer. Calliope music plays from the computer speakers as he pecks his keyboard and maneuvers Pac-Man through the avenues, gobbling little yellow bananas and eluding the blue enemies.

"Here's the Yankee, Sheriff," Deputy Buck says.

"Hang on, dammit," Sheriff Nall says. "I'm on banana level." Pecking frantically, he turns Pac-Man straight into a blue enemy. The calliope music droops to a close and Pac-Man melts.

Wham.

Sheriff Nall slams his keyboard.

"Dammit, Buck! Ya fucked me up. Ya know how hard it is to get to banana level?"

"Sorry, sir." Deputy Buck escorts me to a chair in front of Sheriff Nall's desk. I sit on the edge of the chair to accommodate my hands cuffed behind me.

To my right, by a photograph of Sheriff Nall shaking hands with Ronald Reagan, a window opens onto a patch of yellow mown grass bordered by a razor-wire and chain-link fence. From the blueness of the sky and the sunlight glinting off the razor wire, I guess it's early to mid morning. My head aches from sleeplessness. Apparently I was back in the cell about fourteen or fifteen hours—from about 6 P.M. yesterday until this morning—but it seemed like a week. There were no windows—only dull lightbulbs in the corridor along the cells—so I had no concept of time. At first I yelled for several hours, but no one ever came, so finally I lay down on the cot. But I never fell asleep. I just lay there tossing and turning, wondering what the hell was going on, until this morning when the iron door clanked and Deputy Buck appeared and brought me here.

Sheriff Nall sips a cup of coffee, leans back in his chair, and props his boots on his desk. His straw cowboy hat lies on his desk, and his bare head reveals a hideous hairstyle. Rather than accept his balding condition, he tries to cover it by combing the band of hair around the lower right latitude of his head up and over the top to the left side. His double chin drapes over the collar of his shirt. He stares at me with his beady brown eyes, then suddenly he scowls at Deputy Buck.

"What're ya doin', Buck? Hangin' around like a lost dog?"

"Sorry, sir." Deputy Buck steps from the room and closes the door behind him.

"Sheriff," I say, "could you please tell me what's going on? Why are you doing this to me? What have I done?"

"I toldja. Yer bein' detained fer questionin'."

"On what grounds?"

He wrinkles his brow.

"Whadda ya mean?"

"What do I mean? For God's sake, I'm an American citizen. I'm entitled to rights. If you arrest me, you have to inform me why I'm being arrested, and you have to allow me access to a lawyer."

He slurps his coffee and stares at me with his beady brown eyes.

"Well, 'at's all real perty, smart boy, butchoo ain't arrested. Yer *detained*."

"There's no difference. You can't—"

"Hey!" He points his finger at me. "You just sit there and shut up." He spins around to his computer. "Goduhmighty, I gotta go back to cherry level." He clicks his mouse and starts a new game. Coffee mug in his left hand, he taps his keyboard with his right index finger, directing Pac-Man on another calliope-accompanied fruit-gobbling mission.

The door opens. Don Brock, the banker, steps in, carrying a long white scroll of paper. He wears glossy black wing tips, charcoal slacks, a navy European-cut blazer, ivory shirt, and a maroon silk tie patterned with golf clubs and balls. Although he's bald, too, he seems to accept it with more dignity, sporting a neatly trimmed band of graying hair around the sides and back of his head. He acknowledges me with a cold stare from his steel gray eyes, then steps up to Sheriff Nall's desk.

"Jack."

Sheriff Nall, engrossed in a spree of cherry-gobbling, does not hear him. Don Brock steps around the side of the desk.

"*Jack!*"

Sheriff Nall jumps and spills coffee across his shirtfront.

"Goddam, ya sonofa—" He turns around. His scowl softens. "Oh, *hey*, Don." He stands up, sets his dripping coffee cup on his desk, and wipes his shirt. "Good golly, Don, snuck up on me, didn' ya? How ya doin', buddy?" He smiles and holds out his hand. Ignoring the offer of a handshake, Don Brock lays the long scroll of paper on the desk, grabs a chair, turns it toward me, and sits beside the desk. Sheriff Nall lowers his hand. "Hey, yeah, have a seat, Don. Wanna cup uh coffee or somethin'?"

Don Brock looks at his watch.

"No. C'mon, I've got a director's meeting in forty-five minutes."

"Sure, Don." Gray coffee stain across his stomach, Sheriff Nall waddles around and sits on his desk facing me. Wagging one of his black cowboy boots to and fro, he crosses his arms and props them on his gut. "Ar-ight, boy, let's hear it. What's Merle Luskey up to?"

I look at Sheriff Nall, then Don Brock.

"What do you mean?"

"Don't gimme 'at bullshit. Word is, Merle's gonna drill him a well somewheres. Where's he gonna drill?"

"The location's in the paper this morning, jackass," Don Brock says. He turns and unrolls the long scroll of paper. It's a map. He points to it. "He's drilling right here. Kent County. On the Scheermeyer."

Sheriff Nall looks, then whistles.

"Goddam, 'at's a wildcat, ain't it? Nothin' around 'ere."

"No shit, Sherlock," Don Brock says. He rolls up the map and looks at Sheriff Nall. "I wanna know what he's drilling on."

Sheriff Nall nods.

"Ar-ight." He looks at me. "What's he drillin' on?"

"I don't know what you mean."

Sheriff Nall looks at Don Brock.

"He dudn' know what I mean. Hell, *I* don't know what I mean."

Don Brock rolls his eyes and glares at Sheriff Nall.

"Information, shit-head. What kind of information is he drilling on?"

"Oh." Sheriff Nall looks at me. "*Information*, shit-head. What kind uh information is Merle drillin' on?"

I shrug my shoulders. No way in hell am I going to tell these assholes anything.

"I have no idea," I say. "I just roughneck on one of his rigs."

Sheriff Nall frowns and turns to Don Brock.

"He dudn' know. He just roughnecks."

Don Brock scowls.

"That's bullshit." He looks at Sheriff Nall and points to me. "He's doing all Merle's paperwork."

Sheriff Nall turns to me.

" 'At's bullshit, boy! Yer doin' Merle's paperwork. Ya better sang, Yankee boy. Now c'mon. What the hell's Merle got up 'ere in Kent County?"

I look down at my chocolate lizards and wonder what to do. I definitely don't want to betray Merle. And why should I have to? This isn't Nicaragua. They can't just arrest and extort me like this. Sure, Texas is its own weird fucked-up place, but this is still the United States. I'll get a lawyer and have a field day with these morons. I'll sue the county for every dime in the coffer. I look back up at Sheriff Nall and shake my head.

"I'm not telling you guys anything. This is illegal and you know it. It's extortion. And you both could go to jail for it."

Sheriff Nall's face turns red.

"Listen here, ya lil sumbitch. Don's ar-eady sold 'em drillin' rigs, and if—"

"*Jack!*" Don Brock yells. "Shut up! Jesus."

Sheriff Nall frowns.

"Sorry, Don." He leans down and points his finger in my face. "Ar-ight, boy. Cut the bullshit. What the hell's Merle up to?"

"I'm sorry," I say. "But I'm not giving in to this. This is a crime."

Sheriff Nall stares at me. I stare back. He sighs, turns to Don Brock, and shrugs.

"He won't sang, Don. Whadda ya want me to do?"

"*I* don't know, Jack. Jesus, can't you do anything? What the hell do we pay you for, anyway?" Don Brock stands up.

"Now wait, Don," Sheriff Nall says. "Good golly. Just gimme a chance here." He turns back to me and squints his beady eyes. "Ar-ight, Yankee boy. *Buck!*"

The door opens. Deputy Buck steps in.

"Buck," Sheriff Nall says, "where's 'at dope we found on Yankee boy, here?"

"What dope, sir?"

Sheriff Nall sighs.

"Goddam, Buck, brayng me some dope."

"Uh, what kind, sir?"

"Hell if I know. Whadda we got back 'ere?"

"We got a lot uh pot. And some cocaine."

Sheriff Nall looks at me and grins.

"Cocaine, Buck. Brayng me a big ol' sack uh cocaine."

"Uh, sir, I think you have it."

Sheriff Nall sighs again.

"Get out uh here, Buck!" He slides down off his desk, waddles around to a filing cabinet, pulls open a drawer, and brings out a Ziploc bag full of an ivory white chunky substance. He smiles and holds up the bag. "Well lookee here, Don. Look what Yankee boy brung from Yankeeland. A big ol' sack uh cocaine." He opens the bag, sticks his thumb and index finger inside, and pinches one of the chunks, crushing it. His thumb and finger covered with the powder, he puts them to his nostrils and snorts. He arches his eyebrows and nods. "Perty good cocaine, too." He sticks his thumb and finger into the bag again, wiggles them in the powder, puts them to his nose, and snorts. He blinks his eyes and clears his throat. "Damn. *Real* good, as a matter uh fact." He ambles over and holds the bag out to Don Brock. "Wanna toot? It's 'at sweet shit we found in 'at Mexican's gas tank."

Don Brock scowls and pushes the bag away.

"*Jesus*, Jack. Have you lost your fucking mind?"

Sheriff Nall frowns.

"Well good golly, Don. What's wrong?" He zips the bag closed and pitches it in my lap, then sits back on the desk. Gut slung over his belt, he swings his boot to and fro and stares at me. He rubs his nose and sniffs again. "Yankee boy, you may thank ya know who yer fuckin' with, butcha don't. And you can thank all the Yankee thankin' ya want, but here's how it is—we found 'at sack uh cocaine in yer pocket. And yer gonna be charged with possessin' cocaine. Now ya might hire ya a lawyer and try to beat it, and maybe down the road ya will beat it, but I guarantee, yer gonna spend some time down in the state pen. Matter uh fact, I'll have yer ass down 'ere 'fore sundown. And perty as you are, yer gonna make one uh them big East Texas black boys a real sweet lil ol' wife. Now all ya gotta do is tell us what the hell Merle Luskey's up to, and *hell*, boy, you can get up and waltz right out the front door. Now you just figger out fer yerself how it's gonna be."

I look down at the bag of cocaine in my lap. My heart races a thousand beats a minute. I can't fucking believe this. It's like a scene from a Mel Brooks farce, except it's real. I know I could fight and beat this, that with any lawyer at all I could bring this sonofabitch to his knees. But at the same time, the dumbass might lock me away for a while. And after all, what difference will it make to Merle? He already has the lease. It's a done deal. I filed it myself in the Kent County Courthouse. What can they do to him?

"So," Sheriff Nall says, "what's it gonna be, Yankee boy? Ya gonna sang, or ya gonna go down to the big house tonight fer some cornholin'?"

I don't answer.

"Ar-ighty," he says. "If 'at's how ya wannit. *Buck!*" The door opens. Deputy Buck steps in.

"Yes sir?"

Sheriff Nall points to the bag of cocaine.

"Book this cocaine and weigh it. Then draw up some papers on Yankee boy, here. We got us a cocaine pusher, Buck."

"*All right!*" I say. "All right. I'll tell you what I know."

Sheriff Nall smiles and hitches his belt up around his gut.

"Well, I'll be. Yankee boy's gonna sang."

I HOP OUT OF OL' BLUE AND RAISE MY FACE TO THE BRIGHT
blue sky. God, what a night. I can't wait to tell Merle. I go in
through the garage, but the back door is locked. That's weird.
Merle never locks his doors.

I go around across the yard to the front door. It's locked, too.
I knock. Muffled by the door, I hear dogs barking inside. I wait,
then knock again. The barking rises to a frantic yapping. The lock
clicks and the door opens.

It's Tex-Ann. Her blond hair hangs limply about her shoulders
and she has no makeup on. If not for her trademark bosom, I
might not recognize her. Her face, without makeup and fake eyelashes, is so bland. She wears a long white T-shirt that hangs down
to just above her knees—across the front of it, a black cowboy
boot stuffed with red roses. Her calves and feet are tanned and
her toenails are painted bright red. She holds a lighted cigarette
in one hand, a cup of coffee in the other.

The dogs, a small brown swaybacked dachshund and a slightly
larger white poodle with watery black eyes, bark and scamper in
circles around her bare feet.

RAR-RAR-RAR-RAR-RAR.

"There you are," Tex-Ann says, raising her gruff baritone
above the yapping. She slaps her thigh and scolds the dogs.

"Sasha, Snowflake, y'all settle down. This is Erwin. He's our friend."

The dogs bolt past me and sniff in didoes across the yard. Tex-Ann steps out onto the porch.

"Sasha! Snowflake! Don't y'all run off, ya hear me?"

The dogs ignore her and continue sniffing around the yard. The white poodle pauses at one of Merle's pecan trees, hikes its leg, and pisses on it. Tex-Ann puts her cigarette in her mouth and runs her hand through my hair.

"Where've ya been, darlin'? Merle's been worried."

I shake my head.

"Tex-Ann, if I told you, you wouldn't even believe me."

"*Mm-hm.*" She smiles and takes a drag from her cigarette. "That's what I thought. Been out tomcattin', havencha? I told Merle, I said, 'Honey, as good-lookin' as that boy is, he was in town last night, and some lil ol' cute thayng drug him out to the hayloft.'"

I roll my eyes.

"Not quite. But gosh, it's . . . good to see you. I thought you were . . . you know . . . going home. To Dallas."

"Well I was, honey. Then we got there and Merle all uh sudden decided he just couldn' do without me. So . . ." She takes a sip of coffee and winks. "Here I am."

"Well . . . great. That's wonderful. Is this just . . . you know . . . temporary, or—"

"Listen, doll, when ya been to the barn and back as many times as me, ya just take it one whack at a time. Tomorrow we could be the biggest lovebirds ya ever saw, or we could be clawin' each other's eyes out. Ya just never know about these thayngs." She drags her cigarette and winks at me. "Butcha gotta keep tryin', darlin'. Otherwise ya dry up and crumble like an ol' boot."

"Yes. Absolutely. Well, I hope you guys are very happy together."

"Thank ya, darlin'."

"Is Merle here?"

"Sure, doll. C'mon in. He's takin' a lil nappy-poo. But I know he's anxious to see ya. He's been wonderin' about his drillin' permit."

"I have it. It's in the truck."

"Oh, you are so smart. Merle is so proud of you." She puts her arm around me and we start in the house. In the distance we hear a rumble. We turn. A big black cargo truck drives in along the ranch road, kicking up a trail of white dust behind it. "Oh, goody," Tex-Ann says, "there's the furniture. I was hopin' they'd get here 'fore lunch."

"Furniture?"

"Yeah, I told Merle, I said, 'Honey, I just cain't live sittin' around on the floor like an ol' Indian. I gotta have some thayngs, darlin'.' "

The truck pulls up along the front of the house. It has Fort Worth Furniture and Appliance Rental written across its side. The driver rolls down his window.

"Yoohoo!" Tex-Ann hollers and waves. "This is it! Yer at the right place!"

The driver nods and backs toward the end of the sidewalk. When he puts the transmission in reverse, a warning alarm beeps shrilly, setting the dogs off on a yapping frenzy.

RAR-RAR-RAR-RAR-RAR.

"Sasha! Snowflake! Stay back from there! Ya hear me? Stay back! *Back!*"

As the truck beeps, the dogs yap, and Tex-Ann scolds, Merle appears in the doorway. Blinking his eyes from sleep, he wears white boxer shorts and black socks.

"Goddam," he says, "is it nuclear war?"

"There ya are, sugar," Tex-Ann says. "The furniture's here."

"Well, tell 'em to piss-ant it on in. Hey there, boy. Where the hell ya been? Chasin' split-tail?"

"Not exactly."

"Ja get my drillin' permit?"

"Yes. It's in Ol' Blue."

"Attaboy. We gotta go stake 'at location today. Rig's all set to go. Wanna co' beer?"

"Uh . . . no thank you."

Merle turns and disappears back into the house.

"Scuse me, doll," Tex-Ann says. "I wanna go look and make sure where I want ever'thayng." She takes a deep drag from her cigarette, flicks it out into the grass, then goes inside.

Merle comes out. He's bare from the waist up, but he's put on his brown slacks. In each hand he carries a tall sixteen-ounce can of Coors beer. He offers one to me.

"Here ya go."

I don't take it.

"Merle, I don't—"

He shoves it against my chest.

"Aw, drank the sumbitch. It'll keep ya alive."

I take the beer and follow him out along the sidewalk. The furniture truck has backed up to the end of the sidewalk and parked. The driver rolls open the cargo door. Stacked high in the truck, from wall to wall: sofas, chairs, tables, lamps, even several elaborately framed colorful Monet prints.

"So," the driver says, "somebody gonna tell us where this all goes, or—"

"Yoohoo!" Tex-Ann hollers from the doorway. "I'm ready when y'all are!"

The furniture men grab up a long dark-stained colonial-style dining table and start down the sidewalk. Merle props a black-socked foot on the truck's bumper, cracks open his beer, and guzzles a deep swallow. He sighs and watches the furniture men carry the table to the house.

"Goduhmighty, here I go again."

"Jesus, Merle. I know it's none of my business, but this is sort of quick, isn't it?"

He has another swig and watches the furniture men maneuver the table through the front door.

"Well, maybe so. But I tell ya what." He brushes a shock of hair from his eyes and stares at me. "When 'at ol' gal rubs 'em titties on me and talks nasty, by God, my ol' dick gets so hard a cat couldn' scratch it."

I laugh and look down at my chocolate lizards.

"Okay. Well—"

"And I tell ya what, son, when ya get to be my age, 'ere's a lot to be said fer that."

"I understand. Listen Merle, there's something I have to tell you."

"Ar-ighty." He swigs his beer, then points to mine. "You gonna drank 'at damn thayng or just play with it?"

I sigh. I crack open my beer and sip it.

"I . . . uh . . . sort of betrayed you, Merle."

"Betrayed me? What the hell ya talkin' about?"

I tell him the story of my ordeal with Sheriff Nall and Don Brock. He sips his beer, grumbles, curses, scratches his nuts, and listens.

"I'm really sorry, Merle. I guess I was just scared."

"Goduhmighty, reckon so. Sounds like they had ya by the short hair. But hell, what difference does it make? I done got the lease and permit, and I'm gonna be drillin' up in Kent County. 'At ain't Jack Nall's neighborhood. He cain't do a damn thayng to me up 'ere." He finishes his beer and crumples the can flat. He gives me the crumpled can and takes my almost full beer. He burps and swigs my beer. "So ol' Jack Nall let the cat out uh the bag, huh? Don's done sold my rigs."

"That's what he said."

He scowls.

"Well, ol' Don's gonna wake up with his ass in the fire, cuz he ain't gettin' one goddam stick uh iron off none of 'em. Ya hear me? *None!*"

Wham.

He bangs his fist on the side of the furniture truck.

RAR-RAR-RAR-RAR-RAR.

Tex-Ann's dogs come charging around the truck, barking. Both the dachshund and poodle yap and nip at Merle's black-socked feet.

RAR-RAR-RAR-RAR-RAR.

Merle looks down at them, shakes his head, and frowns.

"Goddam, I hope these fuckin' dogs don't kill the deal."

RAR-RAR-RAR-RAR-RAR.

"*Sasha! Snowflake!*" Tex-Ann claps her hands and yells from the doorway. The dogs back off and trot to the house. "Y'all terrible thayngs," Tex-Ann says. "I'm gonna have to putchall in the backyard." She smiles and waves. "Sorry, honey! They just don't know you yet!"

Merle smiles and waves back.

"Fuckin' dogs," he mumbles. He looks at me and points at me with the hand holding the beer. "Remember, son. 'Ere ain't no free lunches."

Å Å Å

Tex-Ann serves lunch on the new dining table in the dining room. Chili and dumplings. It's good, too. It's like a soup with big hunks of meat and dough in a spicy chili sauce. I'm so hungry I wolf my whole serving in about three minutes.

"God, Tex-Ann," I say, "this is delicious."

White paper napkin tucked in his shirt, holding his spoon in his fist like a three-year-old, Merle slurps a spoonful of chili and seconds my compliment with a grunt.

"Uh-*huh.*"

"Well, good," Tex-Ann says. "I'm glad j'all like it. Big Merle dudn' have much to work with in the kitchen. Fact, honey, I'm gonna need to go in town today and buy some thayngs."

Merle slurps another spoonful.

"I know, baby. I know."

Using a coffee cup as a ladle, Tex-Ann serves me another bowl.

"So, Erwin, tell me all about Los Angeles and Hollywood. I never got a chance to ask ya. How long were ya out there?"

"Oh, about four months."

"Well? Is it just fabulous?"

I shrug.

"Yeah. It's sort of crowded, but the weather's really nice."

"And the people, I bet they're just beautiful."

I scoff as I remember the alkies and heroin heads at the Viva Sol.

"Yeah," I say. "Everyone is tan. And healthy. They're real active out there. They all bike or Rollerblade or play volleyball or surf or whatever. It really is sort of like the stereotype. You know, lots of limos and convertibles and palm trees and sunshine and people wearing sunglasses."

Tex-Ann smiles, reaches out, and squeezes Merle's forearm.

"Oh, Merley, dudn' that just sound *wonderful?*"

Merle gobbles a dumpling and grunts.

"Uh-huh."

"And what about Hollywood?" she asks. "That must uh been so excitin'."

I eat a spoonful of chili and wipe my mouth.

"Yeah, it was. Especially for me, because I'm such a movie freak. Seeing the studio museums was pretty cool."

"Did you see any stars?"

"Yeah."

She flaps her hands excitedly.

"*Oh* . . . who?"

"Let's see. I saw Uma Thurman—she was having lunch at the little café where I worked. And Kevin Costner—he was walking along the street in Universal City. And . . . oh yeah, I had a beer with Brad Pitt."

She opens her eyes wide.

"*Oh my God.* Really?"

"Well, he was standing down at the other end of the bar, but—"

She laughs.

"Oh, you."

Merle stares at me blankly, like he doesn't get the joke.

"So," Tex-Ann says, "you were really out there trying to . . . you know . . . act in the movies?"

I shrug.

"Yeah, that was the general idea, anyway."

"Well, angel, I'm sorry it didn' work out. I don't know why they didn' just snatch you right up and make a star out of ya. Yer good-lookin' as they get. And smart. But I've always heard, Hollywood is *so* hard to get into. Who knows? Maybe you'll have better luck down the road."

"Well, no, I'm afraid that chapter is over and done. I gave it a shot, but I got in over my head. I—"

"*Bullshit,*" Merle says. He bangs his fist on the table and gobbles his mouthful of food. "Hell, I betchur the smartest sumbitch in the state uh Texas. And look atcha, goduhmighty, ya look like ol' whistle britches." He looks at Tex-Ann. "What's 'at ol' boy's name, honey?"

"Montgomery Clift."

"Hell yeah. Now if he can do it, by God, why cainchoo?"

The hairs on my neck crinkle. If Merle wants to be a lugheaded alcoholic moron about his own stuff, that's fine. But I don't need him preaching to me. I put down my spoon and wipe my mouth.

"Look, Merle. I appreciate your vote of confidence. But I think this is a little more complicated than you realize."

Merle shovels another dumpling in his mouth.

"Aw hell, quitchur cryin'. You ain't even started tryin' yet. A man's gotta *fight* fer his dream, son."

My face gets hot.

"Goddammit, Merle. Getting a break in film is not like the oil-drilling business. You don't just chug a fucking bottle of Jack Daniel's, then jump in your truck and start smashing into people."

Merle stares at me as brown chili juice drips down his chin. He points his spoon at me.

"I'm gonna tell ya one more time, son. Don't quit on yer dream. You'll go sour inside."

I roll my eyes.

"Whatever, Merle."

FROM THE NORTHWEST CORNER OF SCHEERMEYER'S LAND
we measure east 2,265 feet along the fence. Merle ties a strip of
red plastic ribbon on the barbed wire to mark this spot, then I
set out perpendicularly, or due south, with the end of one-
hundred-feet-long pipe-tallying tape. Merle stands at the fence
until I stretch the tape tight, then I scrape a mark in the dirt with
the heel of my chocolate lizard. Holding the ends of the tape, we
walk in unison straight out from the fence until Merle arrives at
my first mark and stops. I stretch the tape tight, scrape another
mark, and yell, "Two hundred!" In this way we measure out
through the cactus patches and cedar bushes until I arrive at a
clearing of wiry gray grass which should be—if I've correctly compared the seismic data with the maps—the optimum spot to drill.

"This is it! Two thousand two hundred and sixty-five feet from
the west line, and one thousand three hundred and forty feet from
the north." I gouge an X in the grass and dirt with my heel. Merle
drops the tape and walks to where I stand. Holding a long wooden
stake, he looks down at the X, then around at the tall gray grass
and scrubby dark green bushes waving in the wind. He smiles.

"Can ya feel it?"

"What?"

"Oil, boy."

I lift my nose to the wind and smell the sweet rotting smell familiar to Scheermeyer's place.

"I smell cow shit."

He frowns.

"I didn't say *smell*, goddammit. I said *feel*." He drops the wooden stake in the grass, slides up his pant leg, and pulls his flask from his boot. The polished silver glints in the sun as he takes a swig.

"Aw yeah," he says.

In the distance, on the wind, I hear a shrill high-pitched buzz like a chainsaw or leaf blower. It pulses without rhythm, now slowing to a crackle, now revving to a squeal.

Reeeeee. Reee. Reeeeeeeee. Reee.

"What is that, Merle? A chainsaw?"

Enthralled in a mystical assessment of his well site, Merle ignores me. He looks down at the red-dirt X in the grass beside me.

"It's gonna hit, son. I can feel it." He sips his flask again and smiles. "Yes sir, ol' Merle's gonna fill his sack right here."

I shake my head and laugh. The guy kills me. Here he is, literally staking his financial salvation on the work of someone with no background whatsoever in oil. Does this bother him? Hell no. I walk over, grab his flask, and have a sip.

"Look, Merle, I hate to play the cynic, but I'm telling you, you need to have someone look at the maps and seismic and make sure I've picked this spot right. Get a geologist, or a cartographer, or—"

"Aw, bullshit." He jerks his flask away from me. "I toldja, boy. Yer my savin' angel." He sips his flask, caps it, and slips it back into his boot. "Don'choo worry. Ya done fine." He looks around the ground and nods. "Ya set me down right here, and by God, right here's where I'm gonna drill. I ain't no dummy." He picks up the wooden stake and a big flat rock, sets the stake right on the X and starts hammering it in with the rock.

In the distance, the pulsing engine buzz grows louder.
Reeeeee. Reee. Reeeeeeeee.

Now, under the mosquito-like buzz, I hear a dull rumble.

"What *is* that?" I turn and look south. Several hundred yards away, through the wind-waving tops of the cedar bushes, I see Scheermeyer's black cows running toward us. Behind them, over their bobbing heads, a cloud of orange dust swirls in the wind.

"Shit, Merle! The cows are coming!"

"Do what?"

I point south.

"The *cows*. They're stampeding right toward us."

He stops banging the stake with the rock and looks toward the rumbling herd. He shrugs.

"Aw, hell. They're just lil ol' yearlin' heifers."

The cows, apparently the entire herd of nine hundred, are now just yards away, rumbling right at us.

MAAAAAA.

MAAAAAA.

They bellow as they run.

"Fuck, Merle! They'll trample us!"

He keeps hammering the stake in the ground with the rock.

"Aw, goduhmighty. Stand yer ground. Lil ol' yearlin's ain't gonna bother ya."

I step beside him and turn sideways to the oncoming herd. Hopping over cactus and around bushes, they converge. I grab Merle's arm and close my eyes. The ground rumbles, the air swirls with their warm stink, and—*MAAAAAA*—they bellow all around me. I open my eyes. Merle's right. As though we're just another patch of cactus or cedar bush, they part ranks and rumble right past us. Now, amid the rumbling hooves, *MAAAAAA*, bawling complaints, and—*Reeeeeee*—buzzing engine, I hear whistling and yelling.

Thweet.

"*Hai! Yai! Get on, now!*"

Thweet.

"*Hai! Yai!*"

In the herd's dust-swirling wake, whizzing back and forth in quick swerves and zigzags, Scheermeyer rides a tiny fat-tired motorcycle. He wears tall tan cowboy boots with his blue jeans tucked into their tops, a white sleeveless T-shirt, suspenders, leather gloves, goggles, and a sweat-stained wide-brimmed cowboy hat. His white hair hangs down from under his hat around his neck and flutters in the wind.

Reeeeee. Reee. Reeeeeeeee.

His head jerks back as he guns the throttle and veers between the cactus and cedar bushes, whistling and prompting the herd.

Thweet.

"*Hai! Yai! Get on, now!*"

Thweet.

"*Hai! Yai!*"

He veers around a bush and sees Merle and me.

Reeeeeeeee.

He revs his motorcycle toward us and skids to a halt. He reaches down along the motorcycle with his gloved hand and pulls a wire dangling from the engine. The buzz dies, leaving only the fading hoof rumble and rustling wind.

Scheermeyer pulls his dust-coated goggles down around his chin. Around his sky blue eyes are two ovals of fair, wrinkled skin. The rest of his face is coated with orange dust. The left side of his face is swollen and round from a big hunk of tobacco packed under his cheek.

"Goddam, boys, I'd uh known y'all were out here, I wouldn' uh run 'em right over ya. What the hell y'all doin'?"

Merle ignores him and hammers the stake with the rock.

"We're staking the well," I say.

Pttt.

Scheermeyer spits a long string of brown juice, then lolls the wad of tobacco in his mouth.

"Hell, ink ain't even dry on the lease yet."

I look at Merle, hoping he will respond to this, but he is absorbed with driving the stake.

"I suppose that's true," I say. "But Merle is . . . anxious to get busy."

Scheermeyer shrugs.

"Well, cain't fault a man fer workin', I don't reckon." He lolls his wad of tobacco and smiles. "Goddam, I sure wanna thank y'all fer brayngin' 'at ol' gal out here the other night. It *was* a lil crooked on y'alls' part, I reckon, not tellin' me y'all was oil people. But hell, she's the goddamdest thayng I ever saw. I wudn' about to let a lil bizness get 'tween me and 'at. *Goddam,* she had a pair uh titties on her like a June sow."

Merle grits his teeth and keeps banging the stake with the rock. Still astride his tiny motorcycle, Scheermeyer laughs with a cackle.

"*Woo-wee,*" he says. "Been a month uh Sundays since I had a piece uh ass like 'at. Used to be a wetback over in Jayton. He'd brayng his wife around ever' so often and letcha have a go at her fer fifty dollars. But she wudn' nothin' to look at. But 'at ol' gal the other night, *goddam,* she—"

"Hey!" Holding the rock in his hand, Merle points to Scheermeyer. "Just ferget her, goddammit! She ain't none uh yer damn bizness no more."

Scheermeyer lolls his tobacco wad and stares at Merle. He leans out and spits.

Pttt.

"What's uh matter, Luskey? Ya gotchur lease, didn' ya?"

"Yes sir, I did. But let the dog die, ar-ight? A gentleman don't go around mouthin' off about stuff like 'at." Merle turns and resumes driving the stake.

"Hell," Scheermeyer says, "I ain't never pretended to be no gentleman." He looks at me. "Lookee here, son. Got me a lil souvenir." He reaches around the back of his motorcycle and, from an old leather pouch strapped to the seat, brings out a Ziploc bag containing some black silky cloth. He holds up the clear plastic bag and smiles. "Got her panties right here."

Merle stops banging the stake and looks. Scheermeyer peels open the Ziploc liner, puts his face into the bag, and takes a deep breath.

"Sweet Jesus!" he says. He grins and holds the opened bag out to me. "Getcha a whiff, boy. 'At'll put some sprayng in yer get-along."

"Goddammit!" Merle yells. "Ya ol' goat-ropin' sonofabitch!" He drops the rock and lunges toward Scheermeyer. I step in front of him and grab him around the chest.

"No, Merle! No!"

Merle keeps lunging, but I dig my heels in the dirt, lean into him, and hold on with everything I have.

"Merle! No!"

"Bullshit. I've had enough uh this." He thrashes and tries to get around me, but I hang on.

"Merle! I'm your saving angel and I say, 'Cut the shit.' Remember your dream. Your drilling rigs. You can't afford to do something stupid, Merle. You don't have time."

He stops struggling. He grits his teeth, stares at me, and backs off.

"Okay," I say. "Just calm down." I turn and look at Scheermeyer. "Alton, please, put the panties away. Merle has developed sort of an emotional attachment to Tex-Ann. Don't get me wrong. He's happy he has the lease. And he's happy that you're happy about it. But let's just put the panties away and not discuss the other night."

Scheermeyer seals the panties in the bag and looks at Merle.

"Sorry, Luskey. Hell, I figgered she was just a . . . well . . . I just wancha to know I appreciate it. I really do." He holds up the sealed panties. "And if ya don't mind, I'll hang on to these." He stuffs his souvenir back in the leather pouch strapped to his motorcycle. Merle picks up the rock and starts banging again on the stake. Scheermeyer spits a string of tobacco juice.

Pttt.

"So 'at's where yer gonna drill yer well?"

"Yep," Merle says, "sure is." He steps back. The stake stands firmly in the ground.

"How much it gonna cost ya to drill it?"

Merle pitches the rock out away from the stake. It lands with a dull thud. He rubs his palms together, cleaning off the dirt from the rock.

"Aw, countin' fuel, bits, mud, and payroll, about fifty . . . sixty thousand."

"Well, why don'cha gimme five hunerd and I'll tell ya right now it's dry."

Merle takes a roll of red plastic ribbon from his shirt pocket and tears off a piece about six feet long.

"Oh? Thank so?"

"Hell yeah. Some outfit drilled one back over across the road when I's a boy. Drier'n a popcorn fart. I don't mean to piss on yer parade, son, but there ain't no oil around here."

Merle ties the red ribbon around the top of the stake. Its two streamers flutter sideways in the wind.

"Good. Then I reckon ya ain't gonna get upset if I spill a lil on the ground."

THE SUN PEEKS EGG-YOLK YELLOW OVER THE HORIZON AND casts long shadows across the rig yard. Wearing his usual attire—straw cowboy hat, short-sleeved white shirt, dark brown pants, and beige cowboy boots—Merle stands on a double-wide trailer under the giant rig substructure of welded I beams.

Thweeet!

He whistles and waves his arm high in the air.

"AR-IGHT, MULE, C'MON! STRAIGHT ON, NOW! STRAIGHT ON!"

RAAAWWW.

Mule revs the diesel truck and backs toward the trailer.

Thweeet!

"HO! HO!"

Ssssssss.

The hydraulic brakes hiss as Mule stops the truck under the massive trailer hitch.

"Ar-ight, Harvard, crank her down."

I crank the trailer jack, lowering the trailer onto the truck. Merle whistles.

Theee-o-weet!

"Ar-ight, you sumbitches! Gather up!"

Sipping coffee and smoking cigarettes, the roughnecks of all three Rig Two crews—morning tour, day tour, and evening tour—

gather along the trailer. Merle pushes up the front brim of his hat, puts his hands on his hips, and looks down at his rough-necks.

"Ar-ight boys, I ain't told y'all yet, cuz I didn' wanna spook ya aboutchur jobs, but I'm in trouble with the damn bank. As y'all know, the bottom's dropped out uh the drillin' bizness here lately, and ... well ... I ain't stayed real steady at payin' my damn loan note. Anyhow, this next sumbitch we're gonna drill is my hole. I own the lease. Or I reckon I should say it's *our* hole, cuz if the sumbitch don't come in, we're all goin' belly-ass under. So here's what I wanna tell y'all. 'At damn reef's either gonna be down 'ere or it ain't. And it's either gonna be full uh oil or it ain't. Ain't nothin' we can do about 'at. 'At's in the good Lord's hands. But by God, my deadline with the bank's starin' me right'n the face, and we're gonna have to drill this damn thayng in high gear. We got less'n two weeks to get down and scratch 'at reef."

"How deep we goin', boss?"

Merle looks at me.

"Where's 'at reef gonna come in, Harvard?"

"Uh, it's supposed to be about eight thousand eight hundred feet down."

The roughnecks cuss and look at one another.

"Goddam, boss," Virgil says. "Ain't no way we can go to eighty-eight in two weeks. It'll take us a good three and a—"

"Bullshit!" Merle's face flushes red. "We're gonna strayng on a dozen extra collars and we're gonna run soup fer mud, and by God, we're gonna bullhead the sumbitch on down. I worked my whole goddam life puttin' together this outfit—" He waves out across the rig yard. "And I ain't gonna lose it just cuz the price uh oil's gone to hell and some chickenshit banker thanks he can drive me under. And another thayng, if this well comes in, ever' damn one uh y'all is gonna get a dollar-an-hour raise. So let's go, boys! By God, Kent County, here we come!"

Ä Ä Ä

From the rig yard we emerge, a massive convoy of rumbling, exhaust-stack-spewing machinery—at the head, Merle and I in his red pickup; next, lying horizontally, the gigantic 120-feet-long white-and-red derrick, commandeered by Shay; then a series of seven Peterbilt trucks drawing long flatbed trailers loaded with equipment. Virgil hauls the red doghouse, along with the three rig engines; Mule, the huge substructure of steel beams, on which the derrick will be stationed; and after Mule, roughnecks of Rig Two's other two crews haul mud pumps, steel tanks for mixing mud, massive spools of rubber hose, pipe racks and the catwalk, hundreds of joints of drill pipe, and a five-thousand-gallon diesel fuel tank. Two winch-and-pole trucks, used to assemble the rig floor and hoist the derrick upright, bring up the rear.

We turn north on the highway out of the yard and drive about a quarter of a mile.

Wee-oh, wee-oh, wee-oh . . .

Wailing sirens rise behind us. Merle looks out at his side mirror.

"What the hell's goin' on?"

WEE-OH, WEE-OH, WEE-OH . . .

In a deafening wail, two red-and-blue-flashing Taylor County Sheriff's Department cars whisk past us. The first swerves in front of us, the other slows and drops back along our left flank. Together, they slow and force us to stop along the side of the road.

As we get out, Sheriff Nall steps from the patrol car in front of us. He adjusts his straw cowboy hat and waddles back toward us. His usual frazzled cigar stub is jammed in the corner of his mouth.

"Mornin', Merle."

"Jack."

Deputy Buck steps from the patrol car to our left. He nods at me and smiles.

"Yank," he says.

I look back along our convoy, which has stopped off in the dirt along the side of the road. Two more Taylor County Sheriff's Department cars, their blue-and-red lights flashing in the morning sun, are parked at intervals alongside us, each with a straw-hatted deputy standing beside it. Our roughnecks step down from their trucks.

"What's the problem, Jack?" Merle asks.

Sheriff Nall hitches his glossy black gun-and-ammunition belt up around his belly.

"Well, Merle, I need to check yer overweight permits. Make sure yer square with the D.O.T."

Merle frowns.

"What the hell, Jack? I been movin' rigs nineteen years around here. Ain't nobody ever asked me fer goddam weight permits."

Sheriff Nall smiles and chews his cigar stub.

" 'Ere's a new policy comin' up from Austin. They're crackin' down." He nods back along the convoy. "Ya got weight-exception permits fer these trucks? I'm gonna need to see 'em."

Merle steps forward.

"Tell me somethin', Jack. How come ya gotchur head so far up Don Brock's ass? What's he do fer you? Huh? Pay ya on the side? Tinker with the votes?"

Sheriff Nall takes the soggy cigar stub from his mouth and holds it between his thumb and index finger.

"I don't know whatchur talkin' about, Merle." He gestures down to the asphalt. "This is a matter uh takin' care uh the roads. Now if ya don't have overweight permits, I'm gonna have to arrest yer drivers and impound all this equipment."

Merle just stares at him. Sheriff Nall smiles.

"Ar-ight, boys! Round 'em up!"

"Bullshit," Merle says. "I figgered you'd pull some kind uh stunt, Jack. I gotchur fuckin' permits."

The smile disappears from Sheriff Nall's pink fat face.

"Yer lyin', Merle. Ya ain't got overweight permits. Nobody ever enforces 'em."

"The hell I don't. I heard whatcha done to Harvard, lockin' him up and bulldoggin' him with 'at sack uh dope. I knew some kind uh bullshit was gonna happen today." Merle smiles. "Thoughtcha had me, Jack, didn' ya?"

Sheriff Nall jams the cigar stub back in his mouth.

"Lemme see 'em, Merle."

"Ar-ight. They're in the knowledge box in the doghouse. I got one fer ever' damn truck." Merle turns and walks back along the convoy. Sheriff Nall motions for Deputy Buck to come along. They follow Merle past the derrick to the third vehicle, where the steel-walled doghouse sits on the trailer. I walk back to where Virgil and Shay stand under the crown of the derrick.

"What the hell's goin' on?" Shay asks.

"Sheriff Nall wants to see some kind of overweight permits. I guess Merle has them in the doghouse. He's going to show them."

Virgil and Shay look at each other, then walk back along the road.

Merle crawls up onto the trailer loaded with the red steel-walled doghouse, then turns and helps Sheriff Nall and Deputy Buck onto the trailer.

"They're in here," Merle says, gesturing to the doghouse. He turns the latch handle, swings open the heavy steel door, and steps inside. Sheriff Nall and Deputy Buck follow him in. Suddenly Merle jumps out, slams the door closed, and locks the latch. He turns and points back to the other two deputies.

"Grab them jackasses!"

Apparently having anticipated Merle's strategy, Shay and Virgil are already in position—Shay beside the first deputy's car;

Virgil, the second's. They pounce. Although the deputies are big broad-shouldered brutes, they are no match for roughneck brawn. Within seconds Shay and Virgil have the deputies in ironlike bear hugs.

Ã Ã Ã

The derrick towers in the lavender sky. Its crisscross ironwork whispers in the breeze and throws a long shadow across the reserve mud pits to the far dike, where a row of Scheermeyer's black cows stand observing Mule and Shay at work on the shale shaker. My team's job—setting the fuel tank, stairs, rails, pipe racks, and catwalk—completed, I sit on the rig floor and watch the sun set over Scheermeyer's trailer house. In this flat terrain, twenty-five feet up off the ground on the rig floor, I can see everything, the gray grass and peach-colored soil, light green cactus thickets, dark green cedar bushes, and Scheermeyer's herd scattered from here around the rig across the north side of his land. Heads down, they swish their tails and wander among the cactus and cedars, grazing on the wiry gray grass.

I hear boot heels clanging up the metal stairs. I hop up, put on my gloves, and start arranging the rat's-ass chain in a neat circle by the dead man. Flask in hand, Merle comes up the stairs and walks out beneath the derrick.

"Harvard."

"Yeah?"

"Yer a star hand, boy."

I continue to wind the rat's ass in a neat circular pile.

"I'm sorry, Merle. I really am."

"What the hell for?"

"For knuckling under and telling Sheriff Nall and Don Brock what you're doing. I told them we were moving the rig this morning. If I'd just kept my mouth shut, none of this would've happened."

"Aw, bullshit. They'd uh found out anyhow." He sips his flask. "A man cain't scratch his ass around Abilene without ever'body knowin'." He looks around the rig floor, then curls up his tongue and whistles.

Theee-o-weeet!

"Ar-ight, boys! Let's turn these sumbitches loose and get to drillin'! We got hole to make. Y'all drag 'em weevils out uh the tanks and brayng 'em up here."

Down below, Shay, Virgil, and Mule pull the two handcuffed deputies from the steel mud-circulation tanks and escort them up onto the rig floor.

Merle knocks on the doghouse door.

Clang, clang, clang.

"Jack?"

"*Yeah,*" Sheriff Nall answers, his voice muffled behind the steel.

"Hell, Jack. Are you in 'ere?"

"*Yeah, Merle. I'm in here.*"

Merle smiles and sips his flask.

"Well I'll be go-to-hell. We been lookin' ever'where fer ya, Jack."

"*Zat right?*"

"Hell, yeah. Thank ya wanna come on out now?"

"*Yeah. It's hot in here, Merle.*"

"Zat right? Well, if I open this door, 'ere ain't gonna be no hard feelin's, is 'ere?"

"*No, Merle. Just let us out uh here. Please.*"

"Ar-ight. I'm gonna letcha out."

"*I sure would appreciate it, Merle.*"

Merle looks back at us.

"Y'all might wanna get ready fer this."

Shay and Virgil shield themselves behind the two handcuffed deputies and aim pistols at the doghouse door.

"Jack?"

"Yeah?"

"We got a shitload uh firepower out here, so I wouldn' try nothin' cute."

"Ar-ight. I won't."

"Ar-ight. Here ya go." Merle unlatches the door and swings it open. Sheriff Nall and Deputy Buck step out. Their shirts are soaked in sweat. Merle lays his hand on Sheriff Nall's shoulder. "Goddam, Jack, it's good to see ya. I been lookin' ever'where fer ya."

Sheriff Nall knocks Merle's hand off his shoulder and glares at him.

"Yer in deep this time, Luskey."

Merle swigs his flask.

"Yeah, well, I'm also in Kent County, Jack."

Sheriff Nall takes off his hat, pats his hair-pasted sweating scalp with a drenched handkerchief, and looks around the landscape. He puts his hat back on, hitches up his gun belt, and points his finger in Merle's face.

"I got news fer ya, Merle. Don's gonna cutchur ass up and sell ya off in lil pieces. Shit, he's done sold yer rigs. And he's gonna getchur ranch, yer house, yer truck, ever' damn thayng ya got, right down to yer boots and hat. And by God, Merle, I wancha to know, I'm gonna thoroughly enjoy watchin' you go ass-up."

Merle sniffs and stares at him coolly.

"Well, Jack, if I were you I wouldn' buy the beer and cigars yet." He points down to the rig floor. "I'm fixin' to cut a fat hog in the ass right here."

Sheriff Nall screws his eyes into a squint and hitches up his gun belt.

"No ya ain't, Merle. Cuz I'm gonna hurtchoo fer whatchoo done to me today."

Staring Sheriff Nall dead in the eye, Merle sips his flask and wipes his mouth with the back of his hand.

"Just brayng it on, fat boy. Just brayng it on."

Ä Ä Ä

Thweeet!

Shay whistles and whirls his gloved hand over his head.

"Fire 'em up!"

Virgil engages the electric starter, and after several shrieks and coughs, the engines roar to life and begin their steady grumble.

RAAAWWW . . .

The cows bolt from the mud-pit dike and trot away to a safe distance, then turn and look back at this awesome growling thing.

Virgil, Mule, and I drag the drill bit down the catwalk, where the kelly lies suspended diagonally out of the derrick, and screw it onto the kelly. Meanwhile, Shay, working the foot-feed, guns the accelerator and tests the engines' response.

RAW-RAW-RAW.

Thweeet!

Virgil whistles and shows the thumbs-up sign, indicating the bit is secure.

RAAAAAWWWWW . . .

Shay revs the engines and engages the draw-works. The massive yellow traveling block rises, hoisting the kelly up along the slanted catwalk. Mule and I dash up the stairs and catch the bit as it swings off the catwalk across the rig floor under the derrick.

REEET.

Shay sets the brake, suspending the kelly in the derrick.

REEET . . . REEET . . . REEET . . .

Working the brake, Shay eases the bit and square-sided kelly down through the square hole in the rotary table and down through the substructure.

REEET . . . REEET—BANG.

The bit hits the ground twenty-five feet down below the rig floor.

"AR-IGHT, SHAY-BOY, LOOK OUT GODDAMMIT!"

We turn. Silhouetted by the orange setting sun, Merle stands at the top of the stairs dressed in old mud-caked steel-toed work boots and bright red Luskey overalls. Atop his head, cocked a little to one side, an old white grease-stained hard hat. Stenciled across the front of it:

LUSKEY

DRILLER

We stare.

"WHAT THE HELL Y'ALL LOOKIN' AT?" he yells. "AIN'CHA EVER SEEN A DAMN ROUGHNECK?" He steps out under the derrick beside Shay at the brake and foot-feed. He unzips his overalls and, from the inside breast pocket, brings out his flask. He has a double swig, then returns his flask to his overalls and zips back up. From his back pocket he brings out a pair of white cotton work gloves. He pulls on the gloves and looks at Shay. "LOOK OUT, WORM."

Shay smiles and moves away from the driller's controls. Merle puts his boot on the foot-feed and guns the engines to a deafening roar.

RAAAAAAAAWWWWWWWW . . .

Black smoke spews from the three engines' exhaust stacks and drifts out across the mud pits.

"AR-IGHT, BOYS!" Merle yells. "BY GOD, LET'S MAKE SOME HOLE!" He jerks the clutch.

CLANK.

The rotary table jumps and whirls.

RAAAAWWWW . . .

The engines roar.

"GODDAM," Virgil yells, chewing a mouthful of ham sandwich and corn chips. He leans over and examines the gory brown filling of Shay's burrito. " 'AT THAYNG'S LIABLE TO KILL YER ASS."

Shay stuffs the burrito in his mouth and drinks from a two-liter plastic bottle of orange pop.

"I KNOW. SUMBITCH IS FULL UH JALAPEÑO."

I sit down by them along the catwalk with my Texas Giant vanilla milk shake and Dairy Queen sack. Since Merle and I have been out here on the rig all night, he let me drive into Jayton this morning to get food. Virgil crams a handful of corn chips in his mouth and eyes my greasy sack.

"WHATCHA GOT, HARVARD?" He snatches my sack away.

"HEY. CUT IT OUT." I elbow him in the ribs and grab it back.

"AW, C'MON, WHATCHA GOT?"

"A BURGER. AND FRIES."

All three—Virgil, Shay, Mule—stare luridly as I bring out a double-meat cheeseburger and large order of fries. I spread out the paper sack, lay the fries on it, then unwrap the paper cover from my burger. Each chewing his own food, they lean and stare.

"SUMBITCH GOT CHEESE ON IT?" Shay asks.

Virgil takes a bite of his sandwich, leans over, and looks at my burger.

"HELL YEAH. DOUBLE MEAT, TOO."

"GODDAM."

They grunt and paw around in their lunch pails. Shay holds up a packaged microwavable burrito.

"HEY, HARVARD, TRADE YA FER HALF 'AT SUM-BITCH."

"AW BULLSHIT," Virgil says. "YOU DON'T WANT NO GOAT-MEAT BURRITO." He holds up an extralong Snickers candy bar. "HOW ABOUT THIS SNICKERS FER HALF?"

I shake my head, slowly stuff the burger in my mouth, and take a bite. Strings of onion hanging down my chin, I smile and chew my burger.

"SORRY, BOYS, BUT I BELIEVE I'LL BE ENJOYING THIS BABY IN ITS ENTIRETY."

Thweeet!

We turn and look past the turning kelly and rotary table. Dressed in mud-caked work boots, red Luskey overalls, and his grease-stained white hard hat, Merle stands at the driller's controls, where, except for an occasional break to pee off the side of the rig, he's been all night long. Although I slept several hours in the truck last night while the evening-tour crew worked, Merle stayed at it. Manually running the engines at a high-RPM deafening pitch (far beyond the range of the automatic control), to everyone's amazement, he has drilled over six hundred feet since starting yesterday at sundown. He motions to me.

"HARVARD!"

I lay my burger on the paper sack by my fries and stand up. I look at Virgil and Shay.

"YOU SONS OF BITCHES BETTER NOT MESS WITH MY FOOD."

They smile. I walk under the derrick to where Merle stands at the controls. His eyes look dull and tired.

"GODUHMIGHTY," he yells, "WHERE THE HELL YA BEEN?"

"I JUST DROVE STRAIGHT TO THE DAIRY QUEEN IN JAYTON AND BACK. YOU SURE YOU DON'T WANT ANYTHING TO EAT?"

"HELL YEAH. I'M WORKIN', SON. HERE. I NEED A RECHARGE." He reaches in his overalls and brings out his flask from the inside breast pocket.

Concerned about the security of my burger and fries, I run down to the truck and refill his flask from his backseat bottle. I can't believe he hasn't crapped out yet. This is about the fifth time I've refilled his flask since he started drilling.

I dash back up to the rig and give it to him. With his mud-caked work boot still pressing the foot-feed, he takes off his gloves and uncaps his flask. He swigs it and sucks air through his teeth.

"AW YEAH." He recaps the flask, slips it inside his overalls, and zips them up to his neck. "THANKS, SON."

"NO PROB."

I walk back under the derrick to the catwalk where my colleagues sit, lunch pails, aluminum foil, cellophane food wrapping, and plastic pop bottles scattered around them. On my Dairy Queen sack, beside my milk shake, where I left my fries and burger, I find a microwavable burrito and a Snickers bar.

"OKAY, YOU JERK-OFFS. WHERE'S MY FOOD?"

Virgil burps and rubs his big gut.

"HELL, YA SAID YA WANTED TO TRADE."

"I DID NOT. WHERE'S MY BURGER, GODDAMMIT? I DROVE ALL THE WAY TO—"

Shay smiles. From the other side of him, behind his lunch pail, he brings out my burger and fries. He gives them to me and he and Virgil reclaim their crappy junk food.

As I sit down and resume chowing, Mule grunts.

"UH. UH." He elbows Shay and points—hovering out over Scheermeyer's south fence, a white sleek-nosed helicopter. Beneath it, whipped by its rotor wash, dust swirls and clumps of dry grass and cedar branches bristle.

"WHO THE HELL ZAT?"

"MUST BE THE RANCHER. MAYBE 'AT'S HOW HE WORKS HIS COWS."

"BULLSHIT. SUMBITCH DRIVES A MINIBIKE. HE AIN'T GOT NO HELEECOPTER."

The helicopter rotates sideways and slowly circles around to the west. Painted above a broad gold stripe along its side—Taylor County Sheriff's Department. As it glides in over the fence, kicking up dust and rustling the grass, Scheermeyer's cows scramble away to the far perimeters of his land.

Thweeet!

"HEY, MERLE!" We point to the helicopter.

RAAA-aaawww . . .

The rig engines decelerate and the kelly and rotary table slow to a clanking turn as Merle releases the foot-feed and sets the controls to automatic. He steps out under the derrick, puts his gloved hands on his hips, and watches the helicopter. Out west of the rig, the helicopter stops over Scheermeyer's trailer house, then turns and faces us. Slowly, it tilts down its nose and eases toward us.

POP-POP-POP-POP-POP . . .

Its rotors chop the air as it slides closer to the rig. Cellophane and foil food wrappers, napkins, and paper sacks swirl around us. My fries and paper sack scatter and fly off the side of the rig, but I clutch my burger and milk shake.

The helicopter slowly descends until its cab is at eye level just off the rig floor. Through the olive green windshield I see a pilot wearing a headset and sunglasses and, to his right, in the front passenger seat, Sheriff Nall's smiling fat face. His cowboy hat is tilted back off his forehead, a cigar stub is stuffed in the corner of his mouth, and his fat triple chin hangs over his shirt collar. He raises a radio mike to his face and his voice blares over a loud speaker.

"*MORNIN', MERLE. HOW'S EVER'THAYNG RUNNIN'?*"

Merle steps out to the rig rail and stands immediately beneath the whipping blades, right in front of the olive green windshield. Hands on hips, hard hat cocked to one side, overalls fluttering, he spreads his stance against the swirling air and stares at the helicopter.

"*GOOD,*" Sheriff Nall's voice says. "*WELL, YA LOOK BUSY, MERLE, SO I WON'T KEEP YA LONG. I JUST WANTED TO ASK YA, 'MEMBER WHATCHA DONE TO ME YESTERDAY?*"

Merle points his white gloved hand south toward Abilene.

"*GET THE HELL OUT UH HERE, JACK! THIS IS KENT COUNTY. YOU AIN'T GOT NO BIZNESS HERE.*"

"*AR-IGHT, MERLE. DON'CHOO WORRY. I'M LEAVIN'. BUT 'FORE I GO, I GOT A LIL PRESENT FER YA. I KNOW YA AIN'T GOT A LOT UH TIME TO DRILL YER HOLE, SO I THOUGHT I'D TRY TO HELP YA ALONG OUT HERE. AD-IOS, MERLE. GOOD LUCK ON YER WELL.*"

Sheriff Nall looks at the pilot and nods. The helicopter raises its nose, climbs up to about two hundred feet in the air, and backs out away from the rig. Hovering out over Scheermeyer's trailer house, it rotates sideways. The door behind the pilot opens and a man dressed in black pants, black T-shirt, sunglasses, and a black cap swings his legs out of the door. Secured by a safety harness, he steps down onto the helicopter's skid and stands in the doorway. From behind him, someone gives the black-clad man a scoped rifle.

"*GODDAM, BOSS! HE'S GOT A GUN!*"

Merle looks at us and points to the doghouse.

"*Y'ALL GET'N THE DOGHOUSE!*"

I drop my burger and milk shake and run behind Vigil and Mule into the doghouse. We turn and look out the door. Merle stands at the rail with his hands on his hips. Shay stands beside him, pulling on his arm.

"C'MON, BOSS! HE'S GOT A GODDAM RIFLE!"

Merle yanks free from Shay's grip.

"SHAY-BOY, GETCHUR ASS IN 'AT DOGHOUSE OR YOU AIN'T GONNA HAVE NO JOB."

On the helicopter, the black-clad man leans out on the skid and, steadied by his harness belt, aims the rifle at us. The rifle jerks in his arms and white smoke puffs from its barrel.

Pee-ong.

A bullet rattles off the rig floor and the side of the doghouse.

"GODDAM!"

Shay ducks and scrambles under the derrick into the doghouse. Merle stands at the rig rail facing the helicopter and pointing south.

"GETCHUR ASS OUT UH HERE, JACK. YA HEAR ME?"

Pee-ong.

Another bullet skips off the rig floor.

"BOSS! GET IN HERE."

"GODDAM YOU," Merle yells. He reaches back along one of the derrick's legs and grabs a big greasy thirty-six-inch pipe wrench. He waves the wrench at the black-clad assassin.

"COME ON DOWN AND FIGHT, YA PIECE UH SHIT. I'LL KNOCK YER DAMN HEAD OFF."

Pee-ong.

Pee-ong.

Bullets rattle off the rig's steel floor.

Ping.

Sssssssssss . . .

The engine nearest the derrick gushes steaming water from its radiator.

"YA SONOFABITCH!" Merle yells. He sidesteps along the

rail and stands in front of the engines. "YER GONNA HAVE TO KILL ME 'FORE YA FUCK UP MY ENGINES."

Pee-ong.

A bullet skips off the floor at Merle's feet. He waves the big pipe wrench at the helicopter.

"C'MON DOWN HERE, YA CHICKENSHIT. I'LL BREAK YER GOD—"

As though driven by a wrecking ball, Merle flies back off his feet and falls against the steam-hissing engine. The wrench drops from his hand with a clank and his hard hat tumbles off and rolls across the rig floor.

"SHIT, BOSS!"

Shay and Virgil run out, grab Merle under the armpits, and drag him back into the doghouse. Merle's head and limbs hang limp. At the center of his chest, a dark wet circle blooms across his red Luskey Drilling overalls.

"Aw goddam," Shay says, "he's heart shot." They drag him away from the door and lie him on the floor by the lockers. We kneel around him. His eyes are closed and his Elvis black hair hangs across his forehead. I start to cry.

"Oh God, no, Merle. Jesus. *No.*"

Virgil runs his thick callused hands across Merle's chest. As he searches for the tear in the cloth where the bullet entered, his face folds in a curious expression. He looks around with his buggy bloodshot eyes and sniffs the air. He lifts his hand from Merle's chest and smells his palm.

"Hell, 'at ain't blood. 'At's whiskey."

"What?"

Virgil tears open Merle's overalls. His black-hair-matted chest is unharmed. Shay reaches in Merle's overalls. From the inside breast pocket he brings out the silver flask, mangled and bent from the bullet. He shakes it. It rattles with bullet fragments. Merle moans and opens his eyes.

"Mary's ass. Am I dead?"

"Hell no, ya lucky sumbitch, they shotchur flask." Shay smiles and shows Merle the flask. I laugh and sob at the same time.

"*Oh, Merle. Goddammit, Merle.*"

Merle looks at the mangled flask.

"Those mutherfuckers!" He jumps up and steps to the door. We peek out from behind him.

Although they are still running, all three rig engines squirt steaming water from their radiator panels. The helicopter is still there. Puffs of white smoke burst from the black-clad assassin's rifle.

"WHAT THE HELL'S HE SHOOTIN' NOW?"

Merle leans out the door.

"AW SHIT. HE'S SHOOTIN' UP MY FUEL TANK!"

Down by the mud pits the huge cylindrical Luskey-red fuel tank springs golden diesel from a dozen holes.

"GODDAM, NOT MY FUEL! I GOTTA DRILL. I GOTTA MAKE A THOUSAND FEET 'FORE SUNDOWN." Merle starts out the door, but we grab him.

"NO, BOSS. GODDAM, THEY DONE SHOTCHA ONCE."

"I DON'T GIVE A DAMN. NOT MY FUEL, BY GOD."

"HEY, LOOK. THE OL' RANCHER'S GOT A GOOSE GUN."

We look out through the door under the derrick. Completely naked, armed with his shotgun, Scheermeyer stands on the steps outside his trailer house in a tornado of dust. White hair whipping around his head, he points the gun at the helicopter overhead. The gun jerks and white smoke explodes from the barrel. Suddenly the helicopter gushes black smoke from beneath its body. Cowering, the black assassin throws his rifle in the door and climbs back inside. Scheermeyer fires again. More smoke pours from the helicopter and its body begins to slowly spin beneath its rotors. In a spinning smoke-pouring retreat, it tilts and flies away.

ONE ARM DRAPED OVER MY SHOULDER, THE OTHER CLUTCH- ing his backseat bottle, Merle sways and staggers across the drive-way into the garage. Although I changed clothes in the doghouse (from hard hat, overalls, and rubber work boots to T-shirt, jeans, and chocolate lizards), Merle still has on his overalls and mud-caked boots. I lock my arm under his armpit and hold him up as he stumbles around the garage, kicking off his boots and mutter-ing.

"Go-to-hell sumbitch shoot up my rig, and by God, I'll drill nohow. Ya hear me, Harvard?"

"Damn straight, Merle. I hear you." I spread my stance and hold him tighter, trying to keep him from falling on his ass. He swigs the bottle, slings off his right boot, and starts working on his left.

"By goduhmighty. Nobody gonna shut me down. Honest man. Drillin' a hole. By God. Nobody. Ya hear me, Harvard?"

"Damn straight, Merle. I hear you."

Although I'm getting a little sick of this (I've been listening to his boozy mumbo jumbo for the last two hours while I drove us home), he sure as hell deserves to unwind.

Yesterday, after Sheriff Nall's helicopter assassin shot the hell out of the rig, we all piled in Merle's truck, and, at about a hun-dred and twenty miles an hour, he blasted back to the rig yard in

Abilene. While Virgil, Shay, and Mule robbed radiators off the idle rigs and raced back to the rig in Merle's truck to fix the engines, Merle and I fired up one of the big Peterbilt trucks, winched a new fuel tank onto the trailer, went into town and filled it with five thousand gallons of diesel, and hauled it out to the rig. Within nine hours we were repaired, refueled, and drilling again.

To make up for the setback, Merle manned the driller's controls on through the night and all day today. It was unbelievable. Nipping on his flask the whole time, for another twenty-four hours straight, without a single break for food or sleep, he worked the brake with his gloved hand and the foot-feed with his mud-caked work boot, pushing the engines to their red-line smoke-spewing max. Finally, at sundown today, when the evening-tour crew took over, he relinquished the controls. Despite the rig being shot up by Sheriff Nall (not to mention Merle himself almost getting shot straight in the heart), and being down for nine hours for repairs, he had drilled 1,664 feet.

"By God," he mumbles, "no sumbitch with no heleecopter gun shut ol' Merle down." He swigs his bottle, slings off his other boot, and stumbles forward. "Ya hear me, Harvard?"

"Damn straight, Merle. I hear you. Now c'mon. Walk." I throw open the door.

RAR-RAR-RAR-RAR-RAR.

Sasha and Snowflake yap and scramble through our legs into the garage and out to the driveway. Merle scowls.

"Damn rats."

"Hang on," Tex-Ann says, "I thank they just walked in the door." Wearing red cowboy boots, a short denim skirt, and a pink blouse, Tex-Ann steps into the kitchen/utility room doorway. She holds out the phone to me. "It's fer you, darlin'."

"*Me?* Who is it?"

"Yer daddy."

I stare at the phone. Holy shit. How'd he get the number? I

never gave him Merle's name; I just gave him an address. I shake my head and whisper.

"Tell him I'm not here."

Merle wags his bottle at the phone.

"Aw, bullshit. Talk to him. He's prob'ly worried aboutcha, Harvard. Goddam, son." Merle hiccups and lifts his arm from around me. Tex-Ann holds the phone right in front of my face. I sigh and take it.

"Hello."

"Erwin?"

"Hi, Dad."

"Erwin, what in Christ's name are you doing?"

"Take it easy, Dad. I'm all right."

"Don't you play that with me. Have you lost your mind?"

"Dad, chill out. I'm fine."

"Clearly, Erwin, you are anything but fine. Are you purposefully intending to torment your mother and me? Is that the point of this? After all we've done for you, all the sacrifices, this is how we are repaid? Who are those people you're living with?"

I look at Merle and Tex-Ann, cover the phone mouthpiece with my hand, and clear my throat, suggesting that I would appreciate privacy. They ignore me. Merle, grease marks across his cheeks and forehead, swigs the almost empty bottle of Jack Daniel's and stares at me with ludicrous wobble-headed eye-blinking concentration. Tex-Ann pokes a long 100 cigarette in her mouth, flicks her lighter, and lights it. She takes a deep drag, blows out the smoke, leans back against the kitchen counter, and watches me.

"Erwin? Are you there?"

"Uh, yes, Dad. These people are my friends. Actually, one is my boss and my friend, the other is just my friend."

"They sound like morons, Erwin. Do they wear shoes?"

I look down at my chocolate lizards. I dusted and buffed them with a dry rag this afternoon during some ass time in the doghouse. Their grainy brown lizard hide glistens in the kitchen light.

I think of Dad in his perennial academic garb—tweed jacket, khaki pants, and Nike jogging shoes. I sigh.

"Listen, Dad, just because they're not intellectual prigs doesn't mean they're stupid."

Merle and Tex-Ann glance at each other, then look back at me.

"Well, they speak like morons. That woman, I could not even—"

"All right, Dad, what's your point? Are you just calling to trash me and my friends?"

"Listen here, Erwin, you were already on probation, and in spite of that, in good faith, I loaned you four hundred dollars to settle your debts and come home. So my point is, where *are* you? You are supposed to be home, Erwin. We had an agreement. You were coming home and finding a real job. Remember?"

My scalp tingles and my heart thumps. I turn away from Merle and Tex-Ann and look into the dim garage.

"Dad, I explained in my letter. I found a temporary job here. I'm earning good money. In less than two weeks I'll be coming home like I said, and I should have about three thousand dollars when I get there. So just chill out, all right? You'll get your money back. This is no big deal. I'll be there in a few weeks like I promised, and I'll get a real job. No more acting. No more theater. I swear. I'll—"

Click.

"Heidi," Merle's voice says.

I whirl around. Merle and Tex-Ann are gone from the kitchen.

"Merle. Please. Hang up. This is none of your—"

"Aw, just ease down, boy. Harvard's daddy? Are ya there?"

"Hello? Who is this?"

"This is Merle Luskey. You Harvard's daddy?"

"*Harvard?* Who is Harvard?"

The bottle sloshes as Merle swigs.

"Aw, heck, ya know, Harvard. Yer boy from up 'ere in Boston, New Anglin'."

"Erwin? What's going on? Who is this?"

I smile and listen.

"Anyhow, heidi 'ere, my name's Merle Luskey. What's yers?"

"This is Doctor Maxwell Vandeveer. I don't know you, Mr. Luskey, but I certainly don't appreciate your interrupting my conversation with my son."

"Well god . . . dog, Doc, now I know I ain't no smart sonofagun like you—I'm just an ol' roughneck—but I wancha to know ya got one hell of a fine boy. And I give ya my word, 'ere ain't no need fer ya to worry. I'm lookin' out fer him. I've worked on a rig damn near all my—"

"Mr. Luskey. Who *are* you?"

"I'm a driller. I own a drillin' outfit. I give Harvard a job. I know I ain't kin or nothin', but by gosh I've taken to 'at boy like he's my own."

"But Mr. Luskey, he's not your own. He's mine. Now I don't know what induced Erwin to stop there in Texas, but I certainly hope you're not guilty of some perversity. Because if you are, I assure you I will prosecute to the full extent—"

"Jesus Christ, Dad."

"Honey," Tex-Ann's muffled voice says, "hang up. This ain't none uh yer bizness."

"Naw, hang on," Merle says. "I got somethin' to say." The bottle sloshes. "Now lookee here, Doc, yer prob'ly right, it ain't none uh my bizness, but I'm gonna tell ya a lil somethin'. I don't know whatchoo want Harvard to do fer his life, but I reckon ya know the boy wants to be in the movies. Now the way I see it—"

"*Merle,* hang up."

"Naw, Harvard, hang on. Doc, ya there?"

Dad sighs.

"For Christ's sake, Erwin, make this lunatic hang up the phone. I need to speak with you."

The bottle sloshes.

"Well, ar-ight, Dr. . . . . Fancy-camper, or whoever ya are, you can call me a lunatic if ya want. Hell, I won't even argue with ya. But I tell ya what, yer Harvard's a fine boy, and I sure would like to see him get a full standin' swayng at his dream. I thank ever' ol' boy arta give it hell fer his dream, 'at way he can lay down and die knowin' he gave her his best whirl. Now whether you feel the same way or not, Doc, 'at's yer bizness. But by goshuhmighty, at's how I thank about it. So anyhow, y'all have a good evenin' up 'ere."

Click.

Merle hangs up.

"Erwin? Are you there?"

"Yes, Dad. I'm here."

"Erwin, is that man insane?"

I smile.

"Yes."

AS THE DAYS ROLL LIKE TUMBLEWEEDS ACROSS THE PRAIRIE,
I live the life of a double-tour roughneck.

"Roll out, son! We got hole to make," Merle says every morning at 3:30, and I sit up in the darkness, rubbing my eyes and wondering if I ever actually fell asleep.

Out of the house by four and at the rig by six, we work all day and into the night. Merle sits on his throne, an upside-down plastic bucket on the floor outside the doghouse doorway, overseeing every facet of the operation. I roughneck.

Swab the rig with a wire brush and bucket of diesel while the kelly drills down.

Thweeet!

"KELLY DOWN!"

Make connection (i.e., break the kelly off, pick up the joint of drill pipe waiting in the mouse hole, add it to the drill string, resume drilling).

Cat-line a joint from the racks to the mouse hole.

Mix mud.

Thweeet!

"KELLY DOWN!"

Make connection.

Cat-line a joint from the racks to the mouse hole.

Shovel cuttings from the shale shaker.

Thweeet!

"KELLY DOWN!"

Trip out of the hole from 3,560 (i.e. pull the entire drill string out of the hole in three-joint segments at a time, called stands, and rack the stands vertically in the derrick.)

Break off the old bit.

Tong on a new bit.

Trip back in the hole to 3,560.

Fish the kelly and go back to drilling.

Sweep out the doghouse while the kelly drills down.

Thweeet!

"KELLY DOWN!"

Make connection.

Cat-line a joint from the racks to the mouse hole.

Swab the rig.

On through the day tour (6 A.M. to 2 P.M.) and most of the evening tour (2 P.M. to 10 P.M.), we work past sundown. Finally Merle leaves a list of instructions for the morning-tour (10 P.M. to 6 A.M.) driller in the knowledge box in the doghouse, and we drive a hundred miles back home, where I ravage one of Tex-Ann's fabulous "suppers" of broiled T-bones with baked potato and black-eyed peas. Or El Paso enchiladas, pinto beans, and jalapeño corn bread. Or (my favorite) chicken-fried steak, cream gravy, and cowboy-cut french fries. After supper I march like a zombie to the shower, then I crawl into bed and crash, only to be jolted, all too soon, by Merle's cowboy-hatted silhouette in the dark doorway.

"Roll out, son! We got hole to make."

"BULLHEAD HER DOWN, SHAY-BOY." **MERLE POINTS HIS** gloved finger in Shay's face and yells over the engines' roar. A bare lightbulb, dangling from the doghouse ceiling, glares above their hard hats. "And if anythayng goes apeshit, call me on the radio. Pronto. I cain't afford to be down one sayngle minute."

Shay nods.

"Yes sir."

Shay normally works day tour, but because he is Merle's most trusted driller, Merle has ordered him to watch over the less-experienced evening-tour crew tonight.

"Harvard! What the hell ya doin' back 'ere, son?"

I take a deep breath and try not to snap. Merle has been an impossible bastard all day. I raise up from behind the Drillometer instrument with my can of oil.

"I'm oiling these goddam little gears like you told me to do three minutes ago."

He frowns.

"C'mon, son. Let's go." He looks at Shay. "We're gonna run to the house, get a bite to eat, and rest our eyeballs awhile, then shag-ass back out here." He points his finger in Shay's face again. "Bullhead her down, ya hear me?"

"Yes sir."

On the drive home Merle is a grumbling, fidgeting maniac. For although he has drilled and fought and pushed us to the brink of exhaustion, Mother Earth is a rugged opponent. The deeper he drills, the harder she gets. When we left the rig tonight at 7:15, after our thirteenth day of drilling, the Drillometer in the doghouse showed 8,617. If everything goes smoothly, and we continue to drill at our current rate of about four minutes per foot, we should be down to 8,800 (the projected top of the Canyon Reef according to our 3-D seismic) tomorrow morning, which, unfortunately, is Merle's D day, his deadline with the bank in Abilene when Don Brock will legally be authorized to freeze his assets. Because time has become so tight, over the last several days Merle has arranged a deal with the banker at the tiny Citizens Bank in Jayton. Apparently, if Merle can prove a good oil well, for a one-quarter interest in the well, in addition to a lien against Merle's interest, Citizens Bank will loan him the money to pay off Don Brock and save his rigs. But he has to prove the well is good, and he has to do it by tomorrow.

As we approach home and cruise along the highway beside the ranch, I look across the fence at the house sitting back on the dark plain, its downstairs windows little squares of glowing yellow. Then I glimpse it. Standing high over Merle's fence along the road, a brief flash of white as our headlights sweep past. I cringe and hope Merle didn't notice.

URRRRRRRR.

He slams on the brakes and skids to a tire-screeching halt.

"What the hell was 'at?" He shifts the stick to reverse, pops the clutch, and stomps the accelerator. Lurching backward, he cuts the wheel and slings the front of the truck toward the ranch.

URRRRRRRR.

There in the headlights, eight feet wide and six feet tall, mounted above the fence on wooden posts, a freshly painted sign of red and black letters against a white background:

FOR SALE
<u>426 ACRES</u>
BEAUTIFUL 5,500 SQ. FT. HOUSE
<u>W/ SWIMMING POOL</u>
OFFERED BY:
<u>FIRST BANK OF ABILENE</u>

"*Ohhhhhh,*" Merle says. Staring at the sign, he reaches back over the seat and brings up his bottle *du jour*. He uncaps it, swigs, and grimaces in the green glow of the dash lights. He turns to me. "See, Harvard? See what they do, boy?" He grits his teeth. "They crawl on yer dream like goddam ants!" He looks back at the sign. "*Ohhhhh.*" He shifts the stick to first and rumbles forward off the road into the tall dry grass by the sign. He turns off the engine and headlights and opens his door. "C'mon, son."

We step out. The wind rustles the grass and crickets chirp with a lazy pulse. A million stars litter the sky. Merle reaches into the mound of pipe pieces and tools in the bed of his truck and pulls out a red five-gallon diesel can. He sloshes the can and holds it out to me.

"Here."

"What?"

"We're gonna kick 'at lyin' mutherfucker's ass right now, 'at's what."

I laugh and take the can. Merle, still wearing his red overalls and mud-caked work boots, steps up to the sign, leans over, and braces his hands on his knees.

"C'mon. Crawl up and stand on my shoulders."

I set down the can of diesel and start to pull off my chocolate lizards.

"What the hell ya doin'?"

"Taking off my boots."

"What the hell for?"

"Because the heels are sharp and I might hurt your—"

"Aw bullshit. I ain't no goddam chickenlicker. C'mon."

I grab the can of diesel and hop onto Merle's back. I shimmy up his back and, propping one hand on top his head, one by one, I hook the heels of my chocolate lizards across the tops of his shoulders. He grabs my chocolate lizards behind my calves and braces me. Slowly, wobbly, I stand.

"Now soak 'at lyin' piece uh shit down."

I unscrew the cap and douse the sign with the stinking diesel. Merle steps side to side, allowing me to soak the whole sign.

When the last drop shakes out, I pitch the can down into the grass and crawl down Merle's back. He stares at the sign, now dripping with diesel.

"Go light one uh Tex-Ann's cigarette butts in the ashtray."

I crawl in the truck, push in the cigarette lighter, and pluck a bent half-smoked lipstick-stained cigarette from the ashtray. I blow off the ashes and carefully straighten it. I light the butt and take it to Merle. Staring up at the sign, he puts the cigarette to his mouth and drags it until the tip glows bright orange.

"Ya lyin' sumbitch," he says. He tosses the cigarette up at the sign.

WHOOM.

The sign explodes in a rolling ball of flames.

"Jesus!"

I jump back and hide behind the truck. Silhouetted by the bright yellow flames, Merle stands with his hands on his hips and watches the fire.

Å Å Å

Tiny tongues licking my mouth. Warm sour dog breath.

"Jesus Christ." I bolt up and open my eyes.

RAR-RAR-RAR-RAR-RAR.

Sasha, the brown dachshund, and Snowflake, the white

watery-eyed poodle, bark and scramble back and forth across my lap.

"Oh, *shhhh*, you two."

Burning cigarette in one hand, cup of coffee in the other, Tex-Ann stands by my bed in a red satin housecoat. Stirred by my sudden awakening, the dogs continue to yap and scamper across my bed.

RAR-RAR-RAR-RAR-RAR.

Tex-Ann sets the coffee on the table by the lamp and claps her hands.

"*Shhhh*, you two. I mean it."

The dogs stop barking. One at a time, she scoops them up and pitches them to the floor.

"Now y'all just settle down."

They stand around her red-toenailed feet, stare up at her, stick out their tiny pink tongues, and pant.

I blink my eyes and look at the window. Although she recently added curtains here in the downstairs guest room, (along with the bed, nightstand, lamp, and dressing bureau), I see it's pitch dark outside.

"What time is it?"

She drags her cigarette.

"About one-thirty. Merle's anxious to get back out there. He's all wound up in knots."

I yawn.

"Tell me about it."

"Here." She hands me the cup of coffee. "Here's some hot coffee to help getcha goin'."

"Thank you, Tex-Ann."

"Yer welcome, angel. Now you go on and get ready and I'm gonna fry y'all some bacon and—"

"*Goddammit.*" Merle stands in the doorway wearing his white boxer underwear and black socks. A spot of shaving cream dots his Adam's apple. The dogs stare at him and growl. He wrinkles his brow in a pained expression.

"Tex-Ann, where are my overalls?"

"I washed 'em fer ya when ya came in last night. They were filthy. I put 'em in the dryer a few minutes ago."

He stares at her with sheer disbelief.

"Ya mean to tell me the goddam thayngs are *wet?*"

She drags her cigarette and blows a rolling cloud of smoke.

"Merle, honey. They'll be dry in just a minute. And they'll be *clean.*"

He reaches down and scratches his nuts.

"Well goddam. I ain't believin' this. Biggest job uh my whole damn life and my overalls are wet."

"Oh, you ol' sour thayng. A few minutes ain't gonna kill ya. Lemme go see about 'em." Tex-Ann walks past Merle into the hall. The dogs stand around my bed, staring at Merle and growling. They pull back their black lips and bare their tiny needle teeth. He looks down at them.

"What the hell y'all lookin' at?"

They erupt.

RAR-RAR-RAR-RAR-RAR.

Sasha, the floppy-eared dachshund, charges and scampers around his feet. Merle scowls.

"Back off, ya damn rat!" He draws back and kicks the dachshund in the rear with his black-socked foot.

Ur-ur-ur.

The dachshund whines and runs under the dressing bureau. Snowflake, the poodle, hops up on my bed and yaps furiously at Merle.

RAR-RAR-RAR-RAR-RAR.

Tex-Ann barges past Merle into the room. She grits her teeth and looks around the floor.

Ur-ur.

The dachshund whimpers under the dressing bureau. Tex-

Ann looks around for somewhere to put her cigarette, but can't find anywhere. She holds it out to me.

"Erwin, take this, please."

I take the burning half-smoked cigarette. Tex-Ann kneels on the carpet at the dressing bureau.

"Com'ere, sweetheart." Her cigarette-ravaged voice cracks with sweetness. "Com'ere, baby. Com'ere."

Ur-ur.

The dachshund whimpers. As Tex-Ann bends down further and reaches under the bureau, the belt on her satin housecoat slips and her bare breasts flop out. Concerned only with retrieving her dog, she makes no attempt to retie her housecoat belt or cover herself. She pats the carpet with her palm.

"Come to Mama, baby. C'mon. I won't let that mean ol' man hurtchoo."

Tail curled between its legs, the dachshund waddles into her hands.

"*Yee-us.* Sweet thayng. *Yee-us.*" She gathers the dachshund into her arms and stands up. Her entire front—breasts, stomach, brownish red hairy beaver, and thighs—exposed by her parted housecoat, she holds the dachshund at her side like a football and turns to Merle. She grits her teeth. "Listen here, you sack uh shit. You ever kick one uh my dogs again and I'll cutchur goddam balls off." She opens her eyes wide and glares at him. The dachshund squirms under her arm and licks her breast. Merle puts his hands on his hips and sighs heavily.

"I'm sorry, dear. That was wrong. I'm just . . . a lil on edge."

"Well, I understand thayng's are touchy right now, but that dudn' mean ya gotta shit'n yer nest."

Merle hangs his head and nods.

"Yes, dear. I'm sorry."

"And you can getchur own fuckin' overalls. They're in the dryer." Dachshund under her arm, red housecoat fluttering in her wake, she walks past him into the hall.

RAR-RAR-RAR-RAR-RAR.

Snowflake jumps off my bed and shoots between Merle's legs into the hall. He takes a deep breath and looks at me.

"See what I mean, boy? The love fades."

I bite my lip and hold my breath, trying not to laugh. He scowls.

"Now getchur ass out uh bed. We got hole to make." He turns and walks down the hall. I get out of bed, take Tex-Ann's cigarette to the bathroom, and drop it in the toilet. It hits the water with a hiss.

THE END

RAAAAWWWW...

The engines vibrate our iron island and warm the wind with diesel exhaust. Under the bug-swarmed lights in the derrick and across the top of the doghouse, the rig floor glows like a remote film set in the middle of this pitch-dark prairie. And at center stage—dressed in hard hat, Luskey Drilling overalls, and work boots—Merle sits under the derrick on his upside-down plastic bucket, sipping his half-gallon backseat bottle, gnawing on a rag, and mumbling to the kelly.

"Break, baby. C'mon now. Break. C'mon, baby. Break."

Shay, Virgil, Mule, and I stand in the doghouse doorway, drinking coffee and watching the Drillometer instrument, which now reads 8,792. According to our seismic map, we should encounter the Canyon Reef any time now. But according to Virgil, "ALL 'AT GEOLOGY BULLSHIT DON'T MEAN A DAMN THAYNG TILL 'AT KELLY SCREAMS."

As he explains, the first real evidence of an oil-bearing rock, or pay, is a *drilling break*, or a sudden increase in the drilling rate. This rate increase indicates (hopefully) a transition from drilling through a hard, dense rock—like shale—to a soft, porous rock such as sand or limestone reef, which, because of its porosity, may contain oil and/or natural gas. Sometimes, Virgil says, a drilling break is quite dramatic, changing in rate from six minutes per foot to fifteen seconds per foot. Or, as he puts it, "IF'N 'AT PAY'S GOOD, SHE'LL DRILL LIKE A FUCKIN' SNOWBANK."

And so, on through the predawn hours, the engines thunder, the rotary table turns with a rhythmic clank, the kelly grinds down inch by inch, and we watch and wait.

We drill past 8,800 with no break.

8,801.

8,802.

8,803.

Merle keeps his vigil, sitting on his bucket by the rotary table, gnawing the rag, sipping his bottle, mumbling to the kelly.

"Break, baby. C'mon now. *Break.*"

8,804.

8,805.

8,806.

8,807.

8,808.

Nothing. No drilling break.

Thweeet!

"KELLY DOWN!"

We stop and make connection, adding a thirty-three-feet-long joint of drill pipe from the mouse hole to the drill string, then resume drilling.

8,809.

8,810.

8,811.

8,812.

8,813.

8,814.

8,815.

No break. Merle knits his brow in stark anxiety as he stares at the kelly, sips his bottle, and gnaws the rag. His plea now alternates between mumbled coaxing and screaming intimidation.

"C'mon darlin', break on down now. Be good to me and

break. Please, baby, please . . . AR-IGHT, YA COCKSUCKER, BREAK! YA HEAR ME, GODDAMMIT! BREAK!"

Impervious, at an excruciating five minutes per foot, the kelly drills slowly ahead. Nausea and dread creep over us as we stand around, hands in our pockets, watching and waiting.

8,816.

8,817.

The eastern horizon lightens with gray.

8,818.

8,819.

8,820.

8,821.

8,822.

The sky flushes pink as the sun rises and lights the cool breezy landscape of peach-colored soil and light green cactus patches. Mumbling incoherently to the kelly, Merle turns back toward the doghouse.

"HARVARD!"

I step out beside him under the derrick.

"YEAH?"

He stares at me with pained disbelief.

"WHERE'S 'AT REEF, HARVARD?"

I shrug.

"I DON'T KNOW."

"WHADDA YA MEAN, YA DON'T KNOW?"

"SHIT, MERLE. I TOLD YOU, I DON'T KNOW ANYTHING ABOUT OIL. I JUST DID WHAT YOU TOLD ME TO DO."

He stares at me blankly.

"HERE, SON." He holds out his bottle of whiskey and his gnawing rag. I take them.

Whump.

He clutches my throat with both hands and grits his teeth in red-faced rage.

"YA DUMB YANKEE SONOFABITCH. YA STAKED ME IN THE WRONG SPOT, DIDN' YA?" He drives me to my knees with his choke hold. My hard hat tumbles off and bounces across the rig floor. He shakes my head. "WHERE'S 'AT FUCKIN' REEF, HARVARD? YA GOD—"

Virgil and Shay grab Merle's arms and pull him off me. Still holding his bottle and rag, I fall back against the doghouse, coughing and trying to catch my breath. Merle drops to his knees, beats his hard hat with his fists, and wails.

"Please, Lord, not my rigs. I know I'm a worthless sumbitch, but—"

Eeee.

The kelly falls several inches, screeching as it slips down through the rotary table. Merle looks.

Eeee.

The kelly drops another several inches.

Eeee.

Another several inches.

Eeee.

Eeeeeeeeeeeeeeeeeeee . . .

Suddenly it's as though we've drilled out the other side of the earth and the drill string is free-falling. The rotary table, driven by the engines, continues to turn, and the square-shaped kelly, turned by the square hole in the rotary table, turns as well, but with each revolution the kelly falls six or eight inches. Just as Virgil described, it's like we're drilling through a fucking snowbank!

Rising above this cacophony of roaring and screeching is Merle: "*YEEHAW! ATTA BABY!* DRILL, YA BEAUTIFUL MUTHERFUCKER! DRILL!" He stands astride the rotary table, arms thrust in the air. "DRILL, BABY! DRILL!"

"MERLE!" Shay yells.

Merle turns from the kelly with a maniacal expression on his face.

"SHE BROKE AT EIGHTY-EIGHT-TWENTY-TWO. WE DONE DRILLED OFF TWELVE FOOT IN TWO MINUTES."

Merle points to the brake.

"AR-IGHT. GET OFF HER, SHAY-BOY."

Shay runs to the driller's controls, grabs the brake, and stomps on the foot-feed.

RAAAAWWWW.

He hoists the drill string up about three feet.

REEET.

He sets the brake and hangs the bit just above the bottom of the hole. The rotary table and kelly continue to turn, but smoothly and quietly, since the drill string is not drilling, but merely turning in the hole. Merle snatches his bottle from me and swigs.

"AR-IGHT, BY GOD, LET'S GO SEE WHAT SHE LOOKS LIKE."

While Shay remains on the rig floor at the driller's controls, Merle, Virgil, Mule, and I go down to the reserve mud pit, where the *returns line* gushes soupy gray mud that has circulated up from the drill bit. Virgil takes a large ragged kitchen strainer and holds it out in the gushing stream of mud. Within seconds the strainer fills with black bits of rock. Virgil scoops up a handful, rubs them across his palm, and examines them.

"SHALE," he yells.

Merle nods and points to the mud stream.

"KEEP CATCHIN'."

Virgil continues to strain the cuttings from the mud and examine them.

Suddenly the cuttings change from black to ivory. Virgil grabs a handful of these ivory pieces, brings them to his nose, and smells. A rotten-tooth grin stretches across his buggy-eyed face.

"GODDAM. GOOD ODOR."

Merle snatches the cuttings from Virgil's palm and buries his nose in them. He tosses the cuttings in his mouth and slowly chews them, contemplating their flavor and texture. He spits the rock bits onto the ground.

"GODDAM, 'ERE'S A SHOW." He sticks out his rock-bit-covered tongue and licks his lips. "GOOD ROCK, TOO."

I scoop up some of the ivory cuttings from Virgil's strainer and smell them. I smell oil. Virgil wipes his palm across the front of his overalls and looks at Merle.

"WANT ME TO CALL DOWNHOLE TESTERS AND GET A TEST TOOL OUT HERE?"

Merle swigs his bottle and blinks at the horizon. The sun floats fat and blazing yellow over Scheermeyer's land.

"HELL NO. I AIN'T GOT TIME. IT'LL TAKE US ALL MORNIN' TO TRIP A TEST TOOL DOWN 'ERE."

"WELL HELL, BOSS, YER GONNA TEST, AIN'CHA?"

"GODDAM RIGHT, I'M GONNA TEST. C'MON."

We follow Merle up to the floor. He points to the kelly.

Thweeet!

"SHAY-BOY, JERK 'AT LAST JOINT UP."

Shay nods and presses the foot-feed.

RAAAAWWWW...

He hoists up the almost nine-thousand-feet-long drill string. The kelly rises into the derrick and the top joint of drill pipe rises through the rotary table about four feet. Mud oozes down its side and spills onto the floor.

Thweeet!

"HO! HANG HER IN THE SLIPS."

REEET.

Shay sets the brake.

CLANK.

Virgil and I toss the big iron slips down between the drill pipe and the rotary table. Shay lets off the brake and hangs the drill string from the rig floor.

"NOW KILL THE ENGINES."

Virgil and Shay turn off all the engines around the rig. The wind gusts and rustles the grass. For two weeks this has been a scene of deafening thunder. The relative quiet of the gusting wind is eerie.

Maaaaaaa.

One of Scheermeyer's cows bellows in the distance.

Merle takes a sloshing swig of Jack Daniel's and points to the connection between the kelly and the last joint of drill pipe about four feet above the rotary table.

"Break her out right here, boys."

I grab the backup tongs and—*CLANK*—set them around the drill pipe, then pull the rat's-ass chain toward the dead man. I wait for Virgil to set his hydraulic tongs around the kelly and break the connection, but he just stands and stares at Merle.

"Let's *go*, Virj!" Merle says.

Virgil opens wide his big buggy bloodshot eyes.

"Shit, boss, we ain't hardly got any mud in the hole. We just cut a helluva show. What if she blows out?"

In the distance . . .

Pop-Pop-Pop-Pop-Pop . . .

We look. A helicopter hovers far out on the southern horizon.

"Goddammit, Virj!" Merle yells. "Break her open!"

Virgil shakes his head and sets the tongs.

"Rat's ass!" I yell.

VRRRRRRT.

Virgil engages the hydraulic tongs and unscrews the kelly. We swing it aside and chain it to the side of the derrick.

The top joint of the drill string now stands open-ended about four feet above the rotary table. Inside it, a circle of gray muddy water quivers in the breeze. Suddenly the water gurgles up from the drill pipe, blows in the wind, and splashes across the rig floor.

" 'Ere ya go, darlin'," Merle says. He looks at us. "Get me a damn orbit valve."

Mule and Shay run in the doghouse and come out carrying a big valve with a round handle on it. They heave it atop the gurgling, splashing drill string and screw it on.

On the horizon the helicopter moves closer and grows louder. *Pop-Pop-Pop-Pop-Pop* . . .

The four of us—Shay, Virgil, Mule, and I—look back and forth between the helicopter and the water-gurgling joint of drill pipe. The fountain of water gains force. It now kicks up about five feet in the air and blows back onto us. Merle, water dripping from the brim of his hard hat, stands by the valve and swigs his bottle.

"C'mon, baby!" he yells. "Blow!"

Suddenly a slug of water rockets up into the crown of the derrick. Virgil ducks and runs to the rail by the rig stairs. Heart pounding, I follow him and stand beside him. The blast of muddy water shatters in the crown and splashes down through the derrick onto Merle and Shay and Mule. Merle swigs his bottle and laughs.

"Atta baby! C'mon and blow fer daddy!" He looks at Shay and Mule. "Y'all get back, dammit. This sumbitch is fixin' to get lovely."

"But boss," Shay says, "what if ya cain't shut her in?"

Merle swigs his bottle.

"Bullshit. I'll shut her in. Get back!"

Shay and Mule join Virgil and me at the top of the stairs. Merle stays under the derrick by the drill pipe. Another column of muddy gray water gushes into the derrick. Merle laughs in the dripping rain.

"Atta baby. Blow! Blow! Blow like solid hell, ya beautiful, sonofa—" Suddenly the fountain of water dies. A cap of water trembles on top of the valve and trickles down its side. Merle stares at it. His voice trails off. "Ya beautiful sonofa . . . sonofabitch." Water dripping from the derrick all around him, Merle stares at the cap of water in the valve. It trembles in the breeze. He looks back to the south. The helicopter is moving in on us. *Pop-Pop-Pop-Pop-Pop* . . .

Beneath the hovering helicopter, six cop cars, flanked by two columns of dark-helmeted, dark-uniformed, rifle-carrying men, creep over the cattle-guard gate onto Scheermeyer's land.

"Y'all get off the rig!" Merle yells. "Ya may have to run for it."

"But boss," Shay says.

"Get off the rig, dammit."

Merle turns and stares at the cap of water trembling in the breeze.

"C'mon, baby." He puts his finger in the water and wiggles it.

"Shit, 'ere's cops ever'where," Virgil says. "Let's get the hell out uh here." He grabs my overalls and pulls. I look back as I start down the stairs. Merle leans down and talks to the disk of muddy water quivering in the valve.

"Here, darlin', have a taste." He raises his bottle and pours a splash of Jack Daniel's into the muddy water. He puts his finger in the valve and stirs. " 'Ere ya go, darlin'. Now c'mon. They're fixin' to take ever' goddam thayng I ever worked for."

"C'mon, Harvard!"

I run down the stairs to the ground. As Virgil, Mule, Shay, and I stand out on the ground away from the rig, the ground rumbles. . . .

We look north toward the rig. Merle still stands under the derrick, looking down into the drill string.

We look south. Red dirt rises in the air. Stirred by the approaching helicopter, shoulder to shoulder in a rumbling rank, Scheermeyer's cows come stampeding in wild-eyed panic.

MAAAAAA.

MAAAAAA.

"Goddam! They're stampedin'!"

MAAAAAA.

MAAAAAA.

A herd of rumbling wide-eyed bellowing terror, they storm toward us. Virgil, Shay, Mule, and I huddle together. The cows part and stampede past us. Their hard coarse-haired bodies bounce us together. They rampage past us, around and under the rig's substructure, through the mud pits, and on to the north across Scheermeyer's land.

In the wake of the herd's dust comes the hovering helicopter and six Taylor County Sheriff's Department cars rolling toward us on the dirt rig-location road. Fanned out on both sides of this column of cars, outfitted in drab green helmets, drab green bullet-proof jackets with bright yellow markings—Taylor Co. SWAT—and bearing military-style rifles, ten men stalk toward the rig, crouching and weaving around the cedar bushes and patches of cactus.

I look back toward the rig and the stampeding herd. From the door of the trailer house, two SWAT assailants emerge with Scheermeyer. Apparently they circled around early and caught him while he napped, for he wears only baggy white underwear. Though his hands are bound behind him and he is in the grips of two much younger and fitter men, he kicks and bites at his helmeted bullet-proof-vested captors as they force a pair of cowboy boots on his bare feet and escort him off his stoop.

Up on the rig, Merle still stands under the derrick looking into the valve on the drill pipe. Nothing, however, flows from the pipe.

The lead patrol car approaches us. Sheriff Nall's pink fat face stares from the windshield over the steering wheel. He brings his radio to his mouth. His whining tenor voice blares from the car's siren/broadcast horn.

"ROUGHNECKS, PUTCHUR HANDS UP. WE GOTCHUR ASSES SURROUNDED."

The SWAT-clad commandos, their military assault weapons aimed at us, advance to the edge of the cleared rig location, kneel, and hold their positions in a wide rank. We put our arms in the air.

The two commandos in charge of Alton Scheermeyer, their rifles strapped across their backs, drag him to the edge of the clearing. Despite his potbellied physique, he squirms in their clutches and kicks at them with his boots.

"Turn me loose, ya goddam Natzi! I whuppedchur ass in France, and by God I'll whup it right here."

They open the door of one of the patrol cars and stuff him in.

"Lemme go, ya dirty Natzi sonofa—"

Clump.

They slam the door.

Dressed in his usual uniform of dark brown pants and khaki shirt, Sheriff Nall steps from the lead patrol car, hitches up his gun/ammo belt, and dons his straw cowboy hat. A frazzled cigar stub hangs in the corner of his mouth. Behind him, Don Brock, the banker, steps from the car wearing a drab green helmet and bulky green Taylor Co. SWAT jacket. One hand on top of his hat to hold it down against the wind, Sheriff Nall waddles around to the front of the car. He pulls a piece of paper from his shirt pocket under his badge and holds it up in the wind.

"Boys, I got a jurisdiction authority signed by the Kent County commissioner right here. So don't gimme no shit." He crams the paper back in his pocket and looks up at the rig, then at me. He smiles. "Well, you boys enjoyin' yer last day?"

Don Brock steps up. His bullet-proof jacket bulges stiffly over his shoulders, his helmet sits low on his head, and a fold of his chin hangs over the chin strap. Blinking against the wind, he stares at the rig.

"What's happening?"

"Don't know," Sheriff Nall says. "But by God, I can sure find out." He looks at me. "Yankee boy, what the hell's goin' on out here?"

"I don't know." I point toward the rig. "I think Merle is trying to evaluate his well."

Still holding his hat down with one hand, Sheriff Nall lolls his cigar stub from one side of his mouth to the other, then turns to Don Brock.

"Merle's tryin' to valyeeate his well."

We all look up at the rig floor. Merle stands by the drill pipe and valve, but the fountain of water is still dead. Nothing at all emerges from the drill string. Sheriff Nall laughs.

"Looks like a helluva well, don't it?" He slaps Don Brock on the back. "Yes sir, ol' Merle drilled him a real barn burner." He laughs again.

"Cut the shit, Jack," Don Brock says. "Go give him those papers and get him off my rig."

Sheriff Nall stops laughing and nods.

"Sure, Don." He starts back toward the car.

Thunder rumbles through the gusting wind. We glance at one another. The cows? I look north, to where they just ran, but I don't see anything.

The thunder grows louder. The ground trembles.

"What the hell is that?"

We look up to the rig. Merle stares at the valve on top of the drill pipe with a wild-eyed lunatic grin. He swigs his bottle of Jack Daniel's, cups his hand around his mouth, and yells.

" 'Ere ya go, darlin'! Getchur ass up here and see Daddy!"

The thunder, deep and guttural, rumbles and rumbles . . .

A dark beam blasts from the drill pipe up through the derrick. At its apex in the sky, about three hundred feet over the derrick, the dark column blossoms and sweeps across the sky in the wind. Suddenly we are drenched in warm black rain. Oil splatters in my eyes and blinds me like burning acid. The vapor is so strong I can hardly breathe. I drop to my knees and shield my eyes with my sleeves. Amid the thundering blast and dripping rain of oil, I hear panic.

"Oh, goddam, my eyes. My eyes. I cain't see nothin'. Don? Don?"

"*Ow.* Goddammit, get off me, you fat ass. Where's the fucking car?"

"It's this way, Don. Yer goin' the wrong way."

"Get out of my way, shit-head."

"Don? It's right here. Here's the car, Don. Over here."

"Ow, goduhmighty. My eyes."

Clump.

Clump.

Two car doors slam.

For several long minutes, as the helicopter pops overheard, I kneel in the drenching warm oil, my head down, covered by my arms. Voices groan and cry out:

"Oh, my eyes. Sonofabitch. My eyes."

Gradually, the rain diminishes, then, *pit-pat, pit-pat* . . . it stops. My work boots, overalls, hands, neck, face, and hard hat are soaked in oil. Frantic to relieve my burning eyes, I unzip my overalls, tear off my T-shirt from underneath, and wipe the oil from my face. After a minute of daubing and blinking, I can finally see. I look around.

A wide patch of some five acres all about me—black. The ground is covered with puddles of black; the bushes, grass, cactus, cars, and men rolling on the ground, soaked with black; in the blue sky, hovering back now some quarter of a mile, a black helicopter.

I hear stirring beside me and turn to see three faces of blinking eyes and oil-smeared, smiling, pink-and-white mouths. One of the mouths opens wide.

"Yeehaw!"

I turn and look. Through a haze of vapor, the rig towers against the sky—the crown, the derrick, the draw-works, the engines, the doghouse, dripping black.

On the ground Merle stumbles and weaves toward us through the shimmering waves of vapor. He, too, is black saturated. His hard hat, cocked crooked atop his head, drips oil. His face is a smear of black and tan. In his right hand, down along his side, his bottle of Jack Daniel's is covered in black. Dragging his feet, weaving slump-shouldered, he stumbles up to Virgil, Shay, Mule, and me. In his black face his eyes are a freakish blinking mix of pink, blue, and white. He swigs his bottle.

"Where are the sumbitches?"

"In that first car."

Merle staggers to Sheriff Nall's black-slimed car.

"Jack!" He tries to open the driver's door, but it's locked. He wipes away the coat of oil and leans his black face down to the window. "Hey, Jack. Whadda ya thank? Thank she might flow?" Teeth and lips smeared with oil, he smiles. "Hey, Jack. Reckon I might be able to get a loan this afternoon?" He swigs his bottle, then steps back, wipes the backseat window, and looks in. "Don? Zatchoo in 'ere, Don? How about it? Thank she's gonna flow? Huh, Don? When ol' Shorty Townes over here in Jayton sees this sumbitch get after it, reckon he's gonna gimme 'at cashier's check? Yeah. 'At's right, you lousy sack uh shit. I'll have yer money by lunchtime. Hell, matter uh fact . . . Hey, Don! How much ya want fer 'at damn bank? Huh? Maybe I'll just buy the damn thayng while I'm—"

"*AR-IGHT, BOYS!*" Sheriff Nall's voice blares from his car's siren/broadcast horn. "*LET'S PULL BACK. TURN THE OLD FART LOOSE AND LET'S GET THE HELL OUT UH HERE.*"

Two oil-soaked SWAT commandos remove Scheermeyer from the second patrol car, and the column of vehicles slowly backs away, followed by the stumbling oil-dripping commandos. Merle swigs his bottle and waves at them.

"Hey, wait! Don't run off. I wanna buy yer goddam bank, Don! Hey!"

Ä Ä Ä

I swing Merle's truck into the ranch. The sun sits red and round on the pink dust-blown horizon. Merle rolls down his window and sings to his field of gold wind-swishing grass.

"*Scratch a rich man's ass,*
a rich man's ass,

*I'm gonna scraaaaaaatch
a rich man's ass."*

As we approach the house our welcoming party comes into view. Tex-Ann, in red high heels, extremely short denim shorts, and an outrageously snug red sleeveless blouse, waves and jumps at the sidewalk. Her blond hair blows about her face and her breasts bounce and jiggle. Red balloons fastened to their collars, Sasha and Snowflake leap up at her legs. Behind her on the sidewalk, between Merle's pair of leafless twiggy pecan trees, a small table is set up and covered with a fluttering white cloth. On the table are several champagne flutes and a pewter ice bucket with a bottle in it.

URRR-URRR.

I honk as we approach. The dogs raise their noses and yap. Tex-Ann waves both her arms, high-kicks her legs, and jumps up and down on her high heels.

"Whoopee! Whoopee fer my hero! Whoopee!"

Merle has thrown his oil-saturated overalls and work boots in the bed of the truck and only wears underwear, but they, too, are soaked with oil and cling to him vulgarly. He sits on a big plastic trash bag to keep from staining his truck seat. A stain of oil covers every square inch of his skin from his head to his toes. I, on the other hand, used a towel and some hand-cleaner goop and wiped myself off in the doghouse. I still have oil in my hair and I'm bare from the waist up and I itch all over, but I have on my jeans and chocolate lizards.

As he was when he marched through the front door of First Bank of Abilene with a cashier's check for $381,000, Merle is completely undaunted by his attire of oily genital-clinging underwear. He hops out, hugs Tex-Ann, and whirls her around.

"Yeehaw! We done slipped in the butter dish, darlin'! We're rich! Ya hear me? Rich!"

"Whoopee! My oil-findin' man!" Tex-Ann kisses Merle and steps back with oil on her lipstick.

RAR-RAR-RAR-RAR-RAR.

Sasha and Snowflake yap and scamper around them in circles.

"Oh, honey," Tex-Ann says, "let's have a toast. C'mon, Erwin. Have a toast with us."

"Damn right," Merle says. "Getchur ass out here, son, and drank some champagne. You done slipped in the butter dish, too, boy. We're all gonna get healed up and haired over on this sumbitch."

I step out of the truck.

"Oh my word," Tex-Ann says. "I always wanted to see Montgomery Clift without his shirt. Com'ere, you muscley thayng." She hugs me as Merle aims the champagne bottle across the yard.

Poop.

He shoots the plastic cork over one of his baby pecan trees, then pours us each a brimming flute of bubbly. We raise our flutes. Tex-Ann smiles.

"Here's to my hero and my darlin'. Merle Luskey. The wildcatter."

"Hear, hear. The wildcatter." We clink flutes and drink. Tex-Ann and I merely sip our flutes, but Merle drains his in one gulping swallow. He pours himself another and raises his flute, which overflows with foam.

"Here's to bein' healed up and haired over."

"Hear, hear. Healed up, haired over." We drink again, and Merle, again, shoots his entire glass. He shivers and throws back his oil-soaked head.

"YEEEEEEEE-HAW!"

RAR-RAR-RAR-RAR-RAR.

Balloons jostling on their collars, Sasha and Snowflake charge him and yap at his bare feet.

"Com'ere, ya god . . . dayng precious fellers." Merle leans down and holds out the champagne bottle.

RAR-RAR-RAR-RAR-RAR.

The dogs jump and bark. He pours out a stream of champagne, and they lap it up in midair.

THE WIND HOWLS. CLOUDS OF DUST SWIRL UNDER THE street lights and the blinking yellow traffic lights swing and bob. A tumbleweed bounds and rolls down the street. It bounces off the pole under the Wildcat Cafe's neon sign, blows over a parked white pickup truck, and blows on down the street, bounding and rolling. Merle swigs his backseat bottle.

"Aw yeah." He wipes his mouth with the back of his hand. " 'Ere it is."

Down at the swinging-light intersection, the silver nose of the bus appears. It turns up the street, sweeps its headlights across us, and pulls in under the bus terminal sign. *Los Angeles,* it says over the dark front window.

Sssssss.

Its brakes hiss as it stops. Merle stares at it.

"Ar-ight now, by God, wha'd I tell ya?"

"Let's see." I grab the bottle from him and take a sip. I shiver as the whiskey burns down my throat. "You said no matter what, I shouldn't allow myself to—"

"Aw bullshit." He frowns and jerks the bottle away from me. "I said *fight,* goddammit. *Fight.*" He balls his hand into a fist and holds it up. "Ya gotta fight with ever' speck uh whup-ass ya got. Ya hear me? *Fight.*"

I smile.

"I hear you."

He pushes up the front brim of his hat, leans across the seat, and squints his eyes. "Cuz lemme tell ya, by God—" He points to himself with his thumb. "I *know* about dreams. I don't give a damn if it's gettin' in the movies or pickin' daisies, ya gotta whup some ass. It may be some other ol' boy's ass, or it may be yer own. But ass whuppin's always in 'ere, and don'choo ferget it."

"Okay, I won't."

URRR-URRR.

The bus honks.

"Well." I grab the door handle. "I guess I—"

"Yeah, goddam, don't wanna miss the sumbitch." Merle takes another swig and puts the bottle in the backseat. We step out into the wind. He gets my suitcase and backpack from the backseat.

Sssssss.

The bus door swings open. Merle sets down my suitcase and backpack and pulls his hat down against the howling wind.

"Well, I'm gonna miss ya, boy."

I smile.

"I'll miss you, too, Merle."

"Aw hell, damn near fergot." He reaches in his back pocket and brings out a thick roll of hundred-dollar bills held tightly together with a rubber band. He holds it out to me. " 'Ere's another thousand. 'At arta help getcha goin'."

I stare at the money. I don't understand. He already gave me a check for three thousand dollars, plus five hundred dollars in cash, which is five hundred dollars more than I was supposed to get.

"Hell, Merle, I can't take that. You already paid me."

"Aw, bullshit. Here." He stuffs the money in my shirt pocket. "Ya know damn well I could uh never done what I done withoutchoo." He smiles. "Yer my savin' angel."

URRR-URRR.

The bus honks again. Merle scowls and turns to the dark open door.

"Aw, settle down, goddammit!" He looks at me. "One more thayng." He reaches down, lifts up his pant leg, and brings out a small flat bottle of Jack Daniel's from his boot. He smiles. "Case ya get lonesome on yer way out 'ere." He kneels down, lifts up my jeans, and stuffs the bottle in my right chocolate lizard. He pulls my jeans down over my chocolate lizard and stands back up. He points to my chocolate lizards. "Don't ferget to put snake oil on 'em sumbitches, or they'll dry up."

"I won't."

URRR-URRR.

I grab my suitcase and backpack and look at him.

"Good-bye, Merle." I step through the dark bus door and up the steps.

"Ar-ight, go on, boy. Getchur ass out uh here. But don't ferget what I toldja. Fight, son, figh—"

Whump.

The bus driver closes the door. I give her my ticket and step up into the dark aisle. The bus is fairly empty. Only a dozen or so passengers sit here and there in the darkness, some listening to Walkmans, some with their heads slumped against a window. I walk to the very back row, throw my suitcase in the rack over-head, and sit down.

Sssssss.

The brakes hiss and we lurch forward with a dull rumble and drive west under the swinging yellow traffic lights. I look back. Merle stands by his red truck, holding his hat down against the wind, watching us drive away.

As we hum out onto the highway I look back and watch the lights of Abilene fade into the wide black prairie. I think of all that's happened since just weeks ago when I was on this road going the other way. Luther, the stinking one-eyed con man.

Merle, with his absurd alcoholic tenacity and his incomprehensible generosity to me. Who knows? Maybe Merle's right. Maybe I *was* his angel, and it was some kind of weird fate that I got shafted out of my money and stepped off the bus in the middle of nowhere. Hell, maybe Merle was *my* angel. It's ridiculous, but still, I wouldn't trade my time with him for anything. As Abilene shrinks into a little inch of light on the horizon, I reach down, pull out the pint of Jack Daniel's, and crack it open.

"Here's to you, big Merle." I sip the sour whiskey. As I tuck the bottle back in my chocolate lizard, I run my hand along the smooth tough strips of hide, the tall blocky heel, and the hard pointed toe. Like Merle's oil blasting into the sky, a crazy joy gushes through me. I smile in the darkness. I know that I have hell to pay, that quite likely my father will disown me, that every agent and casting director in town will slam their door in my face again and again, that I could end up serving garlic-pesto pizzas and curly fries and living in some dump like the Viva for months, maybe years. As Merle would say, I'm bound to get my ass shot off and my head kicked in, but by God, I'm going to swallow my teeth, get back up, and take another swing. And even if I never get a gig, at least I'll keep fighting and be worth my boots.